"This book is i
it and realize t

—Terr
autl

The shotgun roared again and the counter in front of Mojo dissolved into air and wood pulp. Mojo lurched to his feet, dragging Juanita up with him. They bolted through the back door and were wondering what to do next when a brand-new, shiny white Cadillac Seville rounded and rolled up in front of them. The Cadillac had a bumper sticker with GUN CONTROL IS HITTING WHAT YOU AIM AT printed on it. Mojo's uncle was behind the wheel. Mojo didn't hesitate. "Uncle Ort! Thank God you're here!" Mojo rushed to the side of the Cadillac.

This about W.A. 'Ort' Ortfeldt, Mojo's uncle: he had once explained to his wife that the world was divided into two classes of people: solid citizens and scumbuckets. Solid citizens made good grades in school; they worked hard; they grew up to be lawyers, doctors, and independent operators of interstate service stations.

Then there were scumbuckets. Trust and responsibility were foreign concepts to them. Scumbuckets were genetically predisposed to rayon shirts, greasy hair, and tattoos. You could always count on a tattooed person to let you down in the clutch. You could always count on a tattooed person to think of himself first and his friends and responsibility second.

Tattooed people smuggled drugs.

Tattooed people ran off without giving notice.

Tattooed people stole their own relatives' vehicles.

MOJO HAD A BLACK WIDOW ON HIS LEFT BUTTOCK.

DOUGLAS
BELL

This is a work of fiction. All the characters and events portrayed in this book are fictitious, and any resemblance to real people or events is purely coincidental.

MOJO AND THE PICKLE JAR

A Tor Book
Published by Tom Doherty Associates, Inc.
49 West 24th St.
New York, NY 10010

ISBN: 0-812-50880-7

First edition: May 1991

Printed in the United States of America

0 9 8 7 6 5 4 3 2 1

For Lynn, Brendan, Jessica, and Rachel

1

Mojo had a talent for spoons.

Mojo could bend spoons with his mind. It was not a trick he had learned. Even as a child Mojo had been able to bend spoons and open locks and rearrange the position of cards in a deck without even touching it. It was spoons, however, that gathered the other kids around him at recess and made him popular in spite of his lopsided smile and bad homelife. It was spoons that allowed Mojo to grow up straight and tall and proud instead of bowed and bent and weasel-eyed like the other children whose mothers had "Make Love, Not War" tattooed on their thighs. It was spoons that first introduced Mojo to the wonder of girls.

Mojo had a talent for girls.

From the seventh grade on girls flocked around Mojo like so many cooing doves. Mojo could talk that sweet talk. It was the sweet talk that attracted the girls, and it was the sweet talk that led to his nose being broken by Emilio Esperanza, the brother of Janie. It was the sweet talk that convinced Mrs. Rothman to give him a C in English instead of the D he deserved, and it was the sweet talk that sent Marcie Glover to the Frances Shepherd Home for Unwed Mothers and Mojo to work in his uncle's store.

Mojo had no talent for business.

"I've got this girl name of Juanita," Poteet promised him, leaning so close that his stale cigarette breath blew into Mojo's face. "She's gonna bring the junk across and deliver it to you at your uncle's store. All you gotta do is drive it up to me in Albuquerque and wait while I deal it to a guy I know. Then I'll cut you two grand. Check it: two grand. Easy."

A snap.

A cinch.

A piece of cake.

The girl name of Juanita had long black hair that swung in rhythm to her walk. She walked through the front door of Ortfeldt's Interstate Service Station and Grocery Store at the appointed time carrying a big straw basket like those sold in Mexican markets. The basket, which had a small green burro embroidered on it, was bulging. Her shoulder was sloping under the weight of it. Mojo couldn't take his eyes off the basket.

He was so intent on the basket that he didn't notice she was walking a little too fast as she approached the counter. He didn't notice the fear in her eyes. He didn't notice the way her lips were trying to form silent words that might have been "rear door." He didn't notice the way her lips were trying to form silent words that might have been "rear door." He didn't notice death wearing tight pants and a mauve silk shirt slip in the door behind her.

Death took a shot at Mojo.

The shotgun blast whumped past Mojo's ear and into a rack of potato chips. A cloud of shredded plastic and potato flour swirled about his head, dancing to the kettledrum rattle of the front windows.

Mojo dove for the floor.

The girl named Juanita dove over the counter.

"Quick! Where's the back door?" Juanita demanded, digging her nails into Mojo's shoulder for emphasis.

Mojo pushed her away and scuttled across the filthy linoleum, heading for the cash register. The old man kept a gun under the register.

Two voices whispered, low but insistent, followed by the tick-tack of boots walking slowly towards the counter.

"Answer me! Where's a door?!" Juanita wrapped an arm around Mojo's neck and squeezed. He wondered whether she would be able to choke him to death before the shotgunner got another chance.

"Come out. Out where I can see you." The voice was low, guttural, with a heavy Spanish accent.

"Don't listen to him!" Juanita hissed in Mojo's ear. "He wants to kill us!"

Mojo didn't listen. He didn't give a rat's ass damn for what either one of them wanted. He knew what he wanted. He wanted to get the gun, and he wanted to get the hell out.

The boots stopped in front of the counter. Mojo pulled the snub-nosed .32 from behind the shiny paperback dictionary. No one had ever used the dictionary in his memory. No one had ever used the gun either.

A long cold black barrel snaked over the counter.

Mojo pointed the pistol at it. His hand was shaking and the pistol wavered from the shotgun barrel to a Rolaids display and back again.

A face followed the shotgun: a flash photo of a dark pompadour and narrowed eyes staring down at him from behind the shotgun barrel.

Mojo fired.

A piece of plastic trim flew off the counter edge and into the shotgunner's face. Overhead, the rusted air-conditioner vent twanged and shook in unison with a scream of pain.

The shotgun roared again and the counter in front of Mojo dissolved into air and wood pulp.

"Run!" Mojo lurched to his feet, dragging Juanita up with him, and ran.

He shot out from behind the counter, Juanita in tow, rounded the magazine stand, and bolted for the back door. A shelf of cereal tumbled in his wake. Then some canned goods. Someone yelled something. He turned and fired blindly over Juanita's head, bringing down the front plate-glass window and two overhead fluorescent lights. The yelling stopped.

The back door was unlocked.

Mojo and Juanita bolted through the back door and ran gasping into bright sunlight. They were in a junk-yard of abandoned home appliances and freezer displays and worn-out tires. They were standing there wondering what to do next when a brand-new, shiny white Cadillac Seville rounded the rear corner of the station and rolled up in front of them. The Cadillac had a bumper sticker with "Gun Control Is Hitting What You Aim At" printed on it. Mojo's uncle was behind the wheel.

Mojo didn't hesitate.

"Uncle Ort!" Mojo rushed to the side of the Cadillac. "Thank God, you're here, Uncle Ort!"

This about W. A. "Ort" Ortfeldt, Mojo's uncle: He had once explained to his wife, Ethel, that the world was divided into two classes of people: solid citizens and scumbuckets. Solid citizens were easily recognizable: They made good grades in school; they worked hard; they grabbed the initiative anytime you gave them a chance at it. They grew up to be doctors, lawyers, and independent operators of interstate service stations.

And then there were scumbuckets. Trust and responsibility were foreign concepts to scumbuckets. Scumbuckets could be counted on to slip through school—if they got through at all—to avoid responsibility and personal involvement at every opportunity, and to end up in suitable positions as barmaids, pump jocks, and assorted oil field trash.

Ort even claimed scumbuckets could be recognized from a distance by their appearance. Scumbuckets were genetically predisposed to rayon shirts, greasy hair, and tattoos. And of these telltale signs, tattoos were the most telling. You could always count on a tattooed person to let you down in the clutch. You could always count on a tattooed person to think of himself first and his friends and responsibilities second. You could always count on a tattooed person to shirk his duties.

Tattooed people smuggled drugs.

Tattooed people ran off without giving notice.

Tattooed people stole their own relatives' vehicles.

Mojo had a black widow on his left buttock.

"There's a couple of drunk Mexicans busting up the store, Uncle Ort! I tried to stop them, but I couldn't!"

Uncle Ort's eyes narrowed. "Busting up the store? What the hell do you mean, busting up the store?"

"I mean they're tearing it to pieces, Uncle Ort! They're roaring drunk, and they're tearing your store to pieces!"

"Sonofabitch!" Uncle Ort scrambled out of the Cadillac. "Then what the hell are you doing out here? Why aren't you in there doing something about it?!"

"I didn't know what to do, Uncle Ort. I was afraid they might hurt this lady, so I brought her out here where she'd be safe."

Juanita lowered her eyes demurely.

"You didn't call the police?"

"No, sir." Mojo hung his head.

"You didn't get my gun out from under the counter?"

"No, sir." Mojo's head drooped even further.

"Why, you worthless little dickhead! I leave you in charge for one friggin' afternoon, and look what happens!" Ort's normally red face grew even redder. His eyes bulged. "You wait here!" He jabbed a stubby finger in Mojo's face. "You just wait here. I'll go inside and handle these Mexicans, but I want to see you when I'm finished!"

"Yes, sir." Mojo's chin touched his chest.

Uncle Ort stormed away towards the rear door, his short arms pumping to keep up with his bowed legs.

As soon as the door slammed behind Uncle Ort, Mojo's head snapped up. He grabbed Juanita and shoved her into the Cadillac.

"Let's get the hell out of here," Mojo told Juanita grimly as he slid underneath the wheel.

Mojo burned the Cadillac out past a 1950s washing machine, slid around a butane stove, and bumped over a half-buried water pipe that marked the boundary where the junk ended and the desert began. Mojo floor-boarded her. The Cadillac tore across the desert, bouncing heavily, crushing small shrubs in its path.

"See anything?"

Juanita raised herself on the seat and peered intently through the rear window. "Nothing. Too much dust."

They hit a ranch road a few hundred yards out and Mojo turned west onto it. Now they could see. In the distance the tin roof of the store shone where it wasn't rusted. Nothing else but brush and emptiness.

Mojo sighed in relief. "I guess they're too busy with Uncle Ort to come after us." He felt drained but strangely exhilarated at the same time. "Or maybe they're in there helping themselves to the cash register."

"Maybe you killed that one." She sounded hopeful.

"Maybe." He didn't believe it. A man would have to be awfully unlucky to die from a piece of plastic counter trim.

"What was that all about?" Mojo asked.

"What do you think it was all about? You need a road map? We were trying to steal their dope."

"But how could they have found out? Did you tell them?"

"Me? Tell them? Me?! Are you crazy?!"

''Well, you must have done something to make them suspicious.''

''Hey! I didn't blow this deal, Jack! You did. You or that bigmouthed *pendejo* Poteet.''

Mojo had to admit that Poteet was a noted big talker.

''Well, it might have been Poteet, but it wasn't me,'' Mojo assured her.

''I'll bet,'' Juanita sniffed.

''It wasn't. I swear to God.''

''So what? So what if it wasn't you? You or him, it was still a stupid Anglo *pendejo* who screwed this deal up.''

''Is that right? Well, you're not exactly a genius yourself, are you? To let those guys follow you all the way into the store?''

Juanita looked away without replying.

They rode in an uneasy silence for a few minutes.

''And what about my money?'' Juanita demanded. ''I was supposed to get two thousand dollars. How am I supposed to collect that money with these *pistoleros* running around trying to kill me? I need that money. I need that money bad.''

''Why's that? Is it an emergency? Someone sick?'' Mojo asked solicitously.

''Yeah. Me. I'm sick. Sick of West Texas. I want to go to L.A.''

Mojo nodded. ''Me too. Only I had Las Vegas in mind.''

''Las Vegas?'' She said it as though she had never heard of it. ''Is it as good as L.A.?''

''Better,''Mojo confided. ''More action. Vegas never shuts down. Action twenty-four hours a day.''

''What'll you do there?''

''I'm gonna go to dealer's school,'' he told her. ''Get

a job at one of the big casinos on the Strip. I'll have my own condo. With a pool. And a car. A fast one. Maybe a Trans Am."

"Just bullshit," she sniffed. But he could tell she was impressed.

A distant pop.

Mojo might have ignored it except for the splash of dust in the road just ahead.

"They're there. Right behind us."

Mojo's heart shifted into overdrive. He pressed the accelerator down. The Cadillac began to drift on the slick caliche road. He cursed the old man for being too cheap to buy all-weather tires.

"I can't see anything . . . Wait! There's another car!"

Mojo glanced in the rearview mirror. "A Suburban. They've got a Suburban. Damn."

Juanita got up on her knees on the seat. The dark bulk of the Suburban drifted in and out of the Cadillac's dust plume. "There's a man hanging out one of the windows."

"He's the one shooting at us. You'd better get down."

"No, I'll help you."

"You think you're Patton? Get down!"

"Who's Patton?"

"Get down, damn it!"

"Quit shooting, damn it!" Nuncio stretched a hand across the front seat of the Suburban, his fingers grasping for Frank, who was just out of reach.

"Why? What's wrong?" Frank raised his head from sighting down the rifle barrel. There was a large purple bruise over his right eye.

"I told you not to shoot at the girl! That's what's wrong!"

"I'm not. I'm aiming at the boy," Frank said indignantly.

"And what happens if you hit him? I'll tell you. He wrecks the truck. The truck wrecks, the truck catches on fire. The truck catches on fire, it burns up. The truck burns up, Ray's dope burns up with it."

"Crap. It's not the dope you're worried about; it's the girl. You want some of her. That's why you were so pissed when I shot at her in that store."

"Hey, you're full of it!" Nuncio shouted. "You want me to tell Ray how you burned up his ten kilos? That what you want? 'Cause if that's it, start firing! Blow them away, man, if that's what you want!"

"Okay, okay!" Frank drew the gun back into the Suburban. "I'll wait. I'll wait until you've had your fun."

There are no nice yellow Highway Department signs announcing curves on ranch roads. It is expected that anyone using a ranch road will know where all the curves, washouts, and gates are. And if they don't, then they didn't have any damn business on that road in the first place.

"What the—!" Mojo had known about the curve and slowed enough to get around it. What he hadn't known about was the new barbed-wire gate twenty yards past.

Not that he would have stopped anyway.

"Hang on!"

They flew through the gate as if it weren't there, the Suburban close behind. For a moment Mojo thought that they had somehow missed it altogether. Then a cedar post shot up into the air over the left fender of

Uncle Ort's shiny new Cadillac. It hung there kitelike on several twanging strands of wire before rocketing back down into the hood, crumpling the metal and sending paint and cedar chips flying.

"Uh-oh."

A second post appeared on the right side. Together they began the job of beating in the sides of Uncle Ort's new Cadillac.

Mojo pushed the gas pedal to the floor. There didn't seem to be anything better to do.

The Cadillac flew down the road.

The Suburban flew after it.

The right-side gatepost was working its way back to the front seat of the Cadillac. When it got close enough to crack the windshield, Juanita screamed. When the next blow took the sideview mirror off, she didn't need Mojo to advise her to get down.

Mojo rammed the brake to the floorboard.

The Cadillac whipped around on the slick caliche roadbed, and suddenly they were traveling backwards. Mojo could see the faces of the two men in the Suburban. The one behind the wheel was screaming something at the one in the passenger seat. The one in the passenger seat scooted over and poked a rifle out the Suburban's side window. Just then the gate jumped off the Cadillac's front grille. The gate, a whirlwind of barbed wire and tumbling posts, bounced once off the roadbed before leaping up onto the Suburban. One of the gateposts shot into the air and then straight down, spearing the Suburban in the center of the windshield.

The Suburban swerved.

The rifle retracted.

The Suburban swerved again.

Mojo watched the Suburban swerve back and forth across the road. His hands were white on the wheel. He was afraid to move them. He had never gone seventy in reverse before and wasn't sure how it was handled.

The Suburban slid to the left. One of its wheels caught on a soft sand shoulder. It slid out of control.

The Cadillac was down to ten miles an hour when the Suburban left the road. The Cadillac rolled to a stop as the Suburban crashed through a pocket of bright green creosote, leaped over a small arroyo, and finally centered-out on a sand dune, its rear wheels spinning frantically.

Mojo made an immediate U-turn in the direction away from the Suburban. "Let's," he suggested, "get the hell out of here."

Juanita kept a demon in a jar.

"A demon?"

"Here. I'll show you." She reached into the big straw basket and, using both hands, pulled out a half-gallon glass jar. There was something in the jar.

"What is it?" Mojo leaned over for a closer look. The jar was filled with a clear liquid. A white, fleshy-looking object was floating inside.

"A real demon," she said with pride. "An old woman I know caught it."

"Let me see." Mojo took the jar from her and held it up to the sunlight. They were parked behind an El Paso Natural Gas pumping station a few hundred yards from the interstate.

"She took it out of a sick woman's belly. Tricked it by getting it drunk."

"Really?" Mojo wondered.

"Really. This sick woman had a demon in her belly,

and so she went to the old woman to get it taken out. The old woman is a curer and a witch. She does that sort of stuff all the time. Anyway, the old woman fed this sick woman tequila. Just a few drops of tequila down her throat. After a while the smell of the tequila got to be too much for the demon, and so it crawled up into the woman's throat where it could lick the little drops of tequila caught there."

"Yuk."

Juanita ignored him. "The old witch woman began to pour more and more tequila down the sick woman. When she figured the demon was probably drunk, she stopped and waited. After a couple of minutes the demon's head popped up in the back of the sick woman's throat, demanding more—demons are greedy, you know. The witch woman just laughed and pretended she was drunk too. The demon got real mad; it threatened to kill the sick woman if it wasn't given more tequila. The old woman laughed again and put the bottle to her mouth like she was drinking from it. Then this demon went crazy. It must have thought the old woman was drinking its tequila or something. It charged out of the sick woman's mouth and yanked the bottle away from the old witch woman. But before it could get back into the sick woman, the old witch grabbed it, dropped it into this jar, and screwed down the lid."

"You saw all this happen?" Mojo asked skeptically.

"Well, not exactly. But there's no question about it. This is definitely the demon from that woman's belly."

Mojo rotated the jar and the thing turned with it. It was dead, ghastly white. It was very wrinkled. It looked like an old horseapple left out in the sun. Long tentacles or fingers or something were hanging from it.

"It looks kinda like those things in that alien movie.

You remember those? The ones that jumped on people's faces? It's got the same fingers or tentacles or whatever they were. Only the aliens were a lot bigger and they had a sucker they could stick down your throat."

He turned the jar once more. The lid was printed in Spanish. It promised premium pickles inside. He handed it back to the girl. The thing was creepy-looking.

"It doesn't look like a demon to me. It looks more like a piece of dried fruit or something."

"That's because you don't know anything about demons," she said seriously.

He couldn't argue with that.

"So you have a demon, huh? I can bend spoons with my mind," Mojo said, not to be outdone.

"A trick. I saw it on TV."

"No, no. I can really do it. Just with my mind. I know there are phonies who bend them with their hands, but all I do is think about it and it happens."

"Uh-huh." She didn't sound convinced. Mojo wondered how she could expect him to believe the thing in the jar was a demon when she wouldn't even believe he could bend spoons.

"Listen, Mojo," she said, grasping his arm so he could see she was serious. "We've got to find a place to hide out. Those guys who tried to kill us work for Raymundo Castillo. You know who he is?"

"Yeah. King of the dopers." Poteet had told him all about Machete Ray Castillo.

"That's right. Castillo's a big man. He's got a lot of money and a lot of soldiers working for him. And he's not just going to forget about us. He's not going to forget about us or this dope." She patted the straw basket on the seat. "He'll have the word out on us. And if he finds us he's going to kill us."

Mojo furrowed his brow. She was right. This was a problem. He thought for a long moment . . . "What about Mexico?" Mojo suggested at last. "Couldn't we hide out over there? At least it'd be easy to sell the dope."

"Mexico?" Juanita pursed her lips. Then: "That's not as stupid as it sounds. That'd be the last place he'd think to look. And besides, I've got relatives in Sonora I could stay with. Yeah, I think Mexico's an okay idea. Tell you what, as soon as it's dark, we'll drive to El Paso and cross the border there."

"Great!" Mojo was pleased. "And say, Juanita?"

"Yes?"

"Do you think I could stay with your relatives too? Just for a while? Just until the heat's off? I don't know anybody over there."

Juanita looked straight at him. Her eyes were expressionless. "I don't think that would be a good idea, Mojo," she said. "I don't think that would be a good idea at all."

2

The moon rose ice white and huge over the mountains of West Texas. The ice-white light of the moon flowed down from the mountains and through the streets of Van Horn. It flowed out from Van Horn and over Ortfeldt's Interstate Service Station and Grocery Store and down Interstate 20 heading west, over two cars and an Airstream trailer and a smoking diesel rig with a faded "Hey Ayatollah! Kiss My Assaholla!" bumper sticker. The ice-white moonlight flowed over Uncle Ort's battered Cadillac Seville racing towards El Paso.

"You painted these? All by yourself?" Mojo asked Juanita.

"Yes," Juanita told him proudly. "You like them?"

"Like them? I love them! I mean, you've really got a talent here! These are as good as the ones they sell in K mart!"

"Thanks." She beamed.

Mojo held the Polaroids up to the Cadillac's dim interior light for a better view. Juanita was driving. The Polaroids were of some paintings Juanita had done.

"These are really great. I'd love to have a couple of these to hang on the walls of my room. Maybe after we sell the coke I'll have enough money to buy some from you."

"Really? You like them that much?" Her eyes glittered.

"Sure. I love them."

Mojo hated them. All the paintings were of big-eyed children. They were big-eyed children paintings. Mojo hadn't realized before this that big-eyed children paintings were actually painted. He had supposed that K Mart had a factory somewhere turning them out like cookie cutters.

"Some people don't like them. They say they're too depressing."

"Not me. I think they're cute."

The paintings reminded Mojo of his ex-girlfriend, Leona. Leona from Lubbock. Leona from Lubbock had been a waitress at the same motel in Van Horn where Mojo had rented a room. Leona had had five of the big-eyed children paintings in her bedroom, one for each wall plus an extra in case she ran out. Mojo had felt those big eyes staring disapprovingly at him each time he had crawled into bed with Leona.

"They're called waif paintings," Juanita told him. "There's a big market for them. Especially out West."

"Really? Is that what you were going to do in California? Sell waif paintings?"

"Maybe. I thought about it. I thought I might if they were good enough."

"They are," Mojo told her seriously. "These are as good as any I've ever seen."

Mojo was not exaggerating.

"Thanks." Juanita smiled at Mojo. Her eyes met his. The huge moon shone in Juanita's eyes.

Mojo smiled back at Juanita. Their eyes stayed locked for a few seconds, then Juanita turned quickly back to the road.

"Listen, Juanita, maybe I could come visit you at your relatives' house in Sonora," Mojo said, trying to follow up. "I could bring you some paints and stuff. Just so you wouldn't get out of practice."

"Why is that guy so close?" Juanita frowned at the rearview mirror. "He's practically riding on our bumper."

Mojo turned around and looked back. There was a car behind them with its brights on. The car was so close Mojo could see it was a Suburban with a lot of front-end damage and a basketball-sized hole in the windshield.

Mojo was quick.

Mojo was born quick. In the fourth grade Mojo had ducked a kitchen knife hurled by his mother from less than ten feet away and escaped without a scratch. In the eleventh grade he had escaped Jack Ochoa's Dobermans by leaping a five-foot chain link fence with two hubcaps under each arm. Less than twelve hours earlier Mojo had dodged death in his Uncle Ort's Interstate Service Station and Grocery Store. And now Mojo dodged death again.

Mojo dropped down low in the front seat of the Cadillac pressing his head against his knees. The bullet passed through the rear window, over the seatback, through the vacant space where Mojo's head had been, and out the windshield. The bullet made a flat slapping sound as it passed through the windshield. Tiny shards of glass fell onto the dash, tinkling like chimes.

"Floorboard it!" Mojo yelled at Juanita.

She already had.

"Dead center!" Frank cried triumphantly. He was hanging out the window of the Suburban, his M-16 braced against the sideview mirror.

"Don't tell me!" Nuncio shouted back. "I don't need to hear no fucking running score! Just keep on firing!"

The Cadillac pulled away with a glasspack roar, ghost white in the moonlight. Nuncio stomped the accelerator and went after it.

"Close up on them!" Frank yelled.

"Get the hell away from them!" Mojo shouted.

"I'm trying," Juanita told him calmly.

Mojo unfolded himself and peered back over the seat. The rear window was a spiderweb of glittering cracks with a perfectly round hole in its center. Headlights were coming up fast behind the spiderweb.

Mojo turned to Juanita. "When I yell 'change' you pull over into the other lane. We'll try and throw his aim off."

"Okay." She was bunched up over the wheel, her mouth set in a grim line.

Mojo looked back. The bright headlights were closer.

"Here he comes . . . he's trying to get a bead on us . . . Get ready . . . Okay! Change!"

Juanita wrenched the wheel to the left. Mojo had to grab the seatback to keep from being thrown against the door. She whipped the wheel back in almost the same motion. Tires squealed. They were flying down the left lane.

"Perfect!" Mojo crowed. And then wonderingly: "Where did you learn to drive like that?"

"You almost killed me!" Frank screamed at Nuncio over the roar of the wind. "Warn me before you turn like that! You almost threw me out!"

"Fuck off!" Nuncio snarled back. His eyes were locked on the Cadillac's taillights, rushing away from him down the interstate. He pressed the pedal even harder against the floor.

Mojo flew.

The interstate flickered in the Cadillac's headlights. Shadows leaped out of its way.

Ninety.

One hundred.

One hundred and ten.

The mountains were the same ice white as the moon.

They whipped across a bridge, the silver posts strobing past, the round red reflectors blinking.

One hundred and fifteen.

They shot across another bridge and up a long hill. They were climbing towards a sky ablaze with stars. The speedometer needle wavered, dropped, steadied, wavered, dropped.

One hundred and ten.

One hundred.

Ninety.

Something sizzled under the Cadillac's crumpled hood.

The headlights of the pursuing Suburban grew

brighter. Mojo watched helplessly as the headlights grew as big as a jumbo jet's.

Juanita held an object out for Mojo. "Here, you take this."

Mojo took the object. It was a .22 revolver.

The rear window of the Cadillac exploded in a sparkling shower of glass. The windshield followed. Mojo ducked. Mojo prayed. Mojo could hear someone pounding on the trunk with a hammer.

Mojo was only halfway through the Lord's Prayer when they topped the hill, the Cadillac's headlights soaring up into a black void for an instant, then arcing back down onto a long descent. The hammering stopped. The speedometer bounced up.

One hundred.

One hundred and ten.

Mojo raised his head. He glanced at Juanita. Juanita was still bent over the wheel, her eyes straight ahead and determined. There was broken glass in her hair that flashed blue and white as the Suburban topped the hill behind them. There was moonlight and wind upon her face. She was beautiful. He loved her.

One hundred and twenty.

"What are you waiting for?" Juanita shouted over the wind.

Mojo turned around and fired the .22 out the shattered rear window at the headlights of the Suburban.

The Suburban came on.

Mojo sighted down the barrel, taking a more careful aim, and fired again.

The Suburban came on.

Mojo lowered the pistol. He had a sinking feeling that a .22 pistol wouldn't be enough to stop a car full of dopers armed with automatic weapons.

One hundred and twenty-five.

Blue fire was flashing from the Suburban.

Mojo peered over the dash. They were crossing another bridge, so fast this time that the posts were only a blur. Ahead the interstate curled up a steep hill like a bow in a silver ribbon.

They surged up the steep hill and then the Cadillac began to slow. The sizzling became a shriek.

One hundred and ten.

Ninety-five.

Eighty.

Mojo turned around. The Suburban was coming up behind them like a skyrocket. The blue fire was stuttering outside its passenger side window. Mojo aimed the .22 at the blue fire and fired twice in rapid succession. The blue fire continued to stutter.

Seventy-five.

Fists pounded the trunk again.

A side window cracked like ice under pressure.

Mojo emptied the .22 at the Suburban, the shots no louder than firecrackers. As he fired his last shot the Cadillac swung suddenly to the right. Mojo was thrown on his side. He dropped the pistol. He dug his fingers into seat fabric to keep from being thrown into Juanita's lap. He heard the Cadillac's tires squealing. He felt the Cadillac tilt over and the right-side wheels lift off the ground.

Oh, shit.

For a long, agonizing second the Cadillac hung in the air, balanced on two wheels, the tires screaming in protest. The glove compartment popped open and dropped cassette tapes on Mojo's head. The passenger door creaked threateningly above him.

Then the Cadillac fell back to earth.

The Cadillac struck earth with a jolt that catapulted Mojo up off the seat. He banged his head on the ceiling. He fell back onto the seat again. He doggedly raised himself back up.

Mojo raised himself up and looked out the broken windshield. The Cadillac was bouncing down a rough dirt road that ran through thickets of creosote and mesquite. Its engine was still sizzling. He turned and looked back. The road behind was dark and black beyond the faint pink glow of the Cadillac's taillights. Nothing moved in the darkness. There were no bright headlights following them.

"Sonofabitch," Mojo said in relief.

"It was the demon who showed me this turnoff," Juanita told him matter-of-factly.

"The demon?"

"He summoned a flaming cross to guide me."

"Well . . . that's great . . . I mean, I really appreciate him doing that."

"This isn't the first time he's saved me from danger. He's done it lots of times before. Even back there at your uncle's store. If I hadn't had the demon with me at your uncle's store, I would've been gunned down for sure."

"Is that right? Well, I guess I . . . Oh, shit." Mojo groaned.

"What is it? Is something wrong?"

"Look in the rearview mirror."

Juanita looked. There was a pair of headlights in the darkness behind them.

The dirt road shot straight as an arrow across the desert. The Cadillac shot down it. The headlights followed. The headlights were only small bright dots for a long while. Then the headlights began to grow. Soon they were the size of owl's eyes.

"We're slowing down!"

"It's not my fault. I've got it floorboarded," Juanita told him.

Mojo could smell the Cadillac's engine. It smelled like old tires burning. He glanced over his shoulder. The Suburban was still behind them. Still coming on.

"It's the engine," he told her. "Something's wrong with the engine. Probably the radiator."

"Can't you do anything to fix it?"

"Not without stopping."

"We're not stopping."

The Cadillac coughed. Missed. Coughed again.

"I wouldn't count on that," Mojo said.

Mojo bent over and felt frantically around on the floorboard for the gun. If he was going to have to make a run for it, he at least wanted a gun in his hand. The Cadillac's engine coughed again. Mojo groped under the seat. The Cadillac's engine screeched, a piercing sound, metal on metal. Paused. Screeched again. Mojo got down on the floorboard and jammed his entire arm under the seat.

Mojo had explored most of the floorboard with only a wadded-up Snickers wrapper and a short stack of Willie Nelson tapes to show for it when Juanita suddenly shouted, "Hang on!"

The Cadillac bounced heavily. Mojo had a sense of falling then bouncing then falling again. Juanita slammed on the brakes. The Cadillac jerked to an abrupt halt. Mojo rammed his already battered head against the dash.

The Cadillac's engine screamed, shook once, then died.

"Damn!" Mojo picked himself up from the floorboard. He was holding his head with one hand. The other hand was empty. "Watch it!" he warned Juanita.

Juanita reached over and switched off the headlights.

"Come on." Juanita opened her door and slid out of the front seat and into the night.

"Hey! Where're you going?"

"Come on. Come on if you don't want to die," she told him.

Mojo definitely did not want to die. He opened the passenger door and slipped out of the Cadillac. The car was parked in the middle of the road at the bottom of a shallow arroyo. The road entered the arroyo from a steep bank just behind Mojo, ran across the arroyo's bottom, then exited up another, more gradual bank across from him. The bottom of the arroyo was hardpack, dirt and rock, as flat and unyielding as a board. He could smell gasoline along with burning rubber.

"This way!" Juanita was running away from him up the shallow draw. Mojo looked up to the sandy rim where the road dropped down into the arroyo. The rim was glowing with a light that was too bright to be moonlight.

Mojo turned and ran after Juanita.

Mojo had run no more than thirty or forty yards when the Suburban flew over the lip of the arroyo, hurtled down the bank, and crashed into the rear end of the Cadillac. There was the sound of metal ripping metal, followed by a huge orange fireball that lit the sky, followed by the sound of a thunderous explosion, followed by a blast of hot wind and sand that stung Mojo's face and burned his eyes.

Mojo turned away from the burning wind. Juanita

was just ahead of him, cringing in the orange light. He ran to her.

Mojo took Juanita by the arm. "We've got to get out of here," he gasped. Moonlight shone on his face, flickering orange fire on hers. "They probably saw that all the way over to Van Horn. The law'll be here soon. The . . . ah . . . the . . ."

It was a flash that caught Mojo's eye, a wink of sudden and intensely blue light from deep within the jar Juanita was cradling. Mojo stared into the jar. The wink came again. Even brighter this time. Even bluer this time.

Then faded like a spent match.

"The what?" Juanita asked impatiently.

Mojo shook his head, irritated. A reflection. Of course. Had to be. Just a reflection of the explosion. Of the moon . . . of something.

"The what? What are you talking about?"

"Nothing. I . . ."

A police siren swept across the desert and down into the arroyo, an angry swarming hum. The siren was far away but closing. Coming on.

"Let's go." Juanita yanked her arm away from Mojo and turned up the arroyo. "I think maybe you're right. I think maybe we'd better get out of here before the law shows up."

3

R. K. Narn was the law.

R. K. Narn was a Texas Ranger.

R. K. Narn looked like a Texas Ranger should look. He wore a white Stetson. He wore black boots. He wore a white western yoked shirt with the collar open and tan slacks with a military crease. He had a hard, determined mouth. He had pale blue eyes that watered in bright sunlight and white, bushy eyebrows that turned down when he was angry. He wore a broad leather belt with a silver buckle in its middle and an ivory-handled pistol in a black leather holster on his hip.

R. K. Narn was a big man. He stood six-foot-three without his boots, six-six with them. When he added his Stetson, he brushed the tops of doorways. His shoulders were as broad and square as a filing cabinet. His hands were as hard and flat and worn as railroad chisels. He was sixty-four years old. It was said of Narn that he could track down a fart in a glue factory.

Narn walked slowly up the arroyo, heading west. He flicked on his flashlight and played it over the ground. The footprints were vague and indistinct on the hard-pack: a scuff mark here, a pebble kicked loose there, nothing that actually looked like a footprint, nothing that the men of the Culberson County Sheriff's Department had actually recognized as a footprint earlier.

Narn followed the footprints almost a hundred yards to where the hardpack bottom changed to sand. He stopped and knelt down, examining the footprints more closely. Even here it was difficult to read too much, the soft sand leaving only shallow depressions, but it was enough for Narn: two people, a man and a woman, both average size, wearing athletic shoes, walking fast, heading west.

Narn stood after a few minutes and walked briskly back to where he had parked his Bronco. The two suspects had a three- or four-hour head start, but that was okay. They were on foot, and he was not. He estimated he would have them by sunrise at the latest.

It was still a few hours before sunrise. The sky was still bright with moonlight and a few thousand stars.

"We're in luck," Mojo whispered to Juanita. "Just look over there."

"Where?"

"Over there. Just to the right of that big yucca."

"I don't see anything."

They were crouched behind a mesquite bush in front of a dilapidated shack built of discarded scraps of lumber, tin, and broken drywall. The shack sat alone in the middle of the desert with no road leading up to it other than a two-rutted track. The shack's roof was sagging. It had no yard and no garage. The outhouse had fallen down.

Mojo pulled on his ear and considered. The shack looked abandoned. Probably was. Its windows were dark. There were no sounds coming from inside. There were no smells. It was probably filled with dust and shadows and rats and rattlesnakes.

Or so Mojo hoped.

Then again, you never knew out here in the middle of nowhere. The shack might be filled with sleeping wetbacks or smugglers or bikers or fence riders, all fully armed and ready to charge out and shoot Mojo for attempting to steal their car.

"There's a car?"

"You can just see it there, just to the right of that woodpile."

Juanita peered into the darkness. "I see it. But it looks like it's on blocks."

"No, I can see one of the front tires. It's on the ground."

"Probably a junker, then."

"No, looks pretty good. Tires aren't even flat."

"Hmmm." Juanita peered into the darkness. "You think it might run?"

"Might. It's worth a shot."

"How'll you start it?"

"Hot-wire it. I can hot-wire anything. Come on." Mojo took Juanita's hand. He led her through the tall weeds in front of the shack and around the side to where the car was parked.

The car was an old Chevrolet Impala. Mojo had been right. The tires were good. The rest didn't look too bad either.

"I still can't believe you left the stuff in the car." Juanita shook her head. She was keeping watch as Mojo worked on the ignition switch.

"Me?" Mojo's voice was muffled, his head crammed underneath the dashboard. "What about you? After all, it was your basket."

"It may have been my basket, but it was on your side of the seat." Juanita sighed. "At least I've got my demon."

"Yeah, well, it just wasn't the sort of situation where you check to make sure you've got everything before you get out."

"Still . . ." She let it hang.

"Don't worry. We'll get some cash. We can sell this car over in Juárez for a few hundred easy. Then we can fly down to your relatives' house in Sonora. Or maybe even over to Cancún."

"Cancún?"

"Why not? I figure as long as we're gonna be fugitives, we might as well as be fugitives someplace nice."

"What about the police?"

"Don't worry about the police; the police aren't gonna catch us. Not once I have this sucker started. We'll drive straight to the border, and that'll be that. They won't have any idea where we've gone."

Juanita nodded, but she wasn't that sure.

Narn eased the Bronco forward, his spotlight trained on the dim trail of footprints leading westward across the desert floor. The Bronco crunched down a draw and over a mesquite bush and up a rocky ridge, a cinnamon toothpick jiggling between Narn's lips; then across the ridge and down a gentle slope thick with ocotillo. Beyond the slope the ground flattened and Narn was able to pick up a little speed. He hummed to himself as he drove, a wordless murmur that was a mixture of Willie Nelson and the yipping and yapping of some coyotes to the south.

The old woman's white hair shone in the moonlight. Her hair was festooned with streamers that stood straight on end as if she had either just gotten out of bed or been electrocuted.

"Come out of there," the old woman ordered Mojo, pointing a shotgun at his head so he could see that she was serious about it.

"I'm coming." Mojo sat up straight in the front seat of the Impala and held his hands out. "I'm coming right now. Just be careful with that thing."

"Hurry it up. And don't try to pick up a gun or anything, because if you do I'll shoot the both of you."

"I don't have a gun. I don't have anything. I promise." Mojo opened the door of the Impala and slipped out beside Juanita. He exhibited his empty hands again. "See? Nothing."

"Move over there." The old woman gestured with the gun. "Over there by the hood . . . That's it." The shotgun was too big for her. Too heavy. It shook in her hands. The barrel wavered. The shaking shotgun made Mojo nervous. He was afraid it might go off accidentally and kill someone. Someone like Juanita or himself.

"Listen. Why don't you point that thing down at the ground?" Mojo suggested to the old woman. "It's not safe to point loaded guns at people."

"You should have thought of that before you came sneaking around here trying to steal my car." The old woman's Spanish had a strange accent Mojo was not familiar with. He had to listen carefully to follow what she was saying.

"Trying is right," Juanita muttered.

"What? What was that?" The old woman switched the gun to Juanita.

"Nothing."

"No, you said something. What was it? Are you plotting against me?" The old woman raised the shotgun threateningly.

Juanita didn't flinch. She looked the wild-haired woman straight in the eye. "Listen, old woman, you can't frighten me with that thing. I've got protection. I've got a demon who protects me, and if you try and shoot me he'll turn you into a frog or a stone or maybe even something worse."

"A demon?" The old woman peered quizzically down the shotgun at Juanita.

"That's right. A demon. I've got him right here in my purse." She patted it. "And if you don't watch your step, I'll let him loose on you."

The old woman stared at Juanita.

"Ah, this isn't exactly how it looks." Mojo jumped in hurriedly before the old woman decided they were maniacs as well as thieves. "We weren't really going to steal your car. We were just gonna borrow it for a little while is all. Just so we could go to the police in Van Horn. We're being chased by a gang of dope dealers, you see. We took some of their drugs accidentally, and we were just on our—"

"You really have a demon?" the old woman asked Juanita, interrupting Mojo.

"I said I did, didn't I?" Juanita snapped.

"Then it's no coincidence that you've come to me,"

the old woman said solemnly, lowering the shotgun. "No, no coincidence at all. This has obviously been planned by a higher hand than any of ours. Someone greater than any of us has sent you here with this demon."

"What do you mean: sent me here?" Juanita wrinkled her nose suspiciously.

"I mean it can be no coincidence that you, who possess a demon, have arrived on the doorstep of the greatest single authority on demons in all the world."

"You're an authority on demons?" Juanita peered doubtfully at the old woman.

"The *greatest* authority," the old woman corrected her. "Yes. Those who know, those who possess the power, consider Grandmother to be the greatest single authority on demons who has ever lived."

"I see . . ." Grandmother turned the pickle jar with a liver-spotted hand. The jar sparkled in the light from the kerosene lantern above the table. The dead-white thing in the jar turned with it. "I see now . . . yes . . . very, very interesting . . ." The old woman looked up. "And you say that the woman who sold you this demon claimed to be the very same witch who caught it?"

"That's right," Juanita said.

Grandmother shook her head ruefully. "Child, child, that is almost certainly not true. Any witch fortunate enough to imprison a demon would never sell it. Not for all the gold in the world. There's not a more powerful servant in this world than a demon. A real witch would never sell a real demon. No. Never."

"Well, this one did," Juanita said defiantly.

Mojo took another Oreo from the package Grandmother had set out for them, leaned back in his chair, and crunched it. The shack was surprisingly comfortable inside. Far cleaner and warmer than he had expected. The furniture was old and worn but sturdy enough. There was only a slight breeze blowing through the chinks in the walls.

"No." Grandmother shook her head slowly. "I'm sorry to be the one to tell you this, but you've been cheated. The thing in this jar is almost certainly not a demon."

"It almost certainly is," Juanita shot back. "I should know. It saved my life twice. I should know whether it's real or not."

Mojo noticed the walls of the room were covered with pieces of paper. Colored pictures. At first he assumed they had been pinned up for their insulation value, but then realized the pictures were all of saints: white-faced saints, dark-faced saints, bright, halo-faced saints; young, old, and in-between saints. He peered at the pictures behind the kitchen table where he was sitting. One was of a child in a floppy hat. "Child of Atocha" was printed beneath it. Another was of a strangely dark Christ with Indian eyes: "Our Lord of Izmiquilpan" was his name. Beside him was a similiar, yet slightly different Christ figure entitled "Mystic Visage of Our Lord of Amecameca." Just to the right of the two Lords was a Madonna with a brightly painted heart and black eyes and the caption "Our Lady of Zapopan."

Mojo frowned. Izmiquilpan? Zapopan? He had been forced by his aunt to learn most of the saints, but he'd never heard of any with names like these. On top of that, they didn't look like regular saints. They looked Mexican.

"The fact that this precious object saved your life doesn't make it a demon," Grandmother told Juanita. "In fact, it argues against it. A demon must be coerced into aiding its master. A demon would never do such a thing voluntarily. No, this" —she tapped the jar with a skeletal finger— "is no demon."

Juanita gave Grandmother a puzzled look. "Precious object?"

"Of course it's precious," Grandmother said firmly. "That's obvious."

"But you don't believe it's a demon?"

"No. I'm certain this is no demon. Not only doesn't it act like a demon, it doesn't look like one either. Every demon I have ever seen was red or orange in color while this one is white. It also lacks claws and teeth."

"Well, what could it be, then? If it's not a demon. I mean, what else could have magical powers?"

The old woman leaned across the table towards Juanita. Her dark eyes sparkled in the lantern light. "A most precious and rare thing, my child," she said in a low, conspiratorial voice. "What you have here in this jar is as rare in this world of sorrows as a soul without blemish. What you have here is a sacred heart."

Mojo squinted at the jar. Thought about it. It did look something like a heart. Sort of. If you were to take a heart and leave it out in the sun and let it shrivel up and then maybe kick it around and after you were finished pop it into a jar full of alcohol, then it might look like the thing in Juanita's pickle jar. Might. Then again . . .

"Bullshit." Juanita's eyes were cold. "I'm not buying this heart crap. A heart couldn't have stopped bullets. A plain old heart, sacred or not, couldn't have shown me that side road off the interstate. No way. You're just jealous that I have a demon and you don't. That's all."

Grandmother shook her head. "Oh, no, my child. Not a plain heart. Not at all. You see, I would trade a hundred demons for what you have in this jar. For this heart. For this is no ordinary heart. Oh my, no. Not at all. This is a special heart, a sacred heart, an ancient heart. This, my dear, is the perfectly preserved heart of an ancient saint. And as such, it has the power to perform miracles. Incredible miracles. Saving you was nothing compared to the miracles this heart is capable of performing. Oh, yes. No demon could ever even begin to match the miracles this heart can perform."

"Miracles?" Juanita frowned. "Really? Real honest-to-God miracles?"

"Definitely."

"Greater miracles than a demon?"

"Oh, yes. As I said, this heart is far, far more powerful than any mere demon. Far, far more powerful!"

"More powerful . . . I see . . ." Juanita leaned forward on her elbows. She peered into the jar. She studied the thing floating in the liquid . . . "Yes," she said slowly after a time, "I think I can see what you mean. Now that I know what to look for. It does look like a heart, doesn't it? You know, I think maybe you're right, Grandmother. I think maybe this is the sacred heart of a very powerful saint and not just a plain old demon after all."

Juanita smiled at Grandmother.

Grandmother smiled back.

"Wait a second." Mojo couldn't let this pass. "If this thing is a saint's heart, why would it help people like Juanita and me? I mean, we weren't exactly on a mission from God when those guys in the Suburban were chasing us. Why would it help us?"

"It helped you because you were thwarting the will of Satan. That's obvious," Grandmother told him.

"It is?"

"Of course. Satan is the evil force behind drugs and drug dealers. You thwarted his will when you took the cocaine. It was his henchmen who pursued you. That's why the heart protected you."

"Satan is behind cocaine smuggling?" This was news to Mojo.

"Of course. Who else?"

"Well . . . I've always heard it was the Colombians. Or maybe even Machete Ray Castillo over in El Paso."

Grandmother sighed. Grandmother shook her head scornfully at Mojo's abysmal ignorance. "You're like so many in the world today," Grandmother told Mojo. "You're blind. You can't see past the small evils to the greater evil that stands behind them. You can't see through the illusions to the true source of the evil."

Mojo shrugged. He supposed that might be true. She might be right. He might not be seeing through illusions. After all, he hadn't even known there were any illusions to see through before now.

"But if this is a heart, then whose heart is it? You said it was the heart of a saint. Which saint?" Juanita asked.

"That," Grandmother said, "is a very good question. And one we must answer before we can utilize the heart's full powers. Come with me." She took Juanita's hand, leading her towards a small shrine in the corner of the room. "We'll light candles and pray to the Dark Lady for her guidance in this matter."

While Grandmother and Juanita prayed, Mojo passed the time by reading a yellowed newspaper he picked off a stack underneath the table. The headline in the paper was "Dead Man Fathers Child." Beneath the headline was a grainy black-and-white photograph of a smiling woman dressed in a mu-mu. The woman looked foreign. She had a mole on her chin. She was built like a washing machine. A caption below the woman read, "I Dug Him Up and Did It, Mom-to-Be Says."

Mojo yawned. Glanced over to the far corner of the shack. Grandmother and Juanita were still there, still busily praying at the small, candlelit shrine.

Mojo turned back to his paper. He finished a short article on how to lose weight by eating nothing but candy and ice cream and became bored. Stared off into space. After a time he stood up, pushed his chair back, and stretched. A bone in his shoulder popped. He turned around. Juanita was sitting down on a packing crate that served as an end table for Grandmother's bed. Apparently she had either lost her fervor for praying or was taking a break from it. Mojo walked over and sat down beside her.

"Fun place, huh? How'd you like to live out here full-time with no TV, no movies, nothing?" Mojo asked Juanita. "I don't see how she stands it."

Juanita shrugged. "She's old."

"Nobody's that old." He kicked at a splinter that was protruding from the wooden floor. "What's taking so long, anyway? She's been over there for nearly an hour."

"These things take time."

"Yeah? How much time? Have you forgotten about all that dope we left back in the car? The cops are bound to have the car by now. Or what's left of it anyway."

"Of course I haven't forgotten," she said. "And Grandmother promised to drive us to El Paso. It's just that we have to find out whose heart is in the jar first."

"Why? You didn't even know it was a heart before. How come you suddenly can't go anywhere until you find out its name?"

"You don't understand."

"You're right there. Come on," Mojo pleaded.

"We've got to get going. We can't just sit around here waiting on that crazy old woman forever."

A clap of distant thunder.

"Listen." Juanita looked up towards the sagging ceiling.

The thunder came again. Closer this time.

"I hear it. Rain's coming. And how do you think we're going to get out of here after a rain? That isn't exactly a paved road out there, you know. Hell, it's not even a dirt road. And that Impala has street tires. If it rains, we're going to be stuck out here in the middle of nowhere; I can promise you that."

Thunder exploded nearby. The sound was almost as loud as the explosion of the Cadillac had been earlier. The sound struck the shack like a hard wind. The walls quivered. The old, brittle wood creaked. The iron stove rattled. Dust and small pieces of debris fell from the ceiling, drifting down onto Mojo's shoulders as softly as a light snow.

"Damn!" Mojo jumped up from the packing crate. "The roof's gonna go!"

But even as Mojo raised himself onto the balls of his feet, poised to make a run for it, the thunder faded. The walls stopped quivering. The stove stopped rattling. The ceiling stopped raining debris. The quiet returned as quickly as it had left.

"A sign!" Grandmother called from the shrine, rising unsteadily from her knees. She turned towards Mojo and Juanita, her face bright with triumph and candlelight. "It's a sign! A special sign from Our Dark Lady! From the most holy Virgin of Guadalupe herself!"

"A sign of what?" Mojo asked shakily. Mojo brushed some of the dust off of his shoulders. Tried to recompose himself.

"A sign of her favor. A sign she has heard my prayers."

"Does that mean we can go now?" Mojo wondered.

Some of the brightness left Grandmother. "No. Not just yet."

"No?! Not even after she sent you this special sign?"

"A sign is not an answer. We must be patient. I'm certain we will hear her answer shortly."

"I'll bet," Mojo snorted.

The sky fell in.

The previous clap of thunder was a firecracker compared to this new one. This new clap of thunder was a bomb. The bomb went off right above the shack. The bomb rolled down from the sky and into the shack and struck Mojo. Mojo felt like he was standing inside an iron church bell that was being pummeled by a gang of hunchbacks armed with mallets.

Mojo ducked his head. He threw his hands over his ears. It didn't do any good. His ears still rang. No matter how hard he pressed his hands against his ears, he could still hear the thunder. Feel it.

After a second or two Mojo gave up and raised his head. The wall next to him was shivering. The pictures of the saints were flapping in an unseen wind, their halos bobbing. He glanced at Juanita. Juanita's mouth was open and she appeared to be screaming, though he couldn't hear her, nothing but the thunder. He realized his mouth was open too. The floor began dancing, nails creaking and boards flapping. Blue lights flashed on the far wall. Mojo turned towards the lights.

The iron stove on the other side of the room was crawling with tiny blue snakes. Mojo watched as the blue snakes slithered down the metal roof flue and leaped off onto the hot plates. The snakes popped and leaped and hissed as they cavorted over the stove, their heads forking into miniature lightning bolts that popped like bacon. One of the forked bolts dove off the stove and into the floor near Mojo's foot. A whiff of white smoke marked its passing.

Mojo felt something new shake and looked up. The ceiling above him was quivering like a wet dog. A ten-foot beam swung out and dropped several feet before stopping just above Mojo's head. The beam teetered for a second, then—to Mojo's immense relief—swung back up.

Mojo ducked his head. He had seen enough. It was time to go.

Mojo grabbed Juanita's arm. Yelled "Come on!" even though he was pretty sure she couldn't hear him, and headed for the front door.

There were blue snakes coiled around the doorknob, but Mojo didn't hesitate. He grabbed the knob—his hand tingling like he had stuck it in ice water, blue snakes swimming up the hairs on his forearms—and yanked the door open. He pushed Juanita through, then followed her out into the weed patch that served as the shack's front yard.

Mojo and Juanita ran a good thirty feet before they finally stopped. The thunder was still ringing. Mojo couldn't even hear his own breathing. He paused to catch his breath, then looked over to make sure Juanita was okay. Juanita seemed okay. She was staring up into the sky with her mouth still open. Mojo stared with her. The moon sat in the center of the sky. The moon was surrounded by billions of stars. The stars were surrounded by billions of miles of clear black nothingness. There were no clouds over the moon. There were no clouds over the stars or sky. There were no clouds or rain anywhere. There were no bolts of lightning. There was no storm.

The ringing faded from Mojo's ears. He frowned with puzzlement.

"Come see, come see," Grandmother called as Juanita and Mojo trooped back through the open door. "A miracle! The Dark Lady has granted us a miracle!"

Mojo followed Juanita over to where Grandmother was standing beside the pickle jar. "See it? The heart has been touched by the Dark Lady! The heart has the fire of life!"

Mojo had to lean close to see it, but there really was light if not fire. A dim blue light was flickering on the surface of the ghastly white thing Grandmother claimed was a human heart.

"A blessing! A sign!" Grandmother proclaimed. "A sign that this is indeed the heart of a blessed saint!"

"Static electricity," Mojo suggested. He thumped the jar lightly with his forefinger and the blue light danced. Bubbles rose in a small cloud. He could smell ozone.

"This is the most wondrous thing in the world! The most fabulous miracle of our age! A living saint's heart!"

"Living? Let's not get carried away here," Mojo cautioned her. "Just because it's got a blue glow doesn't mean it's alive. You could zap a piece of baloney with a bolt of lightning and it would glow."

"And it beats!" Grandmother went on, ignoring him. "It's still weak yet, but there's no question. The heart is beating!"

"Let me see." Juanita pushed Mojo aside and leaned over the table, pressing her face so close to the jar that blue reflections flickered on her cheeks.

Mojo sighed and moved away. Shook his head. Mojo was just about to suggest that they could play with the heart later but now it was time to get the show on the road when he heard something.

Mojo walked quickly to the shack's single window and looked out. The desert was still in the moonlight. Nothing moved. He couldn't hear anything. The sound—if there had been a sound—had stopped.

Then he heard it again. Very faint and far away. Muted and indistinct. The sound faded out. In. Out. Mojo waited. The sound came again, a little clearer this time, a little stronger. It had a rising, falling quality. An animal of some kind? An animal howling? No, not howling . . . That wasn't it. It was . . . deeper than howling, more like . . . baying. Like a dog. Like a pack of dogs. Like . . .

"Bloodhounds!" Mojo whirled around. "It's bloodhounds!"

"It moved! I saw it! It moved! It really did!" Juanita could hardly contain herself. "It was like a . . . a fluttering, you know? Just a little flutter along its side. Not more than a twitch. But I saw it! I really did! You're right, Grandmother! It's beating! My magic heart is really beating!"

Juanita turned to the old woman and hugged her. Her eyes were shining. "This is the most wonderful thing that's ever happened to me!" Juanita bubbled. "The most wonderful thing in my whole life! A living heart! Just think! A real living heart! And it's mine!"

This about Juanita Vásquez: She was missing something.

At first Juanita believed what she was missing was the right shade of skin. This was when she was growing up dirt poor in Presidio, Texas, watching her mother and father scratch out a living picking cantaloupes. She felt then if only she had the right shade of skin—and the language to go with it—she wouldn't be missing anything. That she would be complete.

But later—after she had seen a little more of the world—Juanita decided it wasn't skin color she was missing after all, but money. It was because she believed it was money she was missing that she went to work for Nuncio smuggling drugs across the Rio Grande.

But now Juanita wasn't so sure about skin color or money, either one. It had come to her as she stood at Grandmother's rickety kitchen table holding the pickle jar in her hands that maybe what she was missing was something she had never even thought of before. Not until now. Something more precious than skin or money. Something so rare that it had never even occurred to her that she was missing it: significance.

Mojo hurried back. "We've gotta get out of here fast," he announced breathlessly.

Grandmother frowned. "Wait. I hear something."

"That's what I'm trying to tell you. I think maybe it's bloodhounds. I think maybe it's the law."

"Bloodhounds?" Juanita turned towards Mojo. "You think you hear bloodhounds? Out here?" She peered disbelievingly at him.

Grandmother raised her hand. "Be quiet for a minute and listen."

"Stray dogs," Juanita said after a time, giving Mojo a contemptuous look. "Sounds like a pack of stray dogs to me."

"No." Grandmother shook her head. "Not dogs. The coyotes eat any stray dogs. Not coyotes either."

The baying sound came again. More clearly this time. Deep and throaty.

"See? It is bloodhounds. And they're coming this way."

"No." Grandmother shook her head firmly. "Not bloodhounds. No. These are the cries of . . . something else."

"Something else?" Mojo wondered.

"I think . . . it could be . . . yes . . . it must be. Hellhounds."

"Hellhounds?" Mojo frowned. "What in the world are hellhounds?"

"Demons from the deepest depths of Hell," Grandmother said serenely. "Terrible, black twisted creatures with teeth like daggers. They come up in packs when the moon rises to roam the earth and rip out the souls of those who oppose the Great Deceiver. These must have been attracted by the beating of our blessed heart."

The baying came again. Stronger. Closer. Winding upwards into an angry, piercing scream.

Even Juanita's eyes grew a little larger.

Mojo grabbed Grandmother's car keys off the table and Juanita by the arm.

"Let's motor!" Mojo said.

4

Narn stopped the Bronco on the crest of a low hill and got out. He leaned across the roof on his elbows. The desert stretched away before him, a flat sea frozen by moonlight. He waited, idly twirling his cinnamon toothpick with his lips. He didn't have to wait long.

The baying rose from the mountains to the north, the Sierra Diablo, and floated across the broad plain. The sound was eerily hollow, remote as a freight train. Narn listened for a long minute, then measured the distance by sighting along his thumb. Five miles at least, he estimated. A long way for a sound to carry, even across flat land.

The baying fell.

Rose again.

Narn frowned. It was obviously an animal, but what kind of animal he couldn't imagine. It wasn't wolves or a mountain lion or anything else that could have wandered up from Mexico or down from the Rockies. It wasn't any animal he was familiar with, and Narn was familiar with most every kind of animal.

Narn rolled his toothpick with his tongue and thought about it. Whatever it was, it was a hunter. A hunter following a scent, moving fast.

Too fast.

Narn scowled. Something was wrong here. He marked a line on the Bronco's dusty top between himself and the animal. He waited a minute by the luminous dial on his wristwatch, then marked a new line. He estimated the distance and computed the speed of the creature from triangulation. His scowl deepened. He did another triangulation. Then another. He computed the creature's speed yet again and still wasn't satisfied. Something was off.

Narn spit the toothpick out and crawled back inside the Bronco. He switched on the ignition and pulled out. No animal could move that fast. No animal on the face of the earth. None.

Narn eased the Bronco forward and resumed tracking the footprints. The creature was west and north of him, heading southwest. If the footprints continued due west, he was bound to cross its trail somewhere ahead.

Narn picked up as much speed as he dared.

The eastern horizon was turning to ash grey.

Mojo's hands were white on the steering wheel. He had a queer feeling in the pit of his stomach. Mojo felt like a man driving a Yugo down a one-lane street who has just looked in the rearview mirror and seen a runaway cement truck bearing down on him.

"Slow down!" Juanita ordered as the Impala bounced

out of the rutted track and then back into it. Mojo fought to hold the wheel straight. The sound of brush breaking against the undercarriage was a constant roar.

"I said, slow down!" Juanita repeated angrily. "Are you trying to kill us?!"

"Is something wrong?" Grandmother wondered from the back seat.

Mojo peered into the rearview mirror. The shadow was still there. Still behind them. Still coming on. The shadow topped a distant rise and for an instant Mojo could see long galloping legs. Then the huge shadow was gone, merged back into the predawn murk. Mojo turned back to the road. No question about it. It was gaining.

Mojo pressed the accelerator down as far as he dared. His hands were shaking almost as badly as the Impala.

"What's wrong with you? Have you lost your mind?" Juanita glared at him.

"There's something back there. Following us," Mojo told her grimly, fighting the wheel as the Impala jolted across a chuckhole. "Something big."

Juanita peered over the seatback. "I don't see anything." Then: "Are you sure you aren't imagining things?"

"There's something there. Believe me."

Juanita squinted into the shadows. "Well, I sure don't see it."

The sun rose. A paper-thin sliver of light peeking over the edge of the flat plain to the east. The sunlight glinted off the Impala's windshield. Off the gypsum topsoil. Off the silver creosote and slick mesquite thorns. Something screamed.

The scream rose with the sun. It was long and terrible and very close, not more than a few hundred yards behind them. Mojo's hands jerked involuntarily on the wheel.

"My God!" Juanita's head whipped around. "What was that?!"

"Holy Mother protect us!" Grandmother crossed herself.

Mojo peered into the mirror. The edge of sunlight was sweeping across the desert, a blazing broom incinerating the darkness as it passed. The light intensified. Mojo searched the road behind them, but the shadow was gone. There was nothing behind them now but brush and sky and vast flat emptiness.

Mojo sighed with relief and let up on the gas.

The Impala slowed with a bump.

The rest of the sun came boiling up over the horizon.

By the time Narn had finished searching the shack the sun was already halfway up the eastern sky and the temperature approaching ninety.

Narn wiped the sweat from his forehead as he stepped from the shack's front door. He slipped on a pair of aviator sunglasses. Sniffed the air. He could still smell ozone.

Narn tossed his flashlight onto the front seat of the Bronco and paused to urinate into a clump of tall weeds. He returned to the doorway of the shack and examined a maze of footprints in the dust there.

Narn located the most recent set of footprints and followed them around the corner of the shack. The footprints led to a two-rutted track along the side of the house. There were tire tracks in the ruts. Narn followed the ruts. Found an oil spot where a car had been parked. The footprints ended beside the oil spot.

Narn pulled a notepad from his pocket and made a quick sketch of the tire tracks, using his ballpoint pen to measure tread depth. He replaced the notepad and followed the tire tracks out past the rear of the shack and into the desert. He followed the tracks until he was certain that the car that had made them was heading due south, towards the interstate.

Narn had turned back and was on his way to the Bronco when he noticed a second set of tracks. He stepped over a hedge of creosote to examine them. At first he thought the tracks had been made by a piece of heavy equipment, but the more he looked at them the more unlikely that seemed. There was no piece of equipment that made a perfectly round six-inch depression every six to seven feet. Certainly no animal.

Narn squatted down and poked a finger into one of the depressions and dug out some soil from the bottom. He compared it to some soil from nearer the surface. Damper. The tracks were new, then. Like the tire tracks, they had probably been made earlier this morning. Had yet to spend a day under the Texas sun.

Narn stood up. He turned in a circle, searching the wide horizons. There was nothing to be seen. Nothing to be heard. Nothing moving, even though he could see for miles.

Narn followed the tracks.

He followed the tracks to where they ended on a piece of open ground some fifty feet to the south. The tracks did not turn aside or double back. They just stopped. The tracks stopped as though whatever had made them had vanished into thin air.

Narn kicked at the barren ground where the tracks ended. The ground crumbled easily beneath his boot toe. He squinted and shook his head and then kicked the ground again. He stood quietly for a moment, then began walking in a circle around the spot. Narn walked around the tracks once, then stepped out five long strides and began a new circle. He continued walking in ever-widening circles until he had covered all the ground for over a hundred feet in every direction.

He found nothing.

Narn returned to the strange tracks and sighted the line they made across the desert. The tracks led back towards the northeast. Back towards the Sierra Diablo. They were distinct, easy to follow, two rows of deep, widely spaced, and perfectly round depressions.

Narn stared at the tracks for a while longer, then gave up with a shrug and started back. He shook his head. He popped a new toothpick into his mouth and chewed on it as he walked.

It made no sense.

Narn reached into his pocket and pulled out a white business card he had found stuck inside the freezer compartment of the otherwise empty refrigerator. His only lead.

Narn read the card again. The card was from the Social Services Office of the Archdiocese of El Paso. A priest's name was printed in the lower right corner: Father Jeffrey Huerta.

5

Father Jeffrey Huerta was a chubby little man with rosy cheeks, a stubby nose, and a condescending manner. He reminded Mojo more of a postal clerk than a priest.

". . . and that's why I can only suggest that you take this, ah, ah, thing"—Father Jeff shot a withering glance at the pickle jar sitting in the center of his desk—"over to the biology department at the university. I'm sure they'll be able to tell you what it is."

"Oh, but we already know what it is. It's a heart," Grandmother said. "What we need to find out is whose. Whose heart is it?"

"Whose. I see . . ." Father Jeff tried to look down his nose at Grandmother, but, not having much of a nose to work with, he did a rather poor job of it. Grandmother never noticed.

"That's right." Juanita nodded eagerly. "We've got to find out whose heart it is so we can pray to it."

"Pray to it?" Father Jeff rocked back in his chair. His lips puckered in disapproval. He scowled at Juanita. "Now, see here," he said sternly. "I know you two ladies mean well, but I must warn you. The Church has some very strict rules concerning—"

"Don't you have any books on the saints around here?" Juanita interrupted. "If we had a book on the saints, we could just look through it until we found whichever ones had their hearts cut out and work from there."

"Now, that's a good idea." Grandmother nodded to Juanita. "That way we wouldn't have to bother Father Huerta." She paused for a moment. Then brightly: "I know. There were lots of books out there by the desk of that nice lady who showed us in. The saint we're seeking is probably in one of those books. I'm sure she wouldn't mind if we looked through them. In fact, I think I'll go ask her right now."

Grandmother pushed her chair back.

Father Jeff blanched. "Wait!" Father Jeff held up a warning hand. It was obvious to Mojo that Father Jeff was not thrilled at the thought of Grandmother and Juanita and their heart hanging around his office all day and reading his books.

"Yes?" Grandmother paused halfway out of her chair.

"I just remembered something. I mean, I think I may have an even better idea."

"Oh?" Grandmother sat back down.

"Yes, I don't think my books would be of any help. Not at all," Father Jeff said quickly. "And besides, there is a priest up in New Mexico—an old classmate of mine, actually—who's quite an authority on these, ah, these things. Now, let me look. I know I have his address somewhere . . ." He pulled open a desk drawer and began to rummage through it.

"I don't know about this." Juanita turned to Grandmother. "If this priest here doesn't know about the heart, then why would another one who went to the same school know any more? I think maybe we should look in those books anyway."

"Don't worry," Grandmother said reassuringly. "Father Jeff is a wonderful priest, a true man of God. He comes to my home to make sure that I'm in good health and to bring me the Holy Sacrament at least once every four or five years. If he says this other priest can tell us about the heart, then I'm confident he can."

"Here it is," Father Jeff announced. He had an open address book in his hand. "Simon Fitz. Brother Simon Fitz. He's a monk in the Franciscan Monastery west of Socorro. I only have a P.O. box number for him, but I'm sure someone in Socorro will be able to tell you how to find the monastery."

"And you're positive this guy knows about saints' hearts?" Juanita asked, her nose wrinkling with mistrust.

"Oh, absolutely!" Father Jeff said. "Brother Simon is an authority on religious relics. He's even written a book on pieces of the true cross. Why, you could travel the world over and not find a better man than Brother Simon to show your, er, heart to!"

"He's written a book, huh?" Juanita asked, impressed.

"Yes, indeed. Brother Simon is a noted author."

"Ummh." Juanita thought about it for a moment. "Well, maybe—if he's really an expert—maybe we ought to forget the books for a while and go see him first,'' she said slowly to Grandmother.

''Oh, yes, you should,'' Father Jeff said, leaning across his desk to add weight to his words. ''There's no question, but you should.''

''Then we'll do it!'' Grandmother said eagerly. ''We'll go to New Mexico right away!''

Mojo rolled his eyes, but he went along with it.

This about Joseph ''Mojo'' Birdsong: He could have cut out. He had opportunity. He had the car keys in his pocket. He could have slipped away from Grandmother and Juanita on the way out of the Archdiocese of El Paso building. He could have said to hell with hearts in pickle jars and monks in New Mexico and stolen Grandmother's old Impala from the lot where it was parked. He could have driven the Impala across the border to Juárez and sold it even without a title. He could have taken the money and bought a bus ticket to Cancún or Las Vegas or Cleveland and been long gone from West Texas and Machete Ray Castillo and his Uncle Ort and all the others who were on his tail.

He could have.

But he didn't.

And it wasn't because the thought didn't cross Mojo's mind, because it did. And it wasn't because he was afraid, because he wasn't. And it wasn't because he believed the thing in the pickle jar was a demon or a heart, because he didn't.

It was because of Juanita.

Imagine that.

Mojo stopped at a pay phone in the lobby of the archdiocese on their way out.

The phone rang twice before a gruff voice answered.

"Hello? . . . Hello? . . ." There was a long pause. Then: "Is there anybody there?"

It was Uncle Ort. He was okay.

". . . Mojo? Is that you, Mojo? . . . It is, isn't it?! It is you, you thievin' little ingrate!" Uncle Ort sputtered. "You won't get away with it, boy! No, sir! I've sworn out an arrest warrant on your sorry butt, Mr. Serpent's Tooth! The cops are gonna stomp you flatter than a dead cat in a loading zone, Mr. Doper Dealer! They're gonna throw your scumbucket ass so far back into prison that you'll have to buy a ticket to see the sun! They're gonna—"

Mojo hung the pay phone up.

Mojo whistled as he strolled across the lobby to where Grandmother and Juanita were waiting. He was broke, busted, and on the lam, but at least he wasn't a murderer. Not unless you counted the two creeps in the Suburban.

"You're sure you won't change your mind about this? I'd feel a whole lot safer in Mexico," Mojo said, wheeling the Impala past an El Paso city limits sign followed quickly by a green and white I-25 marker. They were moving through the outskirts of the city now, past the last few hamburger/burrito stands and struggling subdivisions, heading north up the valley of the Rio Grande towards New Mexico.

"No. We have to go to this monastery first. To find out about the heart," Juanita told him firmly.

"Later, then? After you talk to this monk guy?" Mojo pressed.

"Later. Sure. We'll definitely go to Mexico later." She gave him a reassuring smile.

Mojo nodded, but he wasn't all that reassured. He was nervous about this whole deal. He figured New Mexico wasn't much better than West Texas as far as avoiding Ray Castillo was concerned. In fact, New Mexico might even be worse since it was where Poteet had wanted the stuff delivered. There might be even more dopers working for Castillo in New Mexico than in Texas.

Mojo sighed. Maybe he should have stolen the Impala after all.

The last houses fell behind them and they sped through an empty desert bordered by rock-faced mountains on the east and the silver, snaking river on the west.

Grandmother began to snore softly in the back seat.

El Paso passed into New Mexico into a hot, dusty afternoon.

They spent forty-five minutes in Socorro before finding an old woman behind the counter of a 7-Eleven who said she'd heard of a monastery in the mountains west of there and directed them onto the Magdalena Highway.

The sun was low in the west when they passed through the village of Datil and took a left onto a two-lane blacktop that led them up a steep climb across the Continental Divide and into the towering pines of the Gila National Forest.

The sun was just setting into the woods on the crest of a high ridge, feathering the green tops with red and gold and orange, when they pulled off the blacktop and rolled into the gravel parking lot of the Tres Cruces Franciscan Monastery.

6

The Tres Cruces Franciscan Monastery was a large, colonial-style building set well back in the pines. The entry hall, tiled in worn linoleum, reminded Mojo of a county hospital, the kind of big-city welfare hospital with asylum-green walls, scuff-brown doors, and dim, go-blind yellow lighting that no one went to unless desperate, destitute, or within five minutes of death.

The only things in the hallway hinting that this was a monastery were the santos. The hall was lined with wooden statues: dozens of stern saints, anguished Christs, and sorrowing Madonnas staring down at Mojo through icy marble eyes. Almost as many as in Grandmother's pictures. Most of the santos were of the fair-haired, white-skinned European variety, but more than a few were decidedly Mexican-looking: dark, Indian-faced saints, most of them pierced by thorns and daggers and nails and spears and dripping with bright-painted blood.

It was not the sort of decor to put Mojo at ease.

They had been waiting in the entry hall for only a short while when Brother Simon came. The monk was not so old and certainly not so cold as Mojo had expected. He was, in fact, a rather ordinary-looking middle-aged man with thinning hair and a studious look. When Grandmother explained about the heart and how Father Huerta had sent them, Brother Simon invited them into the monastery's library.

"Interesting." Brother Simon turned the jar. He had large, inquisitive eyes. "You know, it does look something like a heart."

"It's sorta tricky. You have to watch it close," Juanita advised him. "It doesn't exactly beat, more like flutters. And it only does that every once in a while."

"I see . . ."

"The blue light is the sign of its beatification," Grandmother volunteered.

"Yes . . ."

They gave him a few moments more to examine the heart. Then Grandmother asked: "Can you tell us whose it is? Which saint?"

"Saint?" Brother Simon looked up at her, the thick glasses perched on the end of his long nose, giving him a scholarly look. "What makes you think it's a saint's heart?"

"Because it is," Grandmother told him simply.

This about Grandmother: She had no doubts. The Virgin, the saints, God Himself, were as real to her as the movie stars on cable TV were to Mojo, as California was to Juanita. Grandmother did not believe. There was no need for that. She knew.

"Yes . . . well . . . you're positive you saw it move?" Brother Simon asked with a frown. "It wasn't just the liquid sloshing?"

"Oh, no. This heart definitely beats," Grandmother said. "Look closer."

"Closer . . . I see . . ." Brother Simon sounded doubtful but he bent down and studied the jar anyway. After a long moment he shrugged. Was just opening his mouth when suddenly he froze.

"What is it?" Juanita asked. "Did you see it?"

"I saw something," Brother Simon said without lifting his head. Then: "There! Like you said! A flutter! A ripple, really. It was subtle, but I'm fairly certain it wasn't caused by wave action." He sounded surprised. Borderline amazed.

"You see?" Grandmother smiled broadly. "I told you. It does beat."

"It does?" Mojo was taken aback. In spite of being a monk, Brother Simon had seemed like a reasonable person. Surely he had made a mistake here. Surely he—

"There!" Brother Simon exclaimed. "Again! A full contraction this time! It's true!" Suddenly the monk was as impassioned as a Baptist preacher passing the hat.

Mojo leaned closer. He felt like a fool since he was pretty certain the thing in the pickle jar was only a piece of salt pork some old woman had conned Juanita into believing was a demon. He eyed the thing. The white lump still had the blue flickering light on its surface which he had to admit was pretty strange since he had once seen a telephone pole struck by lightning and it had quit glowing after only a few seconds. Still, who knew with salt pork or whatever the hell the thing was? Maybe it really was an old dried-up heart, and maybe old dried-up hearts could hold an electrical charge for a long time. Days even. Who knew? Certainly not Mojo. Still, it was crazy, he thought. Just crazy to even consider that—

"Did you see that?!" Brother Simon jerked his head up. His eyes were blazing, his glasses threatening to fall off the end of his nose. "That was even stronger than the last one! And there it goes again!"

"It's beating!" Juanita was thrilled. "It's not just fluttering! It's really, actually beating!"

What the—?! Mojo's eyes widened. He had seen it too. He could hardly believe it, but he had. The thing had contracted! And now it was doing it again! It was getting stronger too. It didn't even looked like a stewed prune anymore.

Mojo rocked back in his chair, amazed. He wasn't sure how Brother Simon had done it, but apparently the monk had flipped the thing's switch.

Juanita threw her arms around Mojo and kissed him. Hard. On the mouth.

Mojo's amazement grew.

"Oh, Mojo," Juanita breathed, pulling back only slightly. "Isn't it wonderful?"

Mojo gazed into her eyes. He had to agree that it certainly was.

Once the excitement had worn down, Brother Simon told grandmother he wanted them to stay overnight so he could consult the library's books for references to miraculous hearts. His eyes were bright as he spoke. His cheeks were flushed. He kept rubbing his hands together. He assured them finding rooms was no problem since there were far more rooms than monks, the monastery having been built in a time when monkdom was more appealing than the present.

Grandmother was agreeable. She told Brother Simon that she hadn't gotten much sleep the night before due to being pursued by hellhounds and that they would accept his offer gladly.

Another monk came, a small but thickset man with a stiff walk, runny eyes, and red hair. He introduced himself to them as the abbot of Tres Cruces. Then led them to a set of three empty rooms near the front entry. The room Mojo was given was small but clean, with a single bed, an ancient two-drawer chest, and a screened window that opened over a narrow walled garden running the length of the building.

As soon as the abbot was gone, Mojo stripped down to his underwear and fell onto the narrow bed. He stretched out and sighed. He closed his eyes. He hadn't realized how tired he was until now.

Mojo rolled over and, tucking the pillow up underneath his head, fell asleep in no time.

Mojo had a dream. In his dream he was standing in the center of a vast marble cathedral, a great hall lit only by a few sputtering candles. At first he thought he was alone. Then, around him, in the shadowy naves, beside the tall pillars, lounging against the white-draped altar table, he saw saints. And not just regular saints either. These saints were all dark-skinned and flat-eyed and bleeding from thorns and daggers and spears and God knew what. Dark Mexican saints like those in the monastery's entry. The saints were watching Mojo. Studying him. Mojo felt as though he was on center stage. Or sitting on a platter in the middle of a banquet table. He could feel the saints' eyes on him, see them gleaming in the half-light.

No, he realized suddenly in the manner of dreams, not just watching, but weighing. The Mexican saints—he could hear the soft drip of their blood on the cold marble floors—were judging him, weighing his soul.

Mojo peered down and saw that his soul was lying in the palm of his hand. It was a small, flimsy thing, brown and crumpled like a wadded-up candy wrapper. Pretty pathetic actually, but heavy as a stone. He understood that the soul was weighing him down, dragging him into the marble floor that was suddenly as soft as muck and pulsating with an angry red glow. His feet had already disappeared. It was as if he was wading in marble.

Mojo, not anxious to be swallowed up by a floor, shook his hand, but the soul stuck to it, clinging as if it had been glued. He shook his hand again, harder this time, but the soul wouldn't let go, sticking to him as tenaciously as the tar baby. He windmilled his arm but that didn't help either. Fear shot through him. He was sinking. He couldn't get rid of the damn thing.

He tried pulling the soul off with his other hand but failed. The soul was slippery, hard to hold, evading his grip as though coated with Crisco. He tried to shout for help but no sound came. He was floundering now, sinking deeper and deeper into the marble. Up to his ankles . . . up to his knees . . . his feet growing hotter . . . and hotter . . .

Mojo awoke with a start.

He opened his eyes. Blinked. Sat up. Rubbed his

face. Moonlight was streaming through a small window beside his head. Damp sheets were tangled around his feet.

For a moment Mojo didn't know where he was. Didn't recognize the room.

Then it came to him.

Mojo shivered once, remembering his dream, then glanced over at the door. He listened but there was only silence.

He shivered again. Late. Middle of the night. Everyone asleep.

Mojo yawned widely. Fell back onto the narrow bed. Closed his eyes again. Faint echoes of the dream came back to haunt him: a glimpse of a vast, shadowy place, of eyes in the dark, of a vague sense of unease. He tried to remember the details of the dream but all he could remember was that it had been one of those deals where you try to run but your feet don't move.

He shook his head, forcing the remnants of the dream from his mind. Was just nodding off again . . .

A sharp click.

Mojo's eyes flicked open. He turned towards the window. Waited. After a few seconds there was another click. A brief, tiny shadow on the glass.

A pebble. Someone was throwing pebbles at his window.

Mojo rolled out of bed and padded over to the window in his bare feet. The world outside was bathed in moonlight and shadows. The tall forest blocked his view less than a hundred feet away. He looked down. Just beyond the narrow garden wall there was a short, cleared area between the monastery and the forest. There was a figure standing there, just at the edge of the forest. The figure was looking up at Mojo's window.

It was Juanita.

She was naked.

Mojo had to look twice before he believed it, but it was true.

Juanita's copper skin gleamed in the moonlight. He could see her face clearly. He could see the dark aureoles of her breasts, the even darker triangle at the base of her stomach.

Juanita saw him looking down and smiled up at him. She tossed her head, her long black hair swinging free across her shoulders. She pursed her lips and threw him a kiss. She made a very small but very suggestive bump with her hips.

Mojo's mouth fell open. Mojo realized Juanita was not just naked, but nekkid, the difference being that a naked person simply has no clothes on while a nekkid person has no clothes on for a very specific purpose.

Juanita waved to Mojo to follow as she disappeared under the shadow of the trees.

Mojo threw some clothes on, even though he was pretty sure he wasn't going to need them.

Mojo pulled the blanket off his bed and opened his door and tiptoed down the long hall to the front door of the monastery.

The front door of the monastery was locked with a bolt, but Mojo was able to ease it back with hardly any sound at all. He slipped out the front door and through the gate and around the garden wall to the side of the monastery that bordered the forest. He walked down the wall, looking for the spot where Juanita had disappeared into the woods.

Mojo was almost to the end of the monastery before

he finally stopped and paused. The forest was an impenetrable black void. He had no idea where Juanita had gone. He stepped towards the forest. He cupped his mouth.

"Juanita?" he called softly.

He waited, but there was no answer. The mountain air was cold. He hardly noticed.

"Juanita?" A little louder.

"Mojo." Her voice was distant. It came from somewhere up in the trees. On the slope above him. It sounded peculiar. Strained.

Second thoughts? Anticipation?

Mojo moved down the tree line in the direction of the voice and found a break in the darkness. There was a narrow footpath leading up into the woods. He took it.

It was pitch-black dark under the trees. Mojo stepped carefully up the path, feeling his way with his feet as much as anything. Limbs and branches brushed against him. He waded through the brush and wondered why Juanita was leading him up into the woods instead of just coming to his room. More romantic, he supposed. Girls were strange about things like that: candles, flowers, nights under the stars . . . girls were crazy about all that stuff. Maybe she had found a meadow up above the woods where they could lie on a blanket in the moonlight. Maybe that was it. Maybe she was leading him up to a beautiful meadow filled with flowers and moonlight. Maybe that was why she a was leading him away from the monastery.

Or maybe she was a screamer.

Mojo picked up the pace. Mojo felt his way around a sharp turn in the path and stopped. There she was.

Juanita. Still nude. Still beautiful. Outlined against the night sky at the top of the trail.

Juanita was standing with her legs slightly parted and her hands on her hips. Her head was held high. The moon shone on her hair and other parts. She was looking down the trail at Mojo. Waiting for him.

"Mojo." Juanita opened her arms as she called his name.

Mojo hurried eagerly up the path towards her. He hadn't gone more than a couple of steps, however, when something large and black detached itself from a tree just ahead of him and came swooping down the path.

Mojo stopped. The thing was coming straight for his head! He ducked.

Juanita hissed.

The flying thing flashed through a shaft of moonlight and Mojo saw that it was only an owl. The owl passed inches above his head, just missing him. He felt the wind from its broad wings across his back.

Mojo stayed crouched down for a second longer, then raised back up and glanced over his shoulder. The owl was gone, swallowed up by the night. The path behind him was a black void.

He turned towards Juanita.

Juanita was still waiting at the top of the trail. She opened her arms to him again. She motioned him forward.

Mojo hesitated. That hiss . . . that sound Juanita had just made . . . He squinted into the darkness.

"Come to me, Mojo. Come," she called urgently.

Mojo hesitated again. Something was definitely wrong. Juanita didn't sound like herself. She sounded more like a creaking door than a woman.

Mojo frowned. Maybe she was just nervous. Or anxious. He shrugged. He took a tentative step forward. Then quickly took it back. He had the strangest feeling . . .

"I . . . said . . . come . . . to . . . me!!"

Mojo gulped. This time there was no question. It definitely wasn't Juanita's voice. It wasn't anybody's voice. He took a quick step back.

The woman who looked like Juanita took a quick step forward. Moonlight caught her face and Mojo could see she was furious. Her nose was flared. Her lips were pulled back from her teeth. Her eyes were slitted.

Then Mojo saw something else. Mojo saw the shadows on either side of Juanita move. Move with her. Rustle across the ground behind her. Part of Juanita? Or what he had thought was Juanita?

Mojo turned and ran.

Something screamed in rage behind him. It wasn't Juanita who screamed. It wasn't even remotely human.

Mojo flew down the path, brush slashing at him. He saw a break in the darkness ahead, a crack of moonlight, and ran for it. He used his hands to fend off the heavier limbs.

Mojo broke through the brush and tore down the hill.

He leaped a final border of two-foot-high pine seedlings and stumbled out into the cleared area in front of the garden wall. He could hear something crashing down the path after him. The something was making an unearthly whirring sound. It was breaking brush and tree limbs as it came.

Mojo raced down the wall towards the front of the monastery. Towards the front door. He heard the thing break out of the undergrowth behind him. He heard it come scrabbling after him across the rocky ground. Whatever it was, it had a lot more legs than he did.

Mojo resisted the temptation to turn around. He drove

his legs as he had never driven them before. His knees churned like pistons. The far end of the wall was just ahead in the moonlight.

Mojo drove for the end of the wall.

And then he could feel it. Smell it. It was a hot, fetid, stinking wind coming up behind him. Coming up like a truck on a freeway. Coming up so fast that he might as well have been sitting down waiting for it. He realized then that he wasn't going to make it, that the thing would have him before he even reached the end of the fence, never to mention the front door.

A pale hand shot out from the wall just ahead of Mojo. Mojo didn't even have time to be surprised. The hand snagged him gafflike as he raced past and jerked him into the wall. Only it wasn't a wall. It was a narrow gate.

Mojo slipped through the narrow gate like a letter through a mail slot.

Something screamed, a huge, angry bellow.

Mojo stumbled to a halt. He was in the walled garden that surrounded the monastery, being held by the shoulder by a shadowy figure in a monk's robe.

"You're safe now." The monk gave Mojo's shoulder a reassuring squeeze. "It can't follow you here. This is consecrated ground. Understand?" Using his other hand, the monk latched the gate with a firm metal click.

Mojo nodded, but he wasn't really listening. His attention was on the thin wooden gate. The flimsy-looking gate. Waiting to see what might come over or under or through it.

Mojo had no confidence in consecrated ground.

Seconds passed without a repeat of the sound of many legs on hard ground or strange whirring noises or anything else. The moonlit top of the garden wall remained empty. The woods beyond the wall remained dark and silent.

Finally Mojo shook off the monk's hand and stepped forward and sniffed the air. It smelled of pine and cold, clear altitude, a faint whiff of roses. Clean as new snow. He moved closer to the garden gate and sniffed again. Still nothing.

It wasn't out there.

The thing had gone without leaving.

"This way." The monk took Mojo's arm and led him up the garden towards the front of the monastery. Mojo, not exactly shell-shocked but close, let himself be led.

They had reached the corner before Mojo had gathered his wits enough to wonder: "What the . . . hell was that?"

"The beast," the monk said grimly. He led Mojo up the front steps and onto the broad lip of the doorway. Mojo could see his face clearly now. The monk had a thin, unlined face with high cheekbones and a long aristocratic nose. The top of his head was shaved and he was wearing a robe of cheap sackcloth with a rope belt. His eyes were a pale blue. He was probably older than he looked.

"Go inside and don't come out before sunrise," the monk instructed Mojo. "The beast fears only light."

He turned to go.

"Wait a minute." Mojo touched the monk's sleeve. "Have I met you before? Were you at dinner tonight?"

"Of course." The monk hesitated on the lower steps. He smiled at Mojo. "I'm always there. But I can see you don't remember me. No matter. Outsiders often think we Brothers all look alike."

"No, I'm sure I would've remembered you," Mojo

protested. ''I would've remembered that robe. That's not the standard issue.''

''Goodbye.'' The monk stepped down off the steps.

''Wait a second! You never did tell me what that thing was. You just said the beast. What kind of beast?''

''Go inside,'' the monk said over his shoulder. He waved as he passed around the corner of the building.

''Hey! Thanks!'' Mojo called after him, suddenly remembering his manners.

Mojo stood quietly, staring at the empty garden for a long moment. It was weird. That wave. That hand. The monk's hand only had two fingers. The thumb and one other. All the rest of his fingers had been cut off cleanly at the bottom joint.

Surely he would have remembered a shabby monk with three fingers missing?

The big entry door behind Mojoe creaked open. Bright light spilled out onto the steps. A plump face peeked around the edge of the door. It was the red-headed abbot. He had a flashlight in his hand.

Mojo turned to face him.

''Mr. Birdsong? What are you doing out here?''

''Well . . .'' Mojo wasn't sure where to begin.

''We heard an animal. It sounded close.'' The abbot eased out the door. Looked cautiously around.

''It *was* close. It was after me,'' Mojo told him.

''After you? Really? How?''

''Well, it's a long story. I was up in my room, see, when I heard this noise at the window. I got up and—''

''Mojo? Is that you?'' Juanita appeared in the doorway. Her face was pale. She looked worried.

''Yeah, it's me.''

''What are you doing out there? Didn't you hear that

scream? Brother Timothy told us it might be a mountain lion. You should come inside, where it's safe."

Mojo shook his head. "It wasn't a mountain lion. I was just telling the abbot here about it. You see, I heard this noise at my window and . . ." He looked into Juanita's eyes. Juanita was staring expectantly at him. Waiting.

Mojo's tongue dried up.

Oh, shit.

What was he going to say next? What could he say? Could he say, "And then I went to the window and saw you down here buck naked doing the bump and grind so I got my blanket and went outside and followed you up into the woods so we could do it only you turned into a monster"?

Not hardly.

"And then?" she prompted.

"And then . . . ah . . . and then I came down to investigate but I didn't find anything," he concluded lamely.

"By yourself? Weren't you afraid?"

"Somebody had to do it." Mojo shrugged. "But don't worry. Whatever it was, it's long gone now."

"You went out there in the dark looking for the lion? By yourself? Oh, Mojo! You could have been killed!"

Mojo didn't say anything but she was right. He had come closer to being killed than she would ever know.

Juanita slipped out the door. Ran down the steps and, before Mojo knew what was happening, threw her arms around him and hugged him.

Juanita pressed herself against Mojo. Tightly. "I'm sorry about all those bad things I said about you," she whispered against his neck.

"That's okay." She felt good. Very good. Soft and

warm. Maybe not as soft and warm as she might have felt lying on a blanket in a meadow underneath the stars, but soft and warm enough.

The long hall was crowded with chattering monks when they returned. Two of the monks moved aside to let Mojo and Juanita through.

"Joseph! I'm relieved to see you." Grandmother came up, pushing her way through the throng. "I've been worried about you. You weren't in your room."

"It's all right, Grandmother," Juanita told her. "Mojo protected us. He went out into the woods and chased the lion away."

Grandmother leaned towards Mojo. "Is this true? You frightened away a lion?"

Mojo wasn't listening. He was staring at a wooden santo of Saint Francis by the entry door. He was staring at Saint Francis' outstretched hand. Three of the hand's fingers were missing, broken off at the bottom joint.

"That santo." Mojo pointed to it.

"Yes?" One of the monks turned to him.

"What happened to its fingers?"

"Its fingers? Oh, now I see. Yes, that's very common with santos from Mexico. Most of them have several fingers broken off. It's what happens when a prayer to the saint goes unanswered."

"You mean somebody broke the statue's fingers because the saint didn't answer his prayer?"

"Exactly."

"They take revenge on a saint? They break his fingers?" This sounded more like the Mafia than religion to Mojo.

"Well . . . yes. But it works both ways. If a prayer is answered, the beneficiary will often bring the santo flowers or maybe even have a *retablo*, a small painting, done in his honor. Reward him for his generosity."

Mojo shook his head. Being a saint in Mexico was apparently a tough business. He resolved he would pick flowers in the morning and take them to the santo of Saint Francis. It was the least he could do.

"You're all up! Good! Good!" Brother Simon came bounding up the hall towards them. He was smiling. "I have something interesting. I think I may have found a reference to your heart!"

7

"I'm sorry, but there's nothing more to tell you. They left early this morning," Brother Simon told Narn.

"They didn't say where they were headed?"

"Not specifically, no."

"The abbot said they asked to see you. That you met with them," Narn persisted.

"Yes. That's right. It concerned a religious matter."

"A religious matter?"

The monk met Narn's level gaze. "That's confidential, of course. Privileged information. A matter between a member of the faithful and a priest."

"You're not a priest. You're a monk," Narn countered.

"Believe me, the relationship is the same. Besides, even if it wasn't, I don't have to tell you anything, do I? The Texas Rangers don't have any legal jurisdiction in New Mexico, do they?"

Narn sighed. He had him there.

"That's true," Narn admitted.

"Then I think you'd better leave." Brother Simon stood up. "As I said before, there's nothing more I can tell you."

"All right." Narn rose slowly to his feet. His Stetson was in his hands. He put it on his head and started for the library door.

"Thanks for your time."

"Of course." Brother Simon watched him go.

"Oh." Narn paused at the door. "If you happen to hear from them, just call the number I left on the table and leave a message."

Brother Simon nodded.

Narn was under no illusion he would do it.

The morning was bright outside the monastery. The sky above a deep, cloudless blue. Narn stopped on the front steps and slipped on his aviator's sunglasses. He walked briskly across the graveled lot towards his Bronco, parked under the shade of a cottonwood.

He passed a small vegetable garden off to the side of the lot. The garden was bordered by a low chicken-wire fence and filled with tall tomato plants tied to stakes. There were some tracks clearly visible in the soft earth beside the fence. Narn went over to examine them.

Narn knelt beside the chicken-wire. Two rows of perfectly round, widely spaced depressions led across one corner of the vegetable garden. It only took him a few seconds to confirm what he had already guessed. The tracks were the same as those at the old Montoya woman's place.

Narn stood up. Brushed the earth from his pants. He

followed the tracks with his eye. The tracks ended on the hard surface of the parking lot, but there was no question where they were going: straight for the monastery.

There was a monk working in the garden. He was carrying a tin pail half full of red ripe tomatoes.

"Morning," Narn called.

The monk look up. Peered at Narn from under his cowl. "Good morning."

"I wonder if you could help me. Did you hear any peculiar sounds last night? Woulda sounded like a big hound baying?"

The monk approached cautiously. He was thin with sunken cheeks and grey lips. He had a large wart on the back of his left hand with a hair growing out of it. "Maybe."

"Maybe?" Narn frowned. "What's that supposed to mean?"

"It means I heard some noises, but I don't know whether it was a hound that made them. It could have been."

"What'd they sound like?"

The monk shrugged.

"Well, did anybody else hear them?"

"Sure. Everybody." He paused a second. "Brother Timothy thought it might have been a mountain lion, but then he's got an active imagination."

Narn eyed the monk. The monk had a cold, pinched face like he had spent time in the catacombs of some government agency or behind the counter of a complaints desk. Not the sort to tell you anything more than he had to, Narn figured. Not unless there was a pressing reason. Narn rubbed his chin. Decided to give him a reason. "Listen, Brother, I'm a Texas Ranger assigned to the El Paso Emergency Medical Agency, and I'm here on an important mission,'' Narn said. ''I'm looking for a Mrs. Ernesto Montoya. I believe she spent the night here last night?''

''Well, we had several guests who stayed over last night. I'm not sure about the names . . .''

''One of them was this Montoya woman. I've already talked to Brother Simon about her.'' Narn nodded confidently as if he and Brother Simon were the best of friends. ''Anyway, we—the Emergency Medical Agency, that is—gave this Mrs. Montoya some heart medicine yesterday, and it wasn't until after she'd already left the building that somebody noticed she'd been given the wrong bottle. The wrong medicine.''

''The wrong medicine? Can't that be dangerous?''

''That's right. Very dangerous. Especially in this case. That's why I was sent up here. To find her and give her the right bottle. And I gotta tell you, all the doctors are really worried. They think she may die if I don't find her quick.''

''Die?''

''That's right. That's why I'm asking around to see if any of you people might have heard her or the people she was with mention where they were going this morning.''

''Well, I did overhear them say something about Punta de Tierra at breakfast,'' the monk said thoughtfully.

''Punta de Tierra? Is that in New Mexico?''

''I think so. I've never been there, but I believe it is.''

''Great.'' Narn allowed himself a smile. ''You've been a big help, Brother. A very big help. I appreciate it.''

"That's all right. I'm always glad to help. I just hope you can find her in time."

"Oh, I will," Narn assured him. "I'll find them. I always do."

They found Punta de Tierra without any trouble. The trouble was, there was nothing there.

"This is it? This is Punta de Tierra?" Mojo wondered. He pulled the Impala off the blacktop onto a dirt shoulder. They were in a small mountain valley hemmed in by piñon-covered hills. A small stream gurgled down the center of the valley, bordering the road.

"That's what the sign said." Juanita motioned back over her shoulder at a metal highway sign.

"But there's no town. No nothing."

"Look. Look back there under those trees." Juanita pointed. "See those old walls? There was a town here. Once."

Mojo put the Impala in park. Off to the right was a flat area overgrown with cottonwoods and brush. Back beneath the trees were several crumbling adobe walls. One with a charred roof beam still mounted over it. "Chuy + Lupe" was spray-painted across its face.

"It's a ghost town," Mojo said. "Nothing left but ruins. We drove all the way from Socorro, and there's nothing here." He turned to Grandmother. "I thought that book Brother Simon gave you said there was a famous church in Punta de Tierra?"

"Yes, but the book is very old. The book says hundreds of pilgrims once came here to seek the sacred heart. But that was back in the seventeenth century. I imagine things have changed in the last three hundred years."

''Yeah,'' Mojo said, peering at the crumbling walls. ''I'd say they'd changed, all right.''

''Maybe there're some people up in the woods,'' Juanita suggested. ''Up that road.''

''What road?'' Mojo craned his neck.

''There. Between those two big trees.''

''You call that a road?'' Mojo wondered. ''Nothing there but two ruts. And check those weeds. They're waist-high. Doesn't look like anyone's been up it in years.''

''We'll see,'' Grandmother said decisively. ''We'll go up and see if anyone still lives in Punta de Tierra.''

No one did.

The ruts ran for only a few hundred feet through the shadowy cottonwoods before dead-ending at a dilapidated old church. There were no houses or people or fields or livestock visible anywhere.

Mojo parked the Impala in front of the church. The church was built of adobe. Its walls were pitted and worn by water erosion. Bird nests protruded from under its eaves. The cross on its steeple had one arm broken. One of the entry doors was hanging open from a broken, rusted hinge.

''Well, this must be it.'' Mojo turned to Grandmother, who was getting out of the car on the other side. ''This must be the famous church of Punta de Tierra, New Mexico, the home of miracles.''

Juanita, who was already out, gave him a dirty look.

Grandmother stood up beside the car and gazed around. ''Yes.'' She nodded serenely after a moment. ''It is beautiful, isn't it? A beautiful place to build a church.''

"What next?" Mojo leaned his hip against the Impala. "Back to the monastery? Santa Fe?"

"Not yet. I want to go into the church and pray first. Perhaps if we pray here, we'll be given guidance."

This sounded pretty dubious to Mojo. He doubted they would be given anything more miraculous than bug bites in the abandoned church.

"Read that passage about the heart again," he said to Juanita. "Maybe we missed something."

"Okay." She pulled an old leather-bound book from the front seat of the car. Opened it to a page marked by a strip of red ribbon. She moved her finger down the page until she found the line she was looking for.

"And in the mountains north of Santa Fe, in the Sangre de Cristo," Juanita read, "there is a small mission called San Diego de Punta de Tierra. In this remote place yet another wonderful gift has been given the Church, a sacred heart that cures all the ailments and afflictions of those who earnestly call upon Our Lady. Hundreds of pilgrims are said to come to the mission each year seeking this heart, and many souls are said to be saved because of it.

"The roads being unsafe, I myself was unable to visit the mission, but an old Indian man whom I met in Santa Fe assured me that the heart exists and that it cured his youngest daughter of a colic that brought her close to death. Also, Father Flavio Esquivel, a brother Franciscan, has assured me that the heart exists and that it is truly a blessing from Our Mother that can cure and heal."

Juanita looked up. "That's all. After that he starts in about some party he went to at the Governor's Palace."

"And when was this written? The seventeen hundreds?"

"Seventeenth century. The date on the letter is 1672."

"Well, there you go. It's probably another heart altogether. I mean, ours sure doesn't look over three hundred years old, does it?"

"The same heart or not, this heart of San Diego de Punta de Tierra is important. I feel certain of it," Grandmother said firmly. "Let's go into the church. Perhaps the Virgin will give us a sign there."

"I'll bring the heart." Juanita reached back inside the Impala and exchanged the book for her purse.

The church was dark. Filled with shadows. The only windows were small and square and set high in the walls. Bird nests blocked most of the light.

Mojo trailed behind Juanita and Grandmother up the center aisle towards the altar. Most of the rough wood pews had been ripped out and the ones that remained were cracked and splintered by age and the dry climate. Other than the few scattered pews the big room was empty. Their footsteps echoed hollowly. It seemed more like an abandoned warehouse than an abandoned church. Several names—including Chuy and Lupe again—had been carved into the soft adobe beside the broken entry door but the interior walls were unmarked. The flagstone floor was streaked with purplish droppings. Bat droppings, Mojo realized with a start.

Mojo hurried after Grandmother and Juanita.

The altar table was chiseled stone and still intact. It was set on a low dais. Grandmother spread her long skirts over the steps and was just about to settle down when a thin voice spoke: "You! You . . . have it!"

Mojo glanced quickly around. It took him a second

to realize the voice had come from just in front of them. From behind the altar table.

"You have the heart!"

It was an old man, barely visible in the dim shadows. He came forward. "You!" He pointed a finger at Juanita. "You're the one!"

Mojo gaped. To say the old man was old was an understatement. He was ancient. Almost mummified, like he'd been stored in an attic. Mojo expected dust to puff from him with every step. His face was gaunt, skull-like, with spotted skin stretched tight over the bones. He looked brittle, as though he might fall apart at the slightest touch. And his eyes . . . Mojo started as the old man stepped onto the altar steps beside them. The old man's eyes were solid white. Eyes like songbird eggs.

"You . . . you there! You have it! I can feel it! You have the heart!" The old man wagged his finger at Juanita.

Juanita placed a protective hand on her purse. She eyed the old man suspiciously. "Maybe."

"Yes! Yes, you do! I can't believe it! After all these years! Come on, give it to me!"

Juanita didn't move.

"Come on, I said! Give me the heart!"

"It's my heart. I'm not giving it to you or anyone else," Juanita said coldly.

"You know about the heart?" Grandmother said, stepping forward eagerly.

The old man ignored Grandmother and remained facing Juanita, his trembling arm outstretched towards her, his hand open. Juanita didn't move.

"You won't even let me hold it?" he asked Juanita

plaintively. ''An old man? You won't even let me touch it?''

''Tell us about it. Tell us about the heart,'' Grandmother said, laying a hand on his arm. ''We came all the way from Socorro to learn about the heart.''

The old man turned his dead white eyes towards Grandmother's voice. Dropped his arm. ''Socorro?''

''Yes. We want to hear everything you know about the heart.''

''You don't know about the heart?'' He sounded surprised.

''No. Only that it is a miracle. Nothing else.''

The old man considered.

''Well . . . perhaps I do know something,'' he said after a time, his voice as dry as his colorless lips. ''I do know some things that might interest you, but my memory isn't what it used to be. It's become foggy lately. Too many years. I can't remember much. Of course, I might if I had something to help remind me. Something real. Something I could touch. Something I could hold on to. Something—''

''Forget it, Jack,'' Juanita cut him off.

''Oh, come on, Juanita,'' Mojo said. ''Let him hold it for a minute. I mean, what could he do? He's old and blind and we're standing right here beside him.''

''What could he do? He could hex it! He could put a curse on it! He could ruin it forever!''

''I think it will be all right,'' Grandmother said gently. ''I think maybe this man values the heart as much as we do.''

''Oh . . . all right!'' Juanita withdrew the pickle jar from her purse. ''I'll let him hold it, then. But just for a minute!''

Juanita thrust the jar into the old man's eager hands.

He grabbed it and hugged it to his chest. Tucked it up under his chin and cradled it. His narrow, cracked face was tinted blue by the heart's glow. Slowly his white eyes closed. He began to rock slowly, his breath coming in soft, rhythmic wheezes, almost a croon.

Grandmother squeezed the old man's arm. "Now you must tell us everything you know about the heart. Will you do that?"

"Of course," the old man said without opening his eyes. "Of course, I'll tell you everything. I have to, you see. I need your help. I need your help to lift the curse."

"The curse?"

"Let me begin at the beginning." The old man continued to rock. "It's always the best place to start."

8

"It was a long time ago. In the early months of 1599. Soon after New Mexico was established as a Spanish colony," the old man began.

"Some soldiers had been murdered that past winter by the Indians of the Acoma Pueblo, and the governor of the colony, a man named De Onate, sent an expedition against them. After a short but bloody battle, the Indians were defeated. The survivors were rounded up and paraded back to the pueblo of Santo Domingo to be tried by Governor De Onate.

The trial was short. The only witnesses were Spanish. The Indians were all found guilty of rebellion against the Crown. The governor passed sentence on them. They were all condemned—every man, woman, and child of them—to give twenty years of personal service. This was the term De Onate used: 'personal service.' The Spanish preferred it to 'slavery' since the

Church forbids slavery, but there was no question about what it meant.

In addition to being enslaved, all men over the age of twenty-five were to have one foot cut off. This accomplished two things: It sent a message to the other Indians who were resisting the governor's rule, and it made escape very difficult since it's hard to run on only one foot."

The old man paused. He hugged the jar even tighter against his chest.

"Once the sentence was read, the Indian men were lined up in chains in the pueblo's plaza. At the head of the line was a blacksmith armed with a short axe and hot tar. Soldiers stood by with cocked firearms and swords. The mutilations began. There was a lot of wailing and sobbing and—from those in the blacksmith's hands—screaming.

At this same time a mule train which had just arrived from Mexico was being unloaded in the plaza. One of the items on the train was a beautiful santo of the Madonna. This santo had come all the way from Spain. She was life-sized, carved from oak, and brightly painted. She had brillant blue eyes and a ruby-red heart. She was a special present to the Franciscan friars from the King of Spain himself.

As the line of condemned Indians moved slowly forward across the plaza, the Madonna was taken from her wagon, unwrapped, and set aside prior to being carried inside the church. No sooner had the Madonna touched ground, however, than one of the Indians jumped out of line and threw himself into the dust at the Madonna's feet. He wrapped his arms around her. He began crying to her to save him.

The soldiers came forward and whipped the Indian

with ropes, but the Indian wouldn't let go of the Madonna. The soldiers pried at the Indian and beat him with their fists, but his grip couldn't be loosened.

The captain was called.

The captain tried to pull the Indian from the santo, but failed just as the soldiers had. The captain decided to take harsher action. He drew his pistol and was preparing to shoot the Indian in the head when a friar ran out of the church and stopped him.

The friar warned the captain that murdering a man who had sought the mercy of the Virgin was a mortal sin.

The captain scoffed.

The friar threatened to excommunicate him.

The captain threatened to jail the friar.

They went back and forth at each other like this until at last a compromise was reached. The captain agreed the soldiers would not touch the Indian as long as the Indian held on to the santo. The friars, in return, agreed not to attempt to move either the santo or the Indian into the sanctuary of their church.

It was a stalemate. But only a temporary one.

For four days and nights the Indian lay in the heat and dust of the plaza without food or water or sleep. For four long days he prayed to the Madonna to save him while the soldiers guarded him in shifts. Inside the church, the friars lit candles and prayed for the Indian's soul and for a miraculous intercession. The intercession didn't come. The Indian's wailing grew weaker and weaker. On the fourth day the captain agreed to let one of the friars go to the Indian and take his confession. The last rites were performed.

Finally, early on the morning of the fifth day, just before sunrise, a soldier went to examine the Indian and found him dead. The soldier dragged the body away and called for help. Several of the friars heard him and came out of the church. Some of the Santo Domingo Indians came with them.

A crowd gathered.

And witnessed a miracle.

As the sun rose it struck the Madonna's face. Her cheeks sparkled in the sudden light. Gasps were heard. The Madonna's cheeks were bright with teardrops, teardrops that sparkled and glittered. Teardrops of gold.

The crowd fell back. Some began to pray.

Then the sunlight dropped to the Madonna's waist and there was even more wonder. The Madonna's heart glittered as well. What had once been a red-painted outline was now a perfectly formed heart that shone as brightly as the tears. A heart of gold.

And that wasn't all. One of the friars shouted and pointed to the santo's eyes. Her eyes, which had been the most brilliant blue, were now dark brown and faintly almond-shaped. Her skin was as dark as her eyes. Her hair was jet black. This Madonna, this blue-eyed Spanish Madonna, had the face of an Acoma Indian. An Acoma Indian with a heart of gold."

Grandmother crossed herself.

"Seeing this miracle, the friars dropped to their knees in the dust. The soldiers joined the friars. Word of the miracle spread like a fire through the pueblo. The crowd in front of the santo grew.

Someone began to ring the church bell.

The captain was called.

The captain ran to tell the governor.

The governor came and was faced with a terrible dilemma. That the transfiguration of the Madonna was a miracle, there was no doubt. It was a miracle, but it was also a rebuke. A direct rebuke of the policies of the governor. It was the governor who had ordered the Indians enslaved. It was the governor who had ordered their feet to be cut off. People in the crowd were already whispering that this miracle was a sign of the Holy Mother's displeasure with the governor.

The governor became frightened as he listened to the whispering. How could he control the Indian if even the Spanish believed God was on the Indians' side? He and his soldiers were hopelessly outnumbered. How long could they survive if the Indians took this miracle as a sign that God was with them and against the Spanish?

The governor knew he had to act fast or lose everything. He gathered the captain and a few trusted men around him. He ordered them to take the Madonna from the friars.

The friars objected, but the captain was quick and decisive. A horse-drawn cart was found. The santo was loaded into it. The captain and his men rode out of Santo Domingo and headed up the river to the pueblo of San Ildefonso.

At San Ildefonso the captain conscripted three friars as well as several converted Indians and a wagonload of supplies. He turned east towards the tiny mission of San Diego de Punta de Tierra.

As they rode up the trail to Punta de Tierra, the captain informed the friars that they had been chosen to establish a new mission, a mission east of Punta de Tierra, a new mission to be located high in the Sangre de Cristo Mountains where there had never been a mission before. The friars objected. There were no pueblos in the mountains, they told the captain. No permanent settlements at all. Not enough Indians to warrant a mission.

The captain ignored their objections. He led the small party through Punta de Tierra and on up into the mountains beyond. They climbed for four days, following trails that were little more than deer paths, until at last they found themselves high in the pine forests and rocky crags, far beyond any Spanish or Indian settlements.

Somewhere near the tree line the captain ordered a halt. He picked out a suitable spot on the edge of a stream beside a meadow and told the friars the new mission was to be built there. He and his men joined in the construction. A tiny church with adjoining rooms for the friars and their servants was raised. Wood for the coming winter was gathered and stacked. Deer were hunted and jerky dried to supplement the cornmeal that had been brought up from San Ildefonso. A wooden altar was carved and the santo set in a place of honor behind it.

Once the friars were safely settled, the captain took his men and rode back. He reached Punta de Tierra just before the first snows fell. He continued on to the river. By the time he reached the governor's headquarters at San Juan he had been gone for over two months and the tale of the Indian Madonna had become little more than a legend. Even those who witnessed the miracle were reluctant to talk about it since the governor had declared the tale a blasphemous rumor punishable by the lash.

The captain resumed his old duties. The governor remained firmly in command. There was no more Indian trouble that winter or in the entire year that followed. The governor—perhaps even the colony—had been saved."

* * *

The old man paused. He reached inside his suit. He pulled out a pint bottle. He took a long swallow. Mojo could smell gin.

"Too much talking. Makes my throat dry," the old man explained.

"Then this Madonna with the golden heart, she wasn't actually here in Punta de Tierra? She was in the mountains above here?" Grandmother asked.

"That's right. And that's where she stayed. The captain never went back. The few people who visited the Madonna after that were all Indians. In fact, the Indians used to meet here, in this very church, for their pilgrimages up into the Sangre de Cristo. Most of them were sick or had relatives who were sick, I suppose. The Madonna was supposed to be able to cure illness. Things like that."

"This is a wonderful story," Grandmother said. "But what does it have to do with our heart? The living heart?"

"A lot." He took another long pull from the bottle. His hand trembled. He wiped his mouth with the back of his sleeve.

"Eighty years passed.

In 1679, or almost eighty years after the Madonna was taken from the plaza of Santo Domingo, a new captain was appointed to head the garrison at San Ildefonso. A man named José María Benegas.

This Captain Benegas was talking to an old Indian woman in the plaza one day when the subject of miracles came up. The Indian woman told him the story of the Miraculous Madonna. The same story I just told you.

The captain didn't believe it, of course. At least not most of it. He thought it was just another legend, just another Indian superstition. But one word did catch his attention. And that word was *gold*. This Captain Benegas was gold crazy. He had the fever. Gold was why he had volunteered to come to New Mexico in the first place. Even though the colony was almost a hundred years old and no gold had ever been found, this captain had faith it was there. Faith he would be the one to find it. Faith he would be the one man to find that Eldorado that everyone believed was out there somewhere. He had this faith even though he had been in New Mexico for nearly three years with nothing more to show for it than the gold buttons on his cavalry tunic.

The captain had faith. And the fever. And now suddenly here was this old woman telling him about a heart of solid gold. A fortune in gold. Enough gold to allow him to return to Spain and live like a don for the rest of his life.

The captain questioned the old woman for a long time. He held her by the arm and wouldn't let her go until he was certain she had told him everything she knew and that he had every detail straight in his mind.

Then he acted.

As soon as his official duties permitted, the captain rode alone to Punta de Tierra. He asked directions from the Fathers there, found the trail, and went up into the mountains. After only a few days he arrived at the tiny mission the Indians called the Weeping Woman's House.

He had supper with the friars—there were only two—and then, after telling them he wanted to give thanks for his safe journey, went to the small log church to see if the old woman's story was true.

It was.

The captain couldn't believe his eyes. After checking to make sure no one had followed him into the church, he went behind the altar and scraped a tiny sliver of gold from the Madonna's heart. He bit the sliver of gold. Rolled it between his fingers. Tested it to make certain. His hands trembled. There was no question. It was pure.

He probed deeper into the heart with the knife, half expecting to find wood, but all he found was more gold. The heart wasn't gilded. No. The heart was as the old woman said it was: pure gold through and through.

A massive lump.

A fortune.

The captain returned to his room and waited until after midnight. When he judged everyone was asleep, he slipped out and returned to the church. He took his knife and, working by the light of a single candle, cut out the Madonna's heart.

The heart was heavy. He could hardly lift it. He brought his saddlebag into the church and loaded the heart into it. He was staggering up the aisle with the saddlebag over his shoulder when one of the friars appeared in the doorway with a lantern.

The friar didn't understand what was happening, never suspected that a captain of the Crown would enter a church in order loot it. He thought the captain had been praying and came forward to greet him. It was his undoing. As soon as the friar was close enough, the captain drew his knife and stabbed him in the chest. The friar struggled, but the captain had him by now, and he continued to stab until the friar slumped to the floor.

The captain put down his load of gold. He went to the room of the other friar and murdered him as well, killing him in his sleep. He considered killing the Indian servants, but decided they would probably run away long before anyone in authority had a chance to question them.

The captain loaded the saddlebag onto his horse and rode off. He made a wide circle around Punta de Tierra and headed for the river. His plan was to carry the gold to Vera Cruz and either sell it there or smuggle it onto a ship bound for Spain.

For six days Benegas rode downriver, avoiding other travelers by hiding in the brush. He was able to buy food from the Indians. He traded for a fresh horse just below Santo Domingo. Things were going well. Each day that passed put him farther from the crime and closer to Spain.

On the seventh night after the robbery he was camped on the bank of the river just above where Albuquerque is today. He had shot a rabbit and was roasting it over a bed of red coals when suddenly he felt a presence.

The captain rolled off his blanket and grabbed his pistol. His eyes searched the darkness. There, just at the far edge of the firelight, was a figure. Benegas raised his pistol. Then lowered it. It wasn't an Indian. It was a woman. Benegas called to her, identifying himself as a soldier of the Guard. The woman stepped forward into the light.

The woman pulled back the side of a long gown she was wearing and displayed a terrible wound. The would was massive. Blood poured from it. The captain gasped. No one could live with such a wound.

The woman dropped the edge of her gown and walked slowly towards the captain, her hands outstretched. Her eyes were filled with sadness, tears glittered on her cheeks. She seemed to be seeking something from him. Beseeching him for something.

Benegas drew back from her. He was terrified. He

thought she was a ghost, an apparition of some sort come to haunt him. Perhaps even a demon. He jumped to his feet. He raised the pistol. He warned her to stop. She didn't. He fired.

When the flash and smoke of the shot cleared, the woman was gone. Simply gone. There was no sign of her, no body on the ground.

For a long time Benegas stood and stared at the place where the woman had been. Then, marshaling his courage, he went forward. He knew that ghosts didn't leave footprints, and he wanted to see if there were any in the soft earth. There weren't. There was something much worse. Blood. The ground was soaked with dark red blood.

Benegas returned to his blankets, shaken and afraid. He added wood to the fire until it was a great blaze. He huddled close to the light. He knew something terrible had just happened, but he wasn't sure what.

Then it came to him.

He ran to the saddlebag and hoisted it. It came up easily. He knew at once that the gold was gone.

Yet the bag wasn't empty. Benegas could feel something lying in the bottom. Something soft and rounded.

Benegas raised the bag higher. Its bottom was wet. A dark stain was spreading across it. Benegas' hand trembled. He dropped the bag. The bag spilled out onto the—''

''Hello!'' The shout reverberated in the empty church. ''Anybody here?''

Mojo turned. Three figures were coming down the aisle. One of the figures pointed at Mojo: ''There they are!''

As the figures drew closer Mojo could see it was

three men. One of them, the one in the lead, was Cesar Romero.

"My God!" Juanita jumped. "It's him!"

"Who?"

"He's found us! Shit!" She whirled around and snatched the jar out of the old man's hands. She crammed the jar back into her purse and snapped it shut.

Cesar Romero and the other two sauntered up to Mojo.

"Good afternoon." Cesar Romero nodded. He had a rich baritone voice. A politician's voice. He had a big smile crowded with amazingly white teeth. He was dressed in a double-breasted navy-blue suit without a wrinkle in it. Every hair was in place.

"I don't believe we've met, but you must be Joseph Birdsong. And this"—he nodded to Grandmother—"must be Mrs. Montoya. Juanita and I are old friends, of course."

Juanita hissed softly. It was the sort of feeble show of defiance a chicken confronted by a rattlesnake might make.

"Who are you?" Mojo asked.

"You don't know? You can't guess?" Cesar Romero asked. His smile broadened. "Then let me introduce myself: I'm Raymundo Castillo. The man whose ten kilos of cocaine you stole. Remember?"

> *This about Raymundo Castillo:* He was the sort of man who would kill you for a dollar and leave a tip. His voice may have been as mellow as a TV game show host's; his face may have been as open and warm as a rich uncle's; his smile may have glowed as comfortingly as a

night-light in a five-year-old's bedroom; but his eyes were as hard and cold as black ice on an overpass at four in the morning.

Mojo gulped. He remembered, all right.

"Pedrito." Castillo nodded casually to one of the others.

The man stepped forward and thrust a cannon in Mojo's face. He flicked Mojo's nose with the barrel. "You give me any trouble, *cabrón*, and I'll blow your brains out," the man told Mojo.

"Now, I want you to all come with me," Castillo said enthusiastically, waving an arm as though inviting them down to the local Dairy Queen for triple fudge sundaes with cherries on top. "We have a little unfinished business to attend to."

"Please, Mr. Castillo. Leave Grandmother out of this," Juanita pleaded. "She doesn't have anything to do with you. The old man either."

Castillo looked puzzled. "What old man?"

Juanita turned around. "This old . . ." But the altar step was empty. There was nothing there but dust.

9

Mojo couldn't move anything but his head.

Mojo and Grandmother were tied to two pine trees. They were wrapped up like mummies. Clothesline was wound around Mojo from his neck to his ankles. The clothesline was tight; it cut into his arms and his chest and his thighs. He doubted whether even Houdini could have escaped from it.

"I'm leaving now," Castillo said, carefully placing the pickle jar on the ground. "It'll be dark soon, and I don't want to be out here after dark."

"Where's Juanita? What'd you do with Juanita?" Mojo demanded to know.

"She's all right. She's back at the car. She'll be going with me when I leave. You see, I have special plans for Juanita." Castillo gave Mojo a toothy grin as he straightened. "She's going to perform a very valuable service for me."

''A service? What kind of service?''

''The service of dying. Of course, you two are going to die as well, but your deaths won't be nearly as important as poor Juanita's.''

''You're wrong. We won't die,'' Grandmother said stoutly. ''We've been chosen by the Lady to be the guardians of her heart. She will protect us.''

''I don't much think so. I don't much think she can.'' Castillo turned to go.

''Wait!'' Mojo called after him. ''You forgot the heart. You wouldn't want to leave without the heart!''

''You keep it,'' Castillo said over his shoulder as he started down the path on the far side of the clearing. ''If you can.''

''Hey! Wait a minute!''

Castillo disappeared into the trees.

Mojo watched him go, then craned his neck to the west. The broken cross of the old mission was just visible through a break in the forest. Rising beyond the mission was a heavily wooded hill. The sun was already below the hill. Its last light was caught in the tops of the highest pines and a few scattered clouds. The clouds glowed: red and purple and yellow and pink. It was a beautiful sunset, but Mojo would have enjoyed it more if it hadn't been signaling his imminent death.

''I'm worried about Juanita,'' Grandmother said. ''I think she must be in some terrible danger.''

''It couldn't be any more terrible than the danger we're in.'' Mojo twisted within his rope cocoon. ''It'll be dark soon, and the beast'll be coming for the heart.''

''You lack faith, Joseph,'' Grandmother said disapprovingly.

''I lack a knife too.'' Mojo wrestled with the clothesline. He got nowhere.

"Our Lady will protect us from the hellhounds."

"It's not hellhounds. It's a beast. One big, ugly mother of a beast. I'm not sure, but I think it may be a giant spider. Or something like a spider."

"It makes no difference. The Lady will aid us against whatever the Great Deceiver sends."

"I hope you're right. But just in case you're not, I wish you'd try to slip those ropes on your own."

"There's no need. She'll come," Grandmother said confidently.

A grey squirrel bounded out into the clearing. It ran scampering through the dead leaves over to Mojo's tree. It paused at his feet, rose up on its hind legs, and sniffed the air.

Grandmother nodded. "See?"

"A squirrel?" Mojo scoffed. "You think a squirrel is gonna get us out of this?"

"Watch."

The squirrel examined Mojo's Nikes. Its nose twitched. It looked up. It studied him with black squirrel eyes.

Mojo studied the squirrel back, not at all certain exactly what the hell was going on.

Suddenly the squirrel leaped up onto Mojo's leg and began climbing him. It climbed onto his stomach and then onto his chest. The squirrel climbed until its black button eyes were almost level with Mojo's blue ones. It clung to the clothesline around Mojo's shoulders and peered into Mojo's eyes. It opened its mouth and hissed threateningly, displaying a large pair of buckteeth.

"Whoa!" Mojo gasped, pulling his chin back into his neck. He felt like a trussed-up turkey on Thanksgiving day.

Another squirrel ran into the clearing. It stopped and

chattered angrily at the squirrel on Mojo's chest. The squirrel on Mojo's chest turned its head.

The second squirrel ran over to Grandmother and then up her. It stopped and turned and chattered at Mojo's squirrel once more. The squirrel on Mojo's chest moved down a short space and began gnawing on the tight coils of clothesline. Mojo could hear its teeth clicking.

"That's it," Mojo said with relief. "Chew the hell out of it." He twisted his neck to the side once again. The colors were fading from the horizon.

By the time the squirrels had chewed through the clothesline and freed Mojo and Grandmother, twilight had descended. The sky was dark except for a pale grey line in the west. Underneath the pines, it was as dark as midnight.

"Let's go." Mojo stripped the last strands of clothesline from around his legs. "Give me your hand and I'll lead."

"We have to find the heart first." Mojo could just make out Grandmother in the murky light, her dim outline.

"The heart? Are you crazy? That's what attracts the beast. You told me so yourself. It might let us go if we leave the heart behind."

"No. We can't leave it."

"Why not?"

"Because it's the Lady's heart. Because we've been entrusted with it."

"Well, let's just dis-entrust ourselves! You don't know what that thing's like!"

As if to prove Mojo's point, a long, horrible howl came from somewhere high above them. From up in the mountains. Mojo froze. The howl rose for a chilling moment, then ended abruptly. Cut off.

Mojo shivered. It was the beast, all right.

"Come on!" Mojo demanded urgently.

"There! I have it!" Grandmother moved towards him in the half-darkness. He could see the pale blue glow of the jar. A shadowy arm reached out towards him. Touched his.

"I'm ready now."

"Then let's vamos. But be careful of where you step. There's lots of loose rock around here."

Mojo led grandmother across the clearing. He could just make out the lighter shadows where the trail cut through the trees. He entered the trail.

The trail was even darker than the clearing. Mojo could hardly see his hands in front of his face. He felt his way down with the tips of his Nikes. The ground was a swamp of blackness.

They descended a steep pitch, then twisted along a narrow switchback, then descended again. The footing was unsure. They inched more than they walked. He was forced to stop a number of times and help Grandmother. It was very slow going.

"We might as well be blindfolded, trying to find our way down in this dark," Mojo grumbled, groping down an incline. "At the rate we're moving that thing'll catch up with us before we get another hundred yards."

"I will ask the Lady for help," Grandmother said.

They hadn't gone another ten steps when suddenly the light from the pickle jar increased in intensity. The blue glow flared and became a blue fire, illuminating the path in front of them.

"You see? The Lady is still with us, still protecting us."

Mojo nodded. He certainly hoped so. He figured they needed all the protecting they could get and then some.

Mojo took Grandmother's hand and helped her down a steep pitch. Her long dress caught in come brambles and he had to climb up to yank it loose. He slid back down beside her. They continued on.

A short time later, as they paused before a rock outcropping, the howling came again. It was definitely lower down the mountain this time. Closer. It had a hungry undertone.

Mojo decided to hell with the footing. He grabbed Grandmother and pulled her down the path.

They rushed around the outcropping and across a small clearing faintly lit by the last hint of dusk. They descended back into the trees.

The trail turned to the left, cutting across the face of the slope, and was level for a time. Mojo tried to jog but Grandmother stumbled almost immediately and he barely turned in time to catch her. He returned to a quick walk. He could feel the beast. He could feel it coming. He could feel it on his skin. It was like an itch he couldn't scratch.

The trail opened, then hooked back to the right, descended again. Mojo helped Grandmother over an exposed tree root. He slipped once, got back up. Grandmother slipped and he pulled her back up. The trail turned, turned back again. There was a faint glow at the bottom this time.

They emerged out of some brush at the foot of the trail and into the big meadow where the old dilapidated church stood. Dusk was almost gone. The church was no more than a hulking shadow in the half-light. Only its broken cross was clearly visible, silhouetted against the soft glow of the horizon. Mojo pulled Grandmother towards it, stumbling through waist-high weeds.

"Hurry! I've still got the car keys. If we can get it started before that thing gets down, we'll have a chance!"

The beast bayed from somewhere above them. It was a long, rolling sound. Challenging. It passed over the meadow and echoed off the opposite hillside. It could have come from the clearing where they had been tied up. Mojo pulled Grandmother through the weeds and up to the front of the church. The old woman was gasping for breath. Mojo looked frantically about, but the meadow was empty except for the weeds and the church and the failing light.

The Impala was gone.

"Damn! Those two creeps must have hot-wired it while they were waiting for Castillo. The cheap bastards! It wasn't worth diddly! You'd think dopers would have enough money, they wouldn't bother with twenty-year-old Chevys!" Mojo said with disgust. He kicked angrily at some weeds. A pungent stench rose up.

"What can we do?" Grandmother asked.

"I don't know . . . Head for the blacktop, I guess. Hope a car comes along. I . . . Hey! Wait a minute! The church!" He turned eagerly around. "I almost forgot! It can't enter consecrated ground! Come on!" Mojo grabbed Grandmother and dragged her towards the church door, his heart soaring.

The door was barred.

"What the—?!" Mojo stood helpless. He couldn't believe it. There was a solid wall of new two-by-fours nailed over the door of the church. He would have needed an axe to get through them.

"This wasn't here before!"

"There's a sign." Grandmother pointed.

Mojo peered closer. A sheet of heavy white paper had been nailed to the two-by-fours. There wasn't enough light to read the fine print, but he could make out the heading well enough. It was printed in inch-high red block letters: "DO NOT ENTER!" and underneath that: "New Mexico State Historical Site."

"Now, where the hell did—"

The beast roared. The sound came from just above and behind them. It was close. Not more than a hundred yards away. Close and deafening loud. Mojo judged the scream as lesser than a banshee's and greater than a football coach's.

"It's here!" Mojo grabbed Grandmother's hand. He didn't hesitate. He turned towards the meadow, towards the stand of cottonwoods at the meadow's far edge and the blacktop beyond. He ran.

Mojo, Grandmother in tow, ran stumbling over the soft, uneven ground of the meadow. Weeds clutched at their legs. Rocks and washouts threatened to break an ankle at every step. They were almost there, the dark line of trees tantalizingly close, when Mojo suddenly felt himself slowing, his legs laboring. It was as though he had stepped into a molasses swamp. His knees were pumping but he wasn't going anywhere. He glanced back. The old woman had stopped running. She was floundering, dragging behind him like a sea anchor. He could hear her wheezing.

He yanked on her arm. "Faster! We've got to get out of the open!"

"I can't!" Grandmother gasped. Then: "Leave me. Save yourself!" She jerked her hand free and stumbled to a halt.

Mojo turned back. "Come on! You can't stop here!"

He grabbed her arm again. ''It's only a little ways further!''

''N-no,'' she gasped, shaking her head. Her breath sputtered, like a lawn mower trying to start. ''I—I'm finished. If you try and take me with you, you'll be finished too. Go on. It's the heart it's after. Leave me and the heart here.''

> *This about Mojo Birdsong:* He had watched too many cable TV movies to even consider leaving Grandmother behind. Would Bogart have left her? Would John Wayne have left her? Rambo? Steven Spielberg?

''Come on,'' Mojo put his arm around Grandmother. ''I'll help you.'' He hoisted her onto his hip and began staggering towards the woods.

''No! Please! You must save yourself!''

''Just hang on. It's only a little ways further.'' Mojo panted, the inviting darkness of the woods looming just ahead.

''Please!''

''Just—a—few—more—feet.'' Mojo's arm was growing numb already. He could hardly feel his right hand. It was amazing how heavy even skinny people were.

''Just—couple—of—more . . .''

They staggered into the shadows beneath the cottonwoods.

Mojo set Grandmother down and turned. The moon rose over the dark mountains to the east. The meadow trembled as the moonlight rushed over it. The meadow was empty. There was nothing moving in its tall grass or against the church at its far edge or under the trees on the hillside beyond.

Mojo sagged against a tree. He rubbed his half-numb arm. The arm tingled as the blood returned. He watched anxiously but the meadow remained still and empty and bright with moonlight.

They were safe. For the moment.

A short time passed with Mojo waiting nervously for the thing to come bounding across the meadow after them. Then Grandmother whispered, "I . . . I think I can walk again. If we don't go too fast."

Mojo peered at her. She looked pale. Her face was drawn. He had forgotten how old she was. She didn't look ready to walk. She didn't look ready for anything more strenuous than a hospital bed.

"Rest a few minutes more," he told her. "Rest, and then we'll go."

"No. We must go now," she said. She touched him. Her hand was cold. "You lead."

"You sure?"

"Just go slow."

Mojo stepped off into the darkness. Grandmother followed.

After a time her breathing became regular.

They had been walking for only a short while when they crossed a broad path leading south. The path was dappled with shadows and moonlight. It was littered with old beer cans and broken bottles. Mojo turned onto it.

The path made several turns under the trees, then passed into an open area where it skirted a couple of crumbling adobe walls. It reentered the woods on the other side of the walls and passed close by a pile of old boards that smelled bad and probably had once held either an outhouse or a pigsty. The path turned and twisted several more times before it finally emerged out of the woods and onto a gravel clearing. The blacktop road was just beyond the clearing.

Mojo left Grandmother and dashed across the clearing and onto the blacktop. He stopped and looked eagerly in both directions, his head swinging from side to side, but there were no headlights coming. He looked up the valley, then down, then into the hills on either side. There were no house lights visible either. No sounds. There was nothing but darkness and silence up and down both sides of the road. There was no place to run.

Mojo walked slowly back to Grandmother. It was as disappointing as a drive-in rejection.

As Mojo and Grandmother stood huddled beside the road, unsure of what to do next, the beast roared once again. The sound was surprisingly distant.

"Hear that?" Mojo asked. "It's still a long way behind us. But why's that?" he puzzled. "I mean, that thing's some kind of fast. It should have caught up by now."

"Perhaps it can't find us."

Mojo thought about it. "No . . ." he said slowly. "I don't think so. It knows where we are, all right . . ." Then angrily: "I get it! It's running us! Playing with us! Well, I may be on the dinner menu tonight, but I'll be damned if I'm gonna provide the entertainment too! If it wants—"

A light flickered in the corner of Mojo's eye.

Mojo was quick. He spun around. The light was coming from underneath a stand of cottonwoods a little farther up the road. The light had the distorted quality of something seen through glass. It took Mojo a couple of seconds to realize what it was: a match, a match flame shining through a car window.

The light winked out.

Mojo's eyes flew open.

"A car!" Mojo whirled to Grandmother. "There's a car up there!"

He turned and bounded up the road. "Follow me!" he called over his shoulder.

Not just a car but cars, a line of dark humps underneath the cottonwoods. It was too good to be true.

Mojo ran to the first car and jerked on the door handle. It was locked. He could hear music pounding. He could see the red glow of a radio dial.

Mojo beat on the window glass.

"Hey! Let me in! This is an emergency!"

There was a flash of naked flesh. A shriek. An angry curse.

Mojo slapped the roof. "Open up! Hurry! This is serious!"

He pounded on the window again.

Car doors were opening. He could hear voices. He looked up and saw interior lights blinking on up and down the line. One of the interior lights was a small crystal chandelier with red-flame light bulbs.

"Come on!" Mojo beat on the roof again.

Dark figures were emerging from the other cars. There was low muttering. Footsteps were coming towards him, crackling on gravel.

Suddenly the car door flew open, knocking Mojo aside. Before Mojo had time to recover, a man leaped out of the door and grabbed him by the throat. The man had a red bandanna tied around his forehead. He slung

Mojo around and pinned him up against the side of the car.

"You want some shit, man? That it? You want some action? Well, you found it. I'm gonna give you some action, man. I'm gonna do you up good!" The voice was deep and menacing. The hand on Mojo's throat tightened.

"No . . . I . . . just—" Mojo found it difficult to talk while being strangled. He struggled, trying to free himself, but the man had an iron grip.

"Bring that flashlight over here. I got a prowler, man. A fucking Peeping Tom."

Mojo was having too much trouble trying to breathe to deny he was a Peeping Tom. He brought both hands up to his throat. He managed to wedge a couple of fingers in between his attacker's hand and his Adam's apple. He drew in a deep gasp of air.

"Right here, man. That's it. Shine it over here." Someone shone a flashlight into Mojo's face. He blinked but then he could see. His attacker was a mean-looking kid. He had a dark, olive face with angry brown eyes and a thin nose. His hair was black and sleek and slicked back. He was wearing a T-shirt with "Los Lowriders Club, Bartolo, N.M." emblazoned across it in red and green letters. His Levi's were unzipped.

"Look! It's an Anglo! An Anglo Peeping Tom!"

A ring of Hispanic faces was growing around the edges of the flashlight beam. None of them looked very friendly. Mojo didn't see a knife, but that didn't mean there wasn't one.

"You don't understand," Mojo wheezed. "I came to warn you. We're in danger. All of us. If we don't get out of here quick, we're gonna have the life expectancy of a used microwave!" Mojo's voice was too high. It was a combination of being half strangled and half terrorized at the same time.

"Shit." The mean-looking kid leaned in closer. "You're the one in danger, man. Your ass is in one deep crack."

"No, really. There's something coming. It'll be here soon. We've got to get out of here right away! All of us!"

"He's from Texas, man. I recognize the accent," a voice from the crowd said.

Oh, shit.

The kid grinned. "Is that right?" The grin grew. "You from Texas, man? You a land grabber?"

Mojo glanced to the side. A girl was hanging out the side window of the car watching him. She had a too-plump face and disheveled black hair. She was chewing gum. There was a long piece of rusted pipe lying on the ground below her.

"So what're we gonna do with him?" The kid consulted his buddies. "What're we gonna do with some Texas *pendejo* who comes sneaking up on us in the middle of the night?"

"Do him up good," a deep voice suggested.

"Let him go!" Grandmother came hobbling into the circle of light. "Let Joseph go!"

The kid turned towards Grandmother. His grip on Mojo's throat loosened for an instant. Mojo broke away. In one swift move he leaped to the side, picked up the piece of pipe, and whirled back around.

The girl shrieked and disappeared inside the car. The kid turned back and, seeing Mojo with the pipe, raised his fists.

Mojo rushed forward. He had the pipe in both hands. He swung the pipe above his head. Someone screamed,

"Look out!" Several alarmed faces dropped out of the circle. But Mojo wasn't even thinking of attacking the Lowriders. He had a much better idea.

At the last moment Mojo spun to the side. He lifted the pipe over the hood of the kid's car and held it there. Poised. Ready to strike. The hood gleamed a deep rich red beneath the pipe.

"Get back!" Mojo shouted. "Get back or I trash the car!"

"Shit!" It was a cry of anguish. "Not my Chevy, man! I got ten coats of lacquer in that finish!"

"I mean it!" Mojo warned. "I'll do it!"

"Shit! Get back!" The kid turned anxiously to the others. "Get back! He's crazy!"

Muttering ominously, the Lowriders moved away from Mojo.

"Show them the heart," Mojo ordered Grandmother. "Show them the heart and explain to them why we've got to get out of here."

"You touch that car and you're dead meat, *pendejo*," the kid warned him. "You put one scratch on that finish and I'm gonna put you in the graveyard, man."

"Just look at the heart," Mojo told him.

Grandmother shoved the pickle jar into the kid's hands.

The kid held the jar for a long time. He held it in front of his face and then at arm's reach and then right under the flashlight beam. He studied it. The heart was in fine form. Mojo could see it bubbling all the way from the car.

Grandmother talked to the kid as he examined the heart. She explained about the beast and how the beast was after the heart but would undoubtedly kill them all since it was already tormenting them by not killing them right away and that the demon was either a giant spider or a pack of dogs but either way was an agent of the Great Deceiver himself.

Mojo didn't know about the kid, but it didn't make any sense to him and he even knew what she was talking about.

After a few more minutes of studying, the kid handed the jar off to a pockmarked boy in a turquoise shirt and turned towards Mojo. The kid had a very serious expression on his face. Mojo assumed the kid was either going to kill him or offer to drive him to the nearest mental hospital.

"I'm Chuy." The kid held out his hand. "Sorry for the misunderstanding, but you know how it is."

"Sure." Mojo dropped the pipe gratefully and shook Chuy's hand.

"That's Lupe." Chuy nodded at the car window. Mojo turned and smiled. Lupe popped her gum and smiled back at him.

Mojo turned back to the kid. "Listen, Chuy, I'm glad to meet you and all, but we've got to get out of here fast," Mojo said. "That thing'll be here any minute."

"The beast?"

"Yeah. That's right. The beast."

"You know, I'm not surprised, man." Chuy looked out into the dark and shook his head. "No, I'm not surprised at all."

"You're not?"

"No. I can see why the devil would be after his heart. I can see it because I never really believed it. No matter what they said, I knew he couldn't really be dead. And this heart proves it, man. This heart is the proof he never really died."

"Who?" Mojo was confused. "Who never really died?"

"The King, man. The King. Elvis. I knew the minute I saw that heart that it was Elvis'." His voice dropped to a conspiratorial level. "I expected it, man. I knew El Rey would be back. I knew they couldn't keep him down."

"Huh . . ."

"Other people might have lost faith, but not me, man. I still got a statue of him on my dash. Procelain, not plastic. Hand-painted. They said he was dead, but I kept the statue anyway. Right next to the Virgin, man."

Mojo started to correct Chuy but then stopped himself. What difference did it make?

"Well, I'm glad you understand, then. Glad you understand how important it is to protect the heart. We've got to move fast, though, if we want to save it. We've got to—"

The beast roared.

The beast roared from the darkness beyond the cars. The sound was so loud that Mojo thought for an instant the thing had slipped up and was standing right next to him.

Mojo jumped. He whipped his head around. Where had it come from? The woods? Yes! The woods! It was just in front of them! They had to move!

"We've got to go! Now!" Mojo grabbed Chuy's arm. "We've got to get out of here!"

Chuy was staring off in the direction of the roar. "That was it, huh? That was the beast?"

"That's right!" Mojo said anxiously. "And now that you've heard it, you can imagine how big it is!"

"Didn't sound that big to me, man," Chuy sniffed. "Not big enough to whip Los Lowriders anyway. No,

I figure if it tries to screw around with us, we'll kick its ass."

"Wha—?" Mojo stepped back. He didn't like the sound of this. Not at all. "Kick its ass? Are you crazy?! It's a demon, for Chrissakes! You can't whip it! We've got to run!"

Chuy turned slowly towards him. He gave Mojo a long contemptuous look. "Los Lowriders don't run from nobody, man. Not never. It's a rule."

Mojo opened his mouth but nothing came out. He was stunned. Without words. This crazy, macho bastard actually thought he could fight a demon!

"Hey!" Chuy waved to the others. "Come over here."

Chuy waited until the other Lowriders were gathered around him. Then: "Look, this beast *cabrón* is coming in after Elvis' heart. Right into Bartolo County like it owned it, man. Now, we can do one of two things: we can turn chickenshit and run like we're a bunch of *pendejos* with no dignity, or we can get our shit together and whip its ass. We gotta decide which."

The following discussion was short. Nobody but Mojo seemed to have any interest in running anywhere. Whipping ass was the unanimous choice.

Mojo stood helplessly by as the meeting broke up and Chuy and his friends went to fetch baseball bats and knives and other assorted weapons from underneath the front seats of their cars.

"Joseph! You can't let them do this thing." Grandmother stepped up beside him. "They'll be killed!"

"You think I want them to do it? If it was up to me, we'd already be halfway to Santa Fe by now. I've had one run-in with this thing already, and I'm telling you, I wouldn't lay odds on Rambo and Dirty Harry put together with half the Marine Corps being able to stop it.''

''There must be something we can do.''

''Well . . . yeah. I've been thinking about that. You stick close to me. Maybe if Chuy and his buddies can slow the beast up for a minute or two, we'll have enough time to steal his car and get away.''

''How can you even think of such a thing? We can't just run away and leave them here to be killed!''

''We can't? Okay, okay, I suppose you're right.'' He held up his hands as she stepped angrily towards him. ''I'll try to think of something else.''

But what, he couldn't imagine.

Then it came to him: ''Hey! Wait a minute! Light! Bright light! The old monk told me it was afraid of the sunlight!''

''But it's night,'' Grandmother protested. ''There's no bright light at night.''

''We can make some! Chuy! Hey! I've got an idea!''

Chuy had just received a long good-luck kiss from Lupe and was climbing out of his car. He had a baseball bat in his hand.

''What is it? You want me to get you a bat? I've got an extra in the trunk.''

''No. I've got something better than a bat. A plan. A plan to stop that thing. Bats won't do it, but I'll tell you what will: light. Headlights. We can blind it.'' Mojo didn't know this for sure, but it seemed like a good assumption.

Chuy pursed his lips. ''Could work,'' he said after a moment. ''I've seen some movies where the monsters are afraid of light.''

''That's right. That's how it usually works,'' Mojo said eagerly.

"But what keeps it from going around behind us and sneaking up on us from the back while our headlights are pointed towards the front?"

Mojo had to think about that one for a moment. "A circle," he said at last. "We'll form a circle. Like the old wagon trains."

"No." Grandmother shook her head. "I have an even better idea. A way to trap the beast."

"What's that?"

Grandmother explained and Mojo was sorry he had asked.

Mojo gripped the jar tightly in his hands. The woods in front of him were dark. Dark and silent. Nothing moved. There weren't even any crickets chirping. He could feel sweat forming on his forehead in spite of the night chill.

Mojo sniffed the air. It was out there. He could smell it. It smelled like an open sewer with burning tires floating in it.

Something rustled in the brush underneath the cottonwood trees and Mojo stopped breathing. The rustling continued for a moment longer, then something darted away into the woods. Mojo took a shuddering breath. A mouse. Or a rabbit.

His relief was short-lived. There was another sound out in the darkness. A crunch. A heavy sound of something breaking. Mojo tensed. It was coming. Sneaking up on him. He knew it. Sneaking up until it was close enough to jump out of the bushes and grab him and—

"Mojo." The voice was not a voice at all. It was a creaking door that formed words. He had heard it before.

Every muscle in Mojo's body went rigid. The voice was less than fifteen feet in front of him. In the bushes.

"Why don't you run? Mojo?"

Mojo took an involuntary step backwards. This was crazy. It was insane. He should have never listened to the old woman in the first place. Where had she gotten this idea from anyway? Staking out lambs for coyotes? He could be killed. Probably would be. And what about the Lowriders? Could he trust a gang of Lowriders? They were probably back there right now passing around joints and making out with their girlfriends.

"Run, Mojo." The bushes shook. Something huge and black and foul was rising up out of the bushes. It rose up until it brushed the overhanging tree branches and then it rose some more. It had glow-in-the-dark eyes. They looked like railroad lanterns.

Mojo would have liked to run, but he couldn't. He was frozen. Still as a Popsicle.

"You won't run? Mojo?" the creaking door creaked.

Mojo opened his mouth to say he'd run if that was what it wanted, but nothing came out.

"Then I will take you here."

The forest trembled then shuddered then erupted. There was a great rattling of bony parts. A wall of blackness surged forward. The yellow eyes surged forward with it.

Mojo unfroze. He stumbled backwards.

"Turn on the lights!" he screamed. "Turn on the friggin' headlights!"

The headlights of the cars behind Mojo flashed on. Not all on high-beam as Grandmother had directed, but enough so that the beast was caught in a blinding glare.

The beast screamed. It twisted in the headlights. It wasn't exactly a giant spider, but it was close. It was a sort of giant centipede-scorpion-spider. The most amazing thing about it was its face. It had more or less human features. If its mouth hadn't been turned sideways and filled with dripping white fangs, Mojo imagined it would have looked something like his Uncle Ort.

The demon screamed again. Coiled and uncoiled. It was even uglier than Mojo had first supposed. Uglier than an old barmaid in broad daylight. Its breath burned like battery acid fumes. Mojo turned and ran behind the nearest car, an old Buick with Cadillac fins welded onto the trunk. Its rear bumper was no more than four inches off the ground. Mojo crouched behind the bumper and peeked over one of the fins. The demon was on fire.

The demon was writhing in blue fire. The blue fire shot off it in long, sparkling streamers. The blue fire had no heat. Mojo was only twenty feet from it and felt nothing but the cool mountain air.

The blue fire grew in intensity. Became brighter and brighter. It swirled around the beast in a burning shell. The shell of blue fire was so bright that Mojo had to squint to see the beast twisting underneath it.

Then poof and the fire was gone and the beast with it. Just poof. Suddenly there was no more fire. No more beast. A few whiffs of grey smoke drifting on the yellow headlights was all.

For a moment there was silence, then someone began honking his horn. In a moment all the Lowriders were honking their horns and yelling congratulations at one another. The sound was deafening.

The front door of Chuy's car opened. Grandmother struggled out. "Joseph?" she called anxiously, raising her voice above the horns and the voices. "Where are you? Are you all right?"

Mojo stood up. "I'm back here. I'm fine."

"You did it, Joseph. The beast is dead." Grandmother hurried to him, her eyes shining. "I'm so proud of you!" She grabbed him and hugged him fiercely.

Mojo, embarrassed, broke away. Chuy was coming around the other side of the car. He was running a comb lazily through his hair as he walked. He had an unlit cigarette dangling from his lips. He sauntered up to Mojo and Grandmother.

"Well, I guess the devil won't be coming around Bartolo County no more after this, man," Chuy said as he reached into his back pocket, pulled out a book of matches, and lit his cigarette. "I guess he's learned his lesson, man; I guess he's learned you don't fuck around with Los Lowriders."

10

Someone was fucking around with Narn.

Someone was playing games.

Narn eased the sheets off his chest. It was pitch-black, can't-find-your-own-ass dark in the motel room. He rolled quitely over and felt on the nightstand for his gun. It wasn't there. He remembered he had left it hanging in the closet.

Narn rolled back. His eyes swept the darkness. There was someone else in the room with him. Narn could feel him. He pulled one leg slowly up out from under the sheets. Then the other.

A tiny light flashed just beyond the end of the bed. A brief sparkle. Than another. Then more sparkles. Then still more until a cloud of sparkling lights as bright as a Christmas tree was growing, pulsating about the foot of the bed. Narn pulled himself up against the headboard, his eyes widening in astonishment. The sparkling could began to coalesce into several soft blue glows. Then the glows into vague figures.

Narn stared as the figures rapidly developed faces and details. He blinked in amazement but the figures didn't go away. Suddenly Narn's bed was surrounded by a ring of tall thin men dressed in white loincloths with crowns of thorns upon their heads. All the men were bleeding or splattered with blood. All had gaping wounds in their palms and sides and anguished looks upon their faces. A few were garden-variety, American-style Jesuses with long blond hair and blue eyes, but most were Mexican-looking: dark, glowering Jesuses with heavy, Indian features, black-eyed Jesuses with streams of bright red blood trickling down their faces.

And they weren't all. Directly behind the Jesuses a second ring of figures was forming, growing out of the first. A ring of women in long, loose robes. These women all had sorrowful faces streaked with tears. Some were holding their hands out in prayerful supplication while still others were pulling their robes open, revealing bright red hearts pierced by silver daggers.

As Narn stared in amazement, one of the Jesuses floated up and over the foot of his bed. The Jesus was bony and angular. He had a radiant white halo over his head. He was black as pitch.

Narn studied him. He was obviously supposed to be Jesus, but he wasn't like any Jesus Narn had ever seen before. In fact, the man wasn't like anyone Narn had ever seen before, period. The man was the purest, deepest, blackest black man Narn had ever seen.

"I must speak with you," the black Christ said in a deep, commanding voice.

"Wh-who are you?" Narn asked hesitantly.

"You don't recognize me?"

"Jesus?" It felt strange to say it.

"I'm called the Lord of Chalma. Sometimes the Lord of Villa Seca. I'm a manifestation of the Christ."

Narn scowled. Narn wasn't much on God or gods, whatever the case might be. When Narn was a child, God—in the form of a corpse-white Sunday School teacher named Mr. Spivey—had taken Narn's last quarter. Narn had never forgiven him for it.

"A manifestation?" Narn wondered. He squinted at the apparition. "You're saying you're not really Jesus?"

"No. I am Jesus. The Jesus who appears as the Lord of Chalma."

"Uh-huh . . ." Narn wasn't too sure about this. "What about all these other guys with you? They all Jesus too?"

"Of course. This is the Lord of Azcapotzalco . . . and the Lord of Ameca . . ." The black Christ glanced over his shoulder.

Narn's eyes narrowed. This was getting to be too much. Narn was raised in a solidly Baptist corner of East Texas. In East Texas there was only one Jesus.

"And this is the Madonna of Juchitán . . . and beside her the Lady of Talpu . . . and—"

"Who are you? Really?" Narn interrupted.

"I just told you. The Lord of Chalma."

"You said you were Jesus."

"The Lord of Chalma is Jesus."

"If you're the real Jesus, then how come you're black?" Narn asked pointedly.

"Many Christs are white, it's true, but not all. There are manifestations of the Christ for every race on earth."

"I'm not talking about manifestations," Narn persisted. "I'm talking about Jesus. The real article. Either you're him or you aren't."

"I am him. I am the real Christ," the black Christ said. "If I weren't, could I appear to you in this manner? Could any of us?"

Narn thought it over, but he had no answer. He shook his head. He had him there.

"We've come to seek your help."

"My help? You want me to help you?" This seemed highly unlikely to Narn, who had never been visited by heavenly apparitions before, but had always assumed they came to help you and not vice versa.

"Yes." The black Christ nodded solemnly. "Will you do it?"

Narn looked around at the rings of Jesuses and Marys, all of whom stared expectantly back at him. Finally he shrugged. "Well, sure," he said. "I mean, how can I refuse?"

"Good. We must move swiftly, then. You are pursuing the ones who carry the heart?"

"The what?"

"You're following the old woman? The one who calls herself Grandmother?"

"The Montoya woman? Well . . . yeah . . . in a way. I'm not after her, though. I'm officially after these two punks she's traveling around with."

"It makes no difference. We need you to help them."

"Help them? You want me to help a couple of dopers? I thought you wanted me to help *you*?"

"It's all the same. We need your help to restore the heart of the world."

"The heart of the world?"

"Listen carefully . . ." the black Christ began.

Sunlight shining through chintz curtains woke Mojo up. He groaned and tried to twist his head away but the light followed him. He groaned again. What time was it? Crack of dawn? He felt like he hadn't gotten more than twenty minutes of sleep in two days. He raised his head and blinked his eyes open. He was in a strange bedroom. He was growing tired of strange bedrooms.

Mojo rolled over. A head of black hair was asleep on the pillow next to him. Cold black, sleek hair. Chuy.

Mojo sat up and rubbed his eyes. There were two cots against the far wall of the bedroom. Both were occupied. From what little Mojo could see, the sleepers had to be children. Probably Chuy's younger brothers. The rest of the room was empty except for a chest of drawers.

Mojo sighed and stretched and remembered the night before and smiled. What a feeling! He was just sorry Uncle Ort couldn't have been there to see it. And Juanita too, of course. Juanita most of all. If only Juanita . . .

Juanita! It hit him then. In his excitement over the demon, he had almost forgotten about Juanita!

Mojo sat up straight. Rubbed his face, trying to get the blood going. They had to find Juanita! And quick! Castillo had said he was going to kill her!

Mojo piled out of bed and scrounged his clothes from the floor. He slipped quietly down a short hall and into a small living room. The living room was neat and bright. One wall was hung solid with photographs. Mojo went to examine them. All of the people in the photographs had brown eyes and dark hair. There was a marine in full dress uniform who looked like he might be Chuy's older brother and a girl in a perfectly white dress who might have been Chuy's sister. Chuy's father was there in an old army uniform. Chuy's car was off to one side, shining lacquer red, with the entire Los Lowriders Club gathered around it. There were dozens of photographs of weddings and first communions and graduations and family ensembles. The largest picture was not a photograph, however. It was a colored print of the Virgin of Guadalupe hung right in the center of the wall with all of the family photographs radiating from it.

Suddenly Mojo smelled something good.

He turned away from the photographs and sniffed the air. His stomach growled. Something was cooking and it smelled delicious. He sniffed again and his stomach rumbled like a freight train over loose tracks.

Surely Juanita could wait until after breakfast?

Mojo let his nose lead him out of the living room and through an open door and into a small but warm kitchen.

"You must be Joseph! Come in. Sit down. I'm Mrs. Garza, Chuy's mother." A short, bubbly little grey-haired woman was standing over the stove, an iron skillet in hand. "Can I fix you some breakfast? I've got scrambled eggs and chorizo. How about some scrambled eggs and chorizo burritos?" She had a plump, smiling face.

Mojo's mouth watered. "Please. That'd be great!"

"And a glass of milk? And some homemade salsa? The tomatoes come right out of my own garden!"

"Both, please." Mojo seated himself eagerly at the breakfast table. The table was Formica with two extra leaves to stretch it out to double length. There were eight chairs spaced around it. He pulled a paper napkin and a metal fork from glasses in the center of the table and set his place. He had apparently hit the jackpot here.

"Mrs. Montoya told me all about last night," the little woman said as she worked the eggs and sausage with a spatula. "About how you brave boys defeated that demon. I was surprised at first. Surprised that such a thing could happen in this day and age. But then she showed me the heart, and of course I could see that it must be true." She paused and pulled up two fat tortillas from a stack on a plate next to the stove and tossed them onto a grill. "These aren't store tortillas either. These are fresh. My sister made them. Two?"

"Yes, ma'am." Mojo's stomach flung itself angrily against his belt buckle.

"It just goes to show that there are still miracles in this world. No matter what anybody says, miracles still do occur. Of course, I guess a demon coming into the world isn't really a miracle. I guess it's really more of a curse." She flipped the tortillas onto a plate and began to fill them. "You want salsa?"

"Please."

Mrs. Garza spooned sausage and eggs onto the tortillas, then ladled salsa from a bowl over them. She deftly rolled the tortillas, poured a glass of milk, and brought both over and set them down in front of Mojo.

It took an extra glass of milk to wash everything down, but in only a few minutes Mojo's plate was sparkling clean.

"More? There's plenty."

"Well . . ."

"Of course you do!"

"Well, maybe one more."

She fixed him two and he ate them both.

Mojo downed the last sip of milk from his glass, then leaned back contentedly in his chair. He let the warm sun from an open window above the sink fall across his face. He could smell roses from the garden just outside. He sighed. Having a full stomach always made him feel better.

"It's frightening," Mrs. Garza was saying, shaking her head as she went to the refrigerator to fetch more eggs. Mojo could hear a chorus of chattering female voices coming from a closed bedroom door. Probably Chuy's sisters.

"Frightening that a demon could threaten you boys like that. I tell you, things just haven't been the same since they did away with the Latin service!"

"Where's Grandmother?" Mojo asked. "Did she go somewhere?"

"Oh, no. She's right outside. Sitting on the front porch with that man."

"Man?"

"I forgot to tell you. He came earlier. He's from El Paso, I think. He was asking about you."

Warning signals went off in Mojo's head. Lights flashed and whistles blew.

"What does he look like? Does he have a moustache and grey hair? Looks sorta like Cesar Romero?"

"Cesar Romero!" Mrs. Garza gave Mojo a puzzled glance. "Oh, no, nothing like him, though I suppose he's old enough to be Cesar Romero."

"I'd better go see him." Mojo pushed back from the table. "Thanks for breakfast. It was delicious."

"Wait until you see what we're having for lunch. Homemade tamales! One of my other sisters is bringing them over. And I'm making a fresh salad from my garden to go with them and . . ."

* * *

Mojo moved cautiously into the living room, then tiptoed over to the front door. Cracked it. He could hear voices. He peeked out. Grandmother was sitting in a porch swing with a strange man. The man was wearing a small-brimmed Stetson. White hair cascaded out from under the Stetson and down the back of his neck. The pickle jar was seated on the swing beside him.

The man in the Stetson turned quickly. His eyes bored into Mojo. His face was as hard as stone. Mojo knew immediately he was the law.

"Joseph!" Grandmother looked up and smiled. "Come out here. There's someone I want you to meet."

Mojo smiled back and strolled out the door as if that was what he had intended to do all along.

"This is Mr. R. K. Narn. He's a Texas Ranger. He's going to help us."

Mojo had to work to keep his smile from collapsing. All of his worst fears were confirmed. Not only a lawman, but a Ranger to boot.

"Birdsong." Narn nodded to him. "I've heard a lot about you. Especially from your uncle."

"I can explain all that," Mojo said hurriedly. "It was all a big misunderstanding. I just borrowed the Cadillac. I was—"

"Cut the crap," Narn said evenly. "You stole that car. You and this Juanita Vásquez woman stole it to transport drugs. I know it for a fact, so there's no point in you trying to lie your way out of it."

A vision of prison swept through Mojo's head. In this vision he was bent over a hard metal table while a long line of large black men formed behind him.

"You've got it all wrong," Mojo protested. "It wasn't like that at all. We—"

"But I'm not here to arrest you."

Mojo paused in surprise."You're not?"

"No. I'm here for something else. This heart deal."

"Heart deal?"

"Mrs. Montoya and I've just been talking about it." Narn nodded to the old woman.

"The Lord of Chalma appeared to Ranger Narn last night!" Grandmother said excitedly. "He sent him here to help us. To help us restore the heart!"

"The lord of who?"

Narn waved it off. "Never mind that. The main thing is, we've got to get the heart back to where it belongs before this demon gets it first."

"You know about the demon?"

"Sure. I oughta know about it; I've tracked the damned thing across half of West Texas and southern New Mexico. I knew it had to be supernatural even before Mrs. Montoya told me about it. Either supernatural or some kind of space alien."

"A space alien!"

"Could have been." Narn shrugged. "Makes as much sense as a demon."

This about R. K. Narn: He was a determined man. He had been determined from the first moment he heard the beast howling in the night. Even more so after he found the tracks. It was why he had followed Mojo and Juanita to New Mexico. He didn't really care about arresting Mojo and Juanita. Was only slightly more interested in Ray Castillo. Couldn't have cared less whether the Lord of Chalma was real or a dream or the aftermath of the bowl of chili verde he'd had for supper. It was the beast Narn was after. He had to see for himself.

"Look, maybe Grandmother didn't tell you everything," Mojo said. "We killed the demon last night. Fried it with light."

"You may have fried it, but it's not dead," Narn told him. "You can't kill it. Lord what's-his-name told me that. Light can send it back to where it came from, but you can't kill it. Not permanently anyway."

Mojo frowned. The demon not dead? This was definitely food for thought.

"But first things first," Narn said. He rose stiffly from the porch swing. "I've been told it's important to snatch this Vásquez girl back from Castillo."

"You're going after Juanita? Good. I'm going with you," Mojo said.

"But how will you find her?" Grandmother asked Narn. "He could have taken her anywhere."

"No. Not just anywhere. He's got a place up here in the mountains. An old hunting lodge. I'm pretty sure that's where she is."

"Will you call the police first?"

"The police? About Ray Castillo? Not likely. Calling the police about Ray is like sending him a telegram you're coming. No, if we were to try and bring the local cops into this thing, then the best we could hope for is he wouldn't have time to dig her grave too deep."

Mojo blanched. "Let's not call them, then."

"I didn't intend to. Now, come on, if you're so hot to trot. My Bronco's parked right out here and we don't have any time to waste." Narn spun away from Mojo and stepped off the porch.

"You coming with us?" Mojo turned to Grandmother.

"No, I'm afraid I'm too old for such things. As I learned last night," she said with a wistful smile. "No, I'll stay here. Mrs. Garza has offered to drive me back up to the old church. I must try and find Captain Benegas again."

"I thought Benegas was the name of the guy who stole the heart?"

"It was," she said. "And is."

"So you think they're the same? That would make the old man . . . what? Three hundred years old?!"

"Strange, isn't it? But that's why it's so important that I find him again."

"You coming, boy?" Narn called. "I haven't got all day."

11

''That's it?'' Mojo asked.

''That's it,'' Narn confirmed.

They were hidden in the shadows of some tall pine trees off to the side of a long, rambling building that resembled a Holiday Inn. A sign in front of the building called it a lodge. The sign said ''Welcome to Los Piñons Lodge.'' They had parked the Bronco a mile or so down the road from the front gates and approached on foot through the woods. They had passed two different trees with ''Chuy + Lupe'' carved into them.

The lodge was built mainly of stone with some wooden trim. It looked old. It had a long front porch and two upper balconies. The wooden trim around the balconies was carved into ornate hearts and deer's heads and hunter's horns and fir trees and other alpine symbols. The trim was painted with bright flowers and curling vines. The lodge looked like something out of an old black-and-white movie. The kind of place where men always wore dinner jackets and women pearls.

"People came here to hunt?"Mojo asked Narn.

"They used to, back in the twenties and thirties. Used to come on the train from back East. But not anymore. It's a private club now. Closed to the public. Castillo's own little private hideaway."

"Look at all those limos." Mojo pointed to several long black cars parked in front of the lodge. "Whose are they?"

Narn shrugged. "Dunno. Friends of Castillo, I guess."

"They must be important friends. Those two guys on the front porch are carrying rifles."

"They're not rifles," Narn said. "They're AK-47s. Heavy-duty stuff. Your nearsighted grandmother could blow your butt off with one of those."

"Then how're we gonna get past them?" Mojo asked.

"Damned if I know," Narn answered.

There was a big black crow perched over a basement window. Mojo looked the crow's way and the crow immediately began to caw loudly. The crow stared directly at Mojo as it cawed.

One of the guards strolled to the end of the porch and peered around the corner. When he saw that it was only a crow making all the fuss, he sauntered back to his post beside the front door.

The crow continued to caw.

"What the hell's wrong with that bird?" Narn grumbled. "I can hardly think with all that squawking."

"Maybe it's trying to tell us something," Mojo ventured.

Narn took a long, slow look at Mojo. "Tell us? You think a bird is trying to start a conversation with you?"

"Could be. An owl saved me just the other night." The crow took wing. It lifted from the top of the basement window and floated over to the pine tree. It landed on a high branch and began cawing and flapping one wing in the direction of the lodge.

"An owl?"

Mojo squinted up at the crow. "I think it wants us to try that rear basement window."

"It wants . . . ? It's a bird, for Chrissakes!"

Mojo looked upwards. "Okay. We'll do it," he whispered to the crow. "Just go back and wait for us."

The crow stopped cawing immediately. It spread its wings and flew back to the basement window. Landed. Cocked its sleek head expectantly towards them.

Narn stared at the crow. Then at Mojo. Then back to the crow.

There were two guards at the rear of the building. The guards were leaning against the wall and smoking cigarettes. They had the same kind of automatic weapons as the two in front.

"Any more bright ideas?" Narn asked Mojo. They were crouched behind a bush opposite the basement window.

"Make a run for it?"

"No good. They'd see us. What we need is a distraction. A diversion."

Mojo thought for a moment. "Like blowing up a car?"

"You've seen too many movies. No, it doesn't have to be that dramatic. Just something to draw their attention away for a few seconds."

"Throw a rock?"

"No, all that'd do would be put them on their guard.

They hear a noise out in the woods, they're gonna be waving those guns in every direction. Including ours.''

One of the guards glanced over towards their bush. They crouched even lower. The guard looked away.

''I can't think of anything else,'' Mojo said.

There was a soft rustling sound near the rear of the lodge. Mojo turned towards it. A deer moved out from under the pines and onto the manicured lawn. A huge buck. He had the biggest rack of antlers Mojo had ever seen. His coat glowed in the dappled light from the forest. The buck sniffed the air and pawed the grass. He stared defiantly at the guards as if daring them to shoot him.

''Look at that,'' Mojo said wonderingly, his eyes glued.

The guards were as mesmerized by the buck as Mojo. After a quick muttered exchange they stood as still as statues. Finally one of them raised his gun. The buck took a step towards the guard and snorted defiantly. The guard pulled an imaginary trigger and made a soft clicking noise with his tongue. The buck tossed his head. The guard grinned and lowered his gun.

''Now!'' Narn hissed. He grabbed Mojo's arm and pulled him from behind the bush. They fled across the lawn to the basement window.

The crow hopped aside.

The window was unlocked.

They were in a small storeroom. The walls were lined with cardboard cases. The cases had names like ''#10 Tomatoes'' and ''Amigo Food Supply, Inc.'' stenciled on them. Mojo shoved the narrow basement window back into place and secured it with a latch. The window was opaque with dirt and grime. There was no danger anyone could look in on them.

Narn motioned. "This way. There's a door over here."

Mojo didn't move. He was waiting for the sound of gunfire. When the sound didn't come he was relieved.

"Come on," Narn called impatiently.

Mojo followed Narn over to the little room's only exit, a heavy grey fire door with a handle instead of a knob. Narn tugged on the handle. The door didn't budge. He looked up. There was a dead-bolt lock set just above the handle.

"Damn." Narn stepped back from the door. "We're trapped. Trapped in this gar-hole. It took a whole menagerie to get us in, and now we've got to go back out and start all over again!"

"Maybe not . . ." Mojo said slowly, eyeing the lock. "Maybe I can pick it."

"Pick a dead bolt?" Narn frowned suspiciously. "You a locksmith? Or is this a little trick you picked up in the doping business?"

"It's just a talent I have," Mojo said defensively. "I'm good at locks, keys . . . all that kind of stuff."

"I'll just bet you are. I—"

Something squealed. Narn glanced down. There was a rat sitting on one of the cases. It was a fat, sleek brown rat with bright black eyes. The rat was staring up at Narn and wagging its pink tail.

Narn eyed the rat critically. The rat squealed again. It raised up on its hind legs and twitched its nose and wagged its tail even harder.

Narn studied the rat for a few seconds longer, then turned to Mojo. "This rat here seems to be acting awfully peculiar for a rat. It's not another one of your little friends, is it?''

"I don't know." Mojo stepped closer. "It could be."

The rat turned and scurried away. It ran to the back of the room and along the wall, leaping from case to case, until it halted underneath an old-fashioned metal coat hook. It turned back to Narn and squeaked loudly. Began hopping up and down.

Narn walked over to the rat. "Okay. I'm here. What next?" Narn asked the rat.

The rat flicked at the wall behind it with its nose. The wall was blank except for the coat hook.

"All right." Narn reached across and pulled down on the hook. Nothing happened. The rat squealed impatiently. Narn pushed up. The hook slid upwards with a groan, exposing a metal track underneath. There was a low grinding noise. A section of the wall a few feet down swung open. There was a descending stairway visible behind the open section.

Narn walked over to the opening and looked inside. "Well, well." He grinned.

Mojo joined Narn. The rat bounded past them across the cases. Scampered through the opening and onto the stairs.

"Lead on, Mr. Rat, lead on," Narn called as he stepped through the doorway.

The rat led them down the staircase and out through a door at its bottom into a long corridor with doorways set off at regular intervals. There was no sign or sound of anyone else.

"Be quiet," Narn warned Mojo as they followed the rat down the corridor. "Just because we can't see anybody doesn't mean they aren't around."

The corridor appeared to have been chiseled rather than built. Its walls were cold damp stone, as was the floor. The rat's toenails and Narn's boots clicked against the stone but Mojo moved silently on his rubber-soled Nikes.

Narn stopped at the first side door and listened quietly before trying the knob. The knob was frozen. He moved on. The next three doors were locked as well. The fifth, and last, turned easily. Narn stepped inside.

After a few moments he emerged again. "Come look at this," he called softly to Mojo.

Mojo went to the doorway and peered in. The room beyond was good-sized. It was filled from floor to ceiling and wall to wall with plump plastic Baggies. The Baggies were filled with white powder. There wasn't much question what kind of powder it was.

"A roomful," Mojo said wonderingly. "A whole room full of dope."

"Something, isn't it? Enough magic powder in here to keep the whole country sniffling for a month. Yeah, I'd say we're looking at the makings for the biggest bust ever." He nodded eagerly, his eyes bright.

"Not yet!" Mojo warned him. "You're not making any bust yet! We've got to get Juanita out of here first!"

"Don't worry," Narn pushed him out and closed the door behind them. "It'll keep. They couldn't move a stash like that with a week's notice. Which is about seven days longer than I intend to give them."

They crept down the corridor. It occurred to Mojo that all the rooms they were passing could be stacked with similar mother lodes of drugs. It was a mind-bending thought.

The rat led them to the end of the corridor and around a corner into a small alcove. There were no doors in the narrow space, only three blank stone walls. The rat went straight to the back wall of the alcove and—rising onto its hind feet—began scratching at the stone.

Mojo and Narn followed it.

"Another door?" Narn ran his hands over the stone, feeling for cracks. He bent down. "What is it, Mr. Rat? Is there another secret door here? Is that what you're trying to tell us?"

The rat squeaked angrily. It swished its long tail in annoyance. It motioned upwards with its nose.

"Something up there? I don't see any . . . Oh, yes. Now I do."

"What is it?" Mojo asked.

"That heating vent." Narn pointed. "That must be it; there's nothing else. He must want us to climb into that duct."

Mojo looked up. There was an old iron grate set high on the wall. The grate was hanging from one screw. Behind the grate was a dark mouth.

"Get in that? Inside it?" This didn't sound like a good idea to Mojo.

"What's the matter? You're not claustrophobic, are you?"

"What?"

"You're not frightened of being closed up in tight spaces, are you? Like elevators? You ever been afraid in an elevator?"

"No. Of course not," Mojo said indignantly. Mojo had never actually been in an elevator.

"Good." Narn reached down and picked up the rat. He dropped the creature into his shirt pocket. Bent over and, putting his hands on his knees, braced himself. "You go first, then."

* * *

The heating duct—like the rooms and corridors—was cut from solid bedrock. Mojo inched his way down it. Mr. Rat was just ahead, his long tail swishing in front of Mojo's nose.

"See anything?" Narn asked from behind.

"Not yet. There's a couple of lights up ahead, though. Probably more vents."

Mojo worked his way to the first vent. Peeked out through the louvered opening. The room beyond was filled with several long, stainless-steel tables covered with lab apparatus. There was metal shelving against the walls. The shelving was stacked with neat rows of unmarked canisters of chemicals. There was a pushcart near the door loaded with the white plastic Baggies.

Mojo crept on.

The next vent opened onto an even larger lab. There were people this time: two men in white smocks standing beside a Bunsen burner. The men were talking quietly together, but their voices were too low to hear. Mojo waited until he was sure they were too preoccupied with their conversation to notice, then squeezed past.

The duct continued another twenty feet in a straight line, then made a sharp turn to the left. Around the turn was a broad shaft heading directly down. Mojo paused at the edge of the shaft and peered over. There was soft light coming up from a hazy bottom far below. There was a column of metal rungs set in the stone walls. The rungs descended towards the haze.

Narn jabbed Mojo from behind. "What're you waiting for?"

Mojo was just about to step off onto one of the rungs when he heard the rat squeak. He glanced to the side. There was a crack in the stone along the back edge of the shaft, just wide enough for a man to squeeze through. The rat was peering out at him from the crack.

Mojo and Narn followed the rat through the crack and down a long descending tunnel. The deeper they went, the cooler the air became, the more cavelike. Just when Mojo was beginning to worry they were going to descend forever, the tunnel opened up into a broad corridor. The corridor was level. It ran perpendicular to the tunnel, back underneath the mountain behind the lodge.

The rat squealed at them and then scampered away up the corridor. Mojo and Narn followed. The corridor finally turned in front of a wall of sparkling granite. Mojo stepped around the turn and found himself in a new, narrower corridor with chalk-white walls.

A tiny pinprick of light was hanging in the corridor just ahead, waiting. Mojo stopped, not sure what to make of it. The light wasn't coming from a bulb or a torch or a candle or anything else. It wasn't attached to anything; it was just there, floating alone in midair. As Mojo watched, the point of light expanded. It grew quickly to the size of a tennis ball. Then even more rapidly to the size of a basketball.

Narn rounded the corner and bumped up behind him.

The light continued to expand rapidly. It became a dazzling white glare that filled half the corridor. Mojo had to squint to see it.

"What the—" Narn began.

Suddenly the ball of light shot forward. Mojo tried to raise his hands to cover his face, but there wasn't enough time. He heard Narn gasp as the ball of light broke over them in a blinding explosion.

Mojo blinked until he could see again. There was a young boy floating ahead of him in midair where the pinprick of light had been. The boy was dressed in a long white gown with ruffled cuffs and a short embroidered cloak. He wore a floppy felt hat with a long purple plume. His face seemed too mature for his plump child's body.

Mojo studied the child for a moment, thinking he had seen him somewhere before. Then suddenly it came to him. That hat, he remembered that funny-looking hat. He had seen it in one of the pictures in Grandmother's house.

Mojo heard something strike the floor behind him. He glanced over his shoulder. Narn was stretched out cold on the stone floor of the corridor. There was another body lying beside his.

Mojo's eyes widened. It was him. It was his body lying next to Narn's. He was looking at himself. He—the second Mojo—was unconscious. His hands were folded neatly across his chest. His chest was heaving softly. He had a smile on his face.

Mojo turned back to the child. He felt strange. Like he was drunk, but not quite. The child floated closer. He held out a hand to Mojo. Mojo looked at the hand. It was transparent. He looked down and saw that his body was transparent too. It was a disconcerting sight. He tried to touch his stomach, to make sure he was still there, but his hand passed right through to his backbone.

The child took one of Mojo's transparent hands in his own. His touch was warm, but more like the warmth of light than flesh. He raised Mojo's hand up, pointing it at the roof of the corridor, and then squeezed it.

A quick shock ran down Mojo's spine.

He began to grow.

12

Mojo sprung like a weed.

In only seconds Mojo grew up to the ceiling of the corridor and then through it. He shot through solid bedrock. Layers of rock strata strobed past his face. Then a crumbling topsoil for an instant before rocketing up into the dappled light of a forest.

Mojo rose up from the forest floor and into the trees. He was growing like the vine in *Jack and the Beanstalk.* His spreading shoulders engulfed an ancient pine, and he felt a tingling current. It took him a moment to realize that the current was a thought. The thought was as slow as sap. It was: "Who?"

Mojo's head broke from the forest and ballooned up into a blue sky. The child was still beside him. They rose into the sky together like twin mushroom clouds. Mojo looked down. The earth was flying away from him. His feet were above ground now. His feet were so large that they covered most of the Sangre de Cristo Mountains. The tip of one shoe was crossing Santa Fe and expanding down the valley towards Albuquerque.

Mojo's head tore through a thin cloud layer and through that into an even thinner layer and through that into a rapidly darkening sky. He had a sense that he was growing at a faster and faster rate. Growing exponentially. A jet buzzed under his nose. He reached out to touch it, but it was already gone, dropping down past his chest like a stone, even though Mojo knew that it wasn't the plane falling, but himself rising.

Mojo left the atmosphere and entered space.

He looked back again as he flew past the moon. The earth was dwindling underneath him. For a moment it looked like the pictures from the space probes, a blue orb wrapped in swirling white clouds. Then it faded to a blue dot. Then to a white dot no brighter than a star.

Mojo mounted up through the solar system. The sun was a shining disk at his feet, the planets revolving around his swelling body. He sparkled as he passed through the rings of Saturn. Comets and meteors too numerous to count shot through him. The child put a hand on his shoulder and gave him a reassuring smile. Mojo could see entire constellations behind the child's smile.

Mojo grew past Pluto—at least he assumed it was Pluto, a small dark planet with nothing near it—and out into the black spaces between the stars.

The sun quickly receded until it was no more than a bright dot. Mojo was going faster now. Ever faster. He passed his first star, a quick blur of light that passed through one of his outstretched hands. Then another. Then ten more. Then a hundred. Stars were whipping past Mojo like highway markers; he couldn't believe there were so many. He stretched out a hand towards a glowing mass of stars that lay far beyond the sun. In seconds his hand reached the mass. Seconds more and his elbow was there. His shoulders were so wide that they stretched across a thousand stars at once.

Mojo rose up out of the sea of stars and into a blackness that was even blacker than the spaces between the stars. He looked down and saw a slowly spinning disk of light at his feet. He recognized the disk as the Milky Way. He tried to see if his feet were still touching the earth, but the earth—if it was still there—was far too small to be seen.

Mojo grew on.

Mojo grew until the Milky Way was no more than a bright blur. He passed through a new galaxy, a great spinning wheel of light. Then a gas cloud that flickered with dozens of colors.

Then more and more.

Soon Mojo was blasting through dozens of galaxies at a time. As far as he could see, there were galaxies. There were millions of them. Maybe billions of them. Maybe more than that. As far as Mojo could see, there were great clouds of stars, some so huge and vast and bright that he could have dropped his own galaxy into any one of them without any more effect than dropping a teaspoon of water into an ocean.

Mojo soared on up through the black night of galaxies. His head was enormous now. It encompassed four galaxies at once. Then eight. Then so many that he couldn't count them all. His body was expanding in every direction. He looked over at the child. The child gave him another reassuring smile.

Mojo grew even larger. As he grew, the galaxies shrank. The galaxies grew ever smaller and smaller relative to Mojo. Soon even the greatest galaxies had dwindled to no more than bright sparks in the universal night. And as these sparks drew closer, ever tighter together, they formed galaxies of their own. Galaxies of galaxies. He saw great spinning wheels of billions of galaxies join together and rush towards him. As he watched these new galaxies form, it struck him that this might be an infinite process. It struck him that if he grew large enough, he might eventually watch these galaxies of galaxies form galaxies of their own and so on out to infinity.

It was enough to make your head swim.

Then even the greatest conglomerations of stars began to dwindle, and he found himself traveling through a fire storm of tiny, close-packed sparks. After a short time the sparks faded, and soon he was in a miasma, a white fog where there was nothing large enough to be seen directly, just a bright hazy light stretching away from him in every direction.

Mojo revolved in the fog. A sense of vertigo seized him. Everywhere he looked, everything looked the same. There was no up, no down, no direction of any kind. Nothing but fog. Infinite white fog. Mojo had grown so big that there was no body in the universe large enough for him to see anymore. Even the galaxies of galaxies had shrunk to no more than faint, diffused light. He had literally outgrown the universe.

Mojo spun in the white fog. Fear shot through him. How would he get back? What if he grew forever out here in this white nothingness with no way to return to earth and Juanita? His eyes darted desperately. Then he felt a touch on his shoulder. He spun around and the child was pointing into the fog ahead of them.

The child was pointing towards an area where the white fog seemed even thicker. At first Mojo couldn't see anything, but then he caught a brief flicker of motion. Something was out there, moving in the fog. Slowly at first, then faster, they approached the area of the motion. Suddenly Mojo realized that it was the fog itself that was moving. The fog was swirling. It was spinning. The fog was spinning around in a great counterclockwise motion like a whirlpool or a tornado.

Mojo and the child drifted deeper into the rapidly swirling fog. The larger they became, the more apparent the motion became. They swelled through the swirling fog and out into an open space. Mojo looked around. They were floating in the still heart of a great vortex. Towering walls of white rushed around them on all sides. Slowly they rose up the funnel of the vortex, up past the white walls, up towards a dim circle of light high above.

In moments they had grown their way out of the vortex and into a pale yellow sky filled with white eggs. At least that's what they looked like to Mojo. The sky was filled with white oval objects that looked exactly like hen's eggs except for small holes in either end which were the mouths of vortexes. Mojo looked down. The vortex they had just come from was on the end of a white egg no different from the rest.

They rose up through the sky of eggs and Mojo saw that many were spinning, their gracefully curved sides dimpling with motion. Some of the eggs were spinning clockwise while others were spinning counterclockwise. Still others, a third variety of egg, didn't spin at all. The eggs were not only spinning but busily dancing around each other as well. They circled one another in intricate and—at least to Mojo—wholly incomprehensible patterns. Here were two eggs revolving around four; there four revolving around two; there eight around four.

Mojo stared dumfounded at the eggs. He couldn't imagine what they were or why.

A few seconds more and they had punched through the last of the eggs and were rising through pale light towards a series of brightly colored bands that reminded Mojo of Saturn's rings except that these rings didn't all lie together on a single plane. These rings arced all around them in great sweeping circles that resembled pictures he had seen of the northern lights. As they drew closer to the rings he could see they were spinning. Spinning and rippling at the same time. Ripples were running around the spinning rings like stockers chasing each other on an oval track. As they pushed through the rings Mojo saw that they were made of billions of the white eggs.

Mojo turned around, staring back past the rings to the white ball the rings orbited, looking for the egg they had emerged from, but it was gone. Swallowed. And then even the white ball and its rings were receding, falling rapidly away from them.

Mojo felt a sense of loss. The earth was back there somewhere. Back in that dwindling white dot down one of those weird eggs through a swirling vortex into a white fog and out into a galaxy of galaxies of galaxies.

Mojo gulped and turned his head away. It made his stomach churn to even think about it.

Mojo and the child swelled up into a sea of white balls. As they grew ever larger the balls began to clump together into groups. Then the groups formed white balls of their own, then even these began to recede until nothing was left but a white haze that was similar to the white fog of the egg yet subtly different.

The white haze began to shade into pink. The child reached over and, without any warning, squeezed Mojo's shoulder. A mild shock ran down Mojo's arm. The pink haze became a red smoke.

Mojo felt different. He tried to figure it out as he drifted upwards through the billowing red smoke. And then he knew. He was slowing. He was still growing, but nowhere near as rapidly as before. He could feel the growing effect running down inside him like a cheap watch.

The red smoke became brown, striated water.

The brown water became a dark, grainy ice.

The dark ice ended and Mojo shot out into bright blue light.

Mojo swam slowly upwards, the child beside him, rising up through the blue light. He was swimming through a heavy liquid that distorted his vision. He emerged from the liquid and floated into clear air. He was rising towards a dark sky. As he rose higher Mojo realized that it wasn't a sky but a ceiling. A ceiling with wooden beams.

Just before Mojo would have bumped into the ceiling the growing effect ground to a halt. Mojo stopped. Suddenly he was no longer rising, no longer expanding. He turned over, his soft transparent body rolling like a water balloon, and looked down.

He was floating above a large, poorly lit room. There was an old white-haired woman seated on a chair directly underneath him. The woman was holding a glass jar in her lap. There was a faint blue light coming from the jar.

Mojoe did a double take. Then another. He couldn't believe it, but it was. It was Grandmother. Grandmother and the pickle jar.

Not only Grandmother. The old man, Benegas, was seated directly across from her. Benegas' lips were moving, but his voice was so low that Mojo couldn't make out what he was saying. Mojo glanced towards the front of the room and there was the entry door hanging from its one hinge. He shook his head in wonder. It was the church. He was back in the old church where they had first met Benegas. He looked down again at Grandmother. At the pickle jar in her lap. There was no doubt about it. They must have come up out of the pickle jar. Out of the blue light. And before that . . .

Mojo felt a hand on his shoulder. He turned. It was the child. The child squeezed Mojo's shoulder for a third time.

Suddenly Mojo was shrinking.

Mojo fell like a stone. He fell across Grandmother. As he passed through her he caught a thought,much as he had with the ancient pine tree. This was a much deeper and faster thought, however. It was: "God help me!"

And then he was through Grandmother and tumbling down towards the glass jar.

Mojo sensed something was wrong and turned. The child was gone. Mojo looked, but couldn't see the child anywhere. He peered down. The jar was closer now, rushing up to meet him.

Mojo windmilled his arms, trying to slow himself, but it didn't work. He continued to fall rapidly. And then suddenly, just before he dropped through the lid of the jar, the child reappeared. Mojo sagged with relief. The child took his arm and resumed guiding him down.

The child directed Mojo through the lid of the pickle jar and down into the liquid. The child pulled on Mojo's arm, guiding him. They swooped around the perimeter of the heart, just catching the edge of the quick blue light. As they curved back, Mojo noticed a large black patch on the heart. The patch ran nearly all the way across the bottom. At first he couldn't figure out what the black patch was, even though he had the feeling he had seen it before. And then, as they drew closer, he knew. As the deep fissures and angry red swelling of the black patch came into clearer focus, he remembered where he had seen such nasty black patches before: in high school, in health class, in the *Perils of Smoking* film Mrs. Benitz had shown them at least a dozen times.

The black patch was a cancer.

They slowed as they curled around the bottom of the heart. They drifted lightly above then onto the surface of the angry black cancer.

Mojo landed on his feet, straddling a fissure that cut so deeply into the heart that he couldn't see its bottom. The child landed beside him.

Suddenly Mojo's feet slipped. He staggered badly. The flesh around the fissure was slick. It was hard and lumpy and contorted. It had a sheen to it like a beetle's shell.

Mojo windmilled his arms. He shuffled his feet looking for solid ground. He didn't find any. He flipped over. He tumbled down into the fissure.

Mojo fell down into the fissure, unable to stop himself. He fell slowly, like sinking in water, even though it was air. It felt creepy. Like being swallowed.

Mojo righted himself. The child was beside him.

Mojo and the child descended deeper into the black fissure. Waves of heat rushed up to meet them. Waves of wet, sweltering heat. Jungle heat. Jungle stench. Mojo felt sweat break out on his face like a sudden rain.

They fell deeper into the fissure. Rough, enflamed ridges of flesh appeared on the walls. There were tiny plants, or what looked like plants, growing on the ridges. The plants were grey and flabby-looking with limp fernlike fronds that trailed the surface. They looked nasty. Diseased. Mojo was glad he was floating free and clear down the center. Even the thought of brushing against one of those mushy-looking plants filled him with revulsion.

The fissure began to narrow ahead. It closed quickly, but it didn't make any difference. As quickly as the fissure narrowed, so did Mojo and the child, growing small enough to slip down it.

Finally, after what seemed like a tremendous distance but was probably only a few millimeters, the fissure closed completely. But that didn't matter either. They fell right on through, down through the floor of the fissure, down a hole between two bubbling black cells.

They exited the hole into a vast grey cavern filled with strange trees. The trees reminded Mojo of fungus. They were even nastier than the fissure plants. A white mucus oozed from pores in the trees' lumpy green leaves and dripped onto the floor of the cavern. The mucus formed slick puddles around the soft sagging trunks. As Mojo and the child drifted down towards the floor Mojo saw something move in one of the puddles.

As they drew closer to the floor the motion grew more pronounced, more agitated. Now Mojo could see other puddles stirring as well. Bubbling trails crossed the slimy surfaces of the puddles. Something popped up directly below. Mojo could see it clearly. It was a worm. A long grey worm. The worm looked up. It had a human face.

"You've come!" the worm shouted. It turned its snout. "Look! He's come! He's come for us at last!"

Other worms began to poke their heads out from beneath the ooze.

"Oh, thank God!" another cried, swinging its head from side to side. It was grinning madly. It had no teeth.

Mojo grabbed the child's arm, trying to turn him in another direction, away from the floor. Mojo didn't know about the child, but this was just about as close as he wanted to come to the worms and their puddles. Just the thought of falling into one of those disgusting puddles of mucus was enough to give him the shivers.

Mojo and the child dropped straight towards the cavern floor. Then, just before they would have splattered into a particularly vile, greenish pocked of ooze, they made a sharp right-hand turn. They shot over the fungus forest, parallel to it, heading for a wide hole in the cavern's wall.

"Wait! Come back!" a worm yelled.

"Don't leave us!" another cried.

"You bastards!" a third screamed.

They passed through the hole into another cavern.

The new cavern was even larger than the last. It was a great, open pit, much like a copper pit, its sides lined by level terraces. The terraces descended like stair steps to a dim bottom far below. Each terrace held rounded mounds of fungus-tree mucus.

They sailed to the middle of the cavern and dropped again. The heat in this new cavern was dry. The jungle sweat evaporated quickly from Mojo's face. They fell swiftly, past terrace after terrace, past mound after mound of mucus.

There were openings in the sides of the cavern. Worms filed in and out of these in columns of two. Each pair of worms slithered to a mound of mucus and spit on it before returning to the opening. It took Mojo a moment to realize it was tree mucus they were spitting.

The worms were carrying mucus in their mouths to the mounds.

They fell deeper into the pit. As they approached the bottom, the heat increased. The mucus mounds here were dried. Crystallized into a granular form like sugar. Gangs of worms were pounding the crystals with rocks, turning them into a fine white powder.

Mojo felt something and glanced to the side. He saw a demon squatting on a ledge.

Mojo grabbed the child's arm in alarm. The demon was ugly as hell. It was similar in some respects to the demon who had chased Mojo and Grandmother the night before, but different in others. It seemed to have more spider in it, less centipede. It had eight legs covered by thick black fur. It had a bulbous head with a wide, gaping mouth and eyebrows that were as hairy as its legs. It had enormous pincers protruding from green, swollen cheeks.

The demon leaped to its feet as Mojo and the child dropped past it. ''Ssstop!'' it buzzed.

Good luck, Mojo thought.

The demon didn't wait to see if they would. It jumped off the ledge and flapped after them on broad dragonfly wings.

Mojo looked down. The cavern floor was coming up fast. That was good. What was bad was that there was only one small area that wasn't covered by a mound of crystallized mucus. If they didn't hit that small area, and if there wasn't a crack or a hole there . . .

''Sssstop!!'' The demon had a voice like an air-raid siren. It made Mojo's ears ring. He could feel the wind from its wings on the back of his head.

As they drew nearer to the floor a tiny crack appeared. Hope surged in Mojo. This could lead to something. It was like the time Betty Gomez had offered to show him the scar on her upper thigh.

Then, just when Mojo was certain they were going to drop through the crack before the demon could catch them, a worm slithered across the tiny opening, blocking it. The worm stopped. Looked up. It had a pudgy grey face with a fat man's tiny eyes.

"Move!" Mojo screamed down at the worm.

The worm's tiny eyes widened.

"Move, damn it! You're in our way!"

The worm gasped. Then: "Help me! Take me with you! I'm not supposed to be here! It's all been a big mistake!"

"Move, damn you!" The worm was coming up fast. Mojo glanced back. So was the demon.

"You have to!" the worm whined. "You have to take me!"

"I said move it!" Mojo squeaked as he shrank rapidly towards the worm. "Move your butt, or I'll move it for you!"

It was an empty threat. The worm was as big as a freight train by now. He could have swallowed Mojo and the child both in one gulp. And if he didn't close his mouth in the next few seconds, Mojo was afraid he just might.

The worm blinked in confusion as Mojo and the child fell towards him. Suddenly his supposed saviors—who only moments before had been giants descending from the sky—were no bigger than bumblebees.

"Why you're . . . you're little!" the worm cried plaintively.

"Move!!" Mojo squealed anxiously.

Then the worm saw the demon. His fat little eyes bulged. His grey face turned even greyer. "No!" the worm wheezed in a suddenly frightened voice. "No! Please!"

Mojo and the child tumbled towards the worm's gaping mouth.

The worm ducked his head and rolled into a protective ball.

Mojo and the child fell past the worm, just grazing his slimy skin, and into the crack in the floor.

The demon screamed.

They plunged through the crack into an ocean of brown, striated water.

Through the water into red smoke.

Through the smoke into a white haze.

Through the white haze into an ocean of tiny white points.

Which quickly became white balls.

Mojo tugged nervously on the child's arm. He was getting worried. They were passing through thousands of the white balls. There were thousands more ahead. How would they ever find the right one when they all looked exactly alike? The one that led back to New Mexico and Juanita.

"Which one?" Mojo asked. "Can you tell?"

The child smiled at him, then turned away without answering.

Mojo shook his head. How would they ever find the right ball? And even if they did, how would they ever find the right spinning egg? And even if they did, how would they ever find the right white speck in the fog of white specks? And even if they did that . . . ?

Mojo sighed. It was too much. He quit trying to think about it.

The white balls grew even larger and fewer.

Suddenly the child pulled Mojo to the left. Then to the right. Then back to the left again.

They were falling towards a single white ball. The white ball mushroomed in size as they approached. Mojo could see its rings rippling. He prayed it was the right one.

They fell through the rings into the white ball.

Through the white ball into an egg.

Through the egg into a white fog.

Through the white fog into a fire storm.

Through the fire storm into a black night of galaxies.

Through the black night of galaxies into the Milky Way.

Through the Milky Way to the earth.

Mojo opened his eyes. He was lying on his back. It took him a moment to realize he was in the stone corridor.

"You okay?"

Mojo looked up. Narn was squatting beside him.

"I think so." Mojo pinched his arm to make sure it was solid. It was.

"Did somebody jump us?" Narn asked.

Mojo hoisted himself up to a sitting position. Rubbed his eyes to clear them. "I had a vision."

"I bet you did. But did you see who it was? The last thing I remember was this big ball of bright light coming straight at me."

Mojo nodded. "Me too. That was right before I left."

"Left?" Narn frowned.

"Well, I'm not sure I left left. At least my body didn't. My body must have stayed here, but my mind definitely left."

Narn studied him for a long moment. ''I can believe that,'' he said finally.

''No, really. I really had this vision. It wasn't a dream or anything. It was real.''

''A vision, huh? Was it the black guy?''

''No, it was a child. I think maybe it was one of Grandmother's saints. He took me on a tour of the universe.''

''The universe like in the moon and stars?'' Narn asked as he rose to his feet. He reached down and took Mojo's hand, helped him up.

''Yeah,'' Mojo said, standing. ''It's big, I can tell you that. Real big. You wouldn't believe how big the universe is.''

''Oh, I might.''

''I think he did it to show me what's in the heart. He wanted me to know how important the heart is; why we have to get it back to the Madonna right away.''

''In the heart? There's something in the heart?''

''Everything's in the heart. You, me, the earth, the whole universe, we're all inside the Madonna's heart.''

Narn peered doubtfully at Mojo. ''The heart in the pickle jar?''

''Yeah. The whole universe is inside the heart in the pickle jar. And it's sick too. He showed me that. That's why we've got to get it back to her as quick as we can.''

Narn stared hard at Mojo for a long time. Finally he shrugged. ''Come on,'' Narn said.

Narn turned on his heel and started up the corridor.

Mojo followed after him.

Mr. Rat was waiting.

13

The rat led Mojo and Narn down the chalk corridor and through an unlocked door into a small, empty room.

"Guardroom," Narn said, looking around. "We must be close. Cells are probably just outside that door."

He walked over to a gun rack and jerked on it. A hasp lock rattled. "Too bad. I'd sure like to have something with a little more stopping power than a pistol."

"I can open it for you," Mojo offered.

"Well, then, don't just stand there, do it."

Mojo pulled a length of stiff wire from his pocket and went to work on the hasp lock. The rat danced away from Narn and over to the door and then back again. It fussed angrily, its long tail slapping the floor.

"Keep your shirt on," Narn told the rat. "It won't do any good to spring the girl if we can't get back out again. And I figure what's in this rack is a direct ticket to the outside.''

Mojo popped the lock. Narn wrenched the rack open and reached in and selected a sawed-off shotgun. He slid the rack's bottom drawers out and began searching through them for shells.

''A shotgun?'' Mojo wondered. ''I figured you'd want one of those automatic rifles.''

''Shows what you know,'' Narn said as he filled his pockets with shells from an open box.

''Here.'' He handed Mojo a rifle. ''You may need this.''

In a few minutes Narn had the shotgun loaded. ''Okay.'' He slammed a shell into the chamber with a sharp clang. He turned to the rat. ''We're ready now, Mr. Rat. Take us to her.''

The rat led them out of the small room and into another corridor. The corridor was empty. There were barred cell doors along both sides.

Mojo followed Narn and the rat slowly up the corridor, his ears open for any sound. He moved stealthily, checking each cell as he passed. All were empty. He tried carrying the rifle cradled in his arms and then slung over his shoulder. It felt uncomfortable both ways. He pulled the rifle off his shoulder and let it dangle by his side. He wished he hadn't taken it. Mojo couldn't shoot straight, and his Uncle Ort had always warned him that it was dangerous for a man who couldn't shoot straight to carry a gun. Someone else might not know it and shoot him first.

Juanita was in one of the middle cells. She was lying on a cot in a corner, fast asleep. Mojo used his wire on the door lock while Narn and the rat stood guard.

Mojo had the door open within seconds. "Juanita?" he whispered. He went to her. Shook her shoulder gently. "Wake up, Juanita."

She was on him in a flash. If Mojo had been any slower, she would have clawed his eyes out. He received a long scratch on his cheek as it was.

"Hey! It's me!" he cried, backing off.

"Mojo!" Juanita suddenly realized she had made a mistake. "Oh, I'm sorry! I thought you were one of them!"

"Keep your voice down," he warned her.

"Oh, Mojo." She threw her arms around him. "I knew you'd come! I knew you wouldn't let those *pendejos* sacrifice me!"

"Sacrifice you?"

"Can you believe it? These creeps were actually gonna sacrifice me to the devil! The devil!"

"Hurry up! Quit screwing around in there!" Narn hissed into the cell.

"Who's that?" Juanita asked.

"Narn. He's a Texas Ranger."

"A what?"

"Later. I'll explain everything later. Right now, we've got to get you out of here before somebody comes along to check on you."

Mojo led Juanita out of the cell and into the hallway.

"This way. After that rat up there."

"Rat?!"

The rat was already halfway up the corridor. It turned and squeaked urgently.

"You want me to follow a rat?" Juanita asked incredulously.

"Not just a rat. *Mister* Rat." Mojo took her arm and started up the corridor.

"Wait." Juanita stopped him. "We've got to get Rocky out first."

"Who?"

"Him."

Mojo turned to where Juanita was pointing. There was a young boy hanging on the bars of a cell across the way. He couldn't have been more than fourteen or fifteen. His hair was wild and unkept. Dirt and filth obscured most of his thin face. He was dressed in jeans and a torn T-shirt with "Metal Rules" emblazoned across the front.

"That's Rocky?"

"Right. They were gonna sacrifice him along with me. Can you help him?"

"No problem," Mojo told her.

Mojo had the door of the second cell open in seconds. The boy was just stepping through when footsteps approached from down the hall. Then the sound of a man's voice.

Mr. Rat squealed in alarm and flew up the corridor.

Mojo grabbed Juanita's arm and raced after Mr. Rat.

Narn and the boy raced after Mojo and Juanita.

Mojo and Juanita skidded around the end of the corridor and fled up another. They were almost to the end when the rat suddenly stopped and began clawing at a stone wall. Mojo looked up. There was another loose grate.

"Too late. We don't have time for that," Mojo told the rat as he shot past him.

Shouts echoed from somewhere behind them. The sound of running feet.

They flew around a second corner and into yet another corridor. There was an open double door just ahead. Mojo ducked into the door, taking Juanita with him. The boy and Narn followed. They sprinted into a vast, open room, their footsteps echoing thinly off distant walls.

Mojo slowed. Then stopped. His eyes darted desperately from side to side, surveying the huge room, which wasn't really a room at all but a cavern with a high arched roof with stalactites hanging from it. Great sweeping walls of washed limestone fell from the roof to a concrete floor.

Mojo heard footsteps behind them, pounding up the corridor. His eyes swept the cavern again but without success.

There were no other exits.

They were trapped.

The cavern was lit by dim, oily torches and filled with folding chairs. Row upon row of folding chairs swept away towards the front. Beyond the chairs, mounted high on the front wall, was a gigantic goat head. The goat head was white, covered by long fur. It had huge red eyes that caught the torchlight. Its horns were golden and hooked. Directly below the goat head was the dark maw of a small cave. In front of the cave was a carved stone altar on a raised dais. In front of the altar were four men. Mojo recognized two of them.

The first man Mojo recognized was the Reverend Jerry Lee Rutt, the semifamous TV evangelist. The Reverend Rutt was pointing angrily at Mojo. He didn't look at all like he looked on television. His cheeks weren't pink. He didn't have a Bible in his hand. He wasn't grinning. If it hadn't been for his hair—a towering black edifice of waves and curls—Mojo wouldn't have recognized him at all.

The second man Mojo recognized was the one pulling a gun from his coat pocket: Machete Ray Castillo.

"Get down!" Mojo yanked on Juanita's arm.

He was just in time.

Narn's shotgun exploded behind them. Fire leaped over their heads. Shotgun pellets, sounding like hail on a tin roof, ricocheted around the altar.

Castillo yelled and dropped his gun and clutched the side of his head. The other three men dove into the first row of folding chairs.

Narn's shotgun roared again. One of the folding chairs next to Castillo did a front flip. Castillo jerked his hand away from his head and dove for the cover of the chairs. Mojo could see Castillo's ear was bleeding. What was left of it.

"This way!" The boy, Rocky, ran past them down the aisle. Mojo had a pretty good idea of where he was headed. The cave. It was the only way out.

Mojo grabbed Juanita and ran after the boy. He could hear Narn's boots pounding the concrete behind them.

They were only four or five rows from the altar when Mojo heard a shout from behind, followed by several gunshots, followed by another thunderous roar from Narn's 12-gauge. An instant later a figure popped up out of the folding chairs to Mojo's right. It was Castillo. His mouth was drawn back in a pained grimace. The shoulder of his expensive suit was soaked with dark blood. His pistol was in his hand. He was taking aim at Mojo.

Mojo blanched. There was no way he was going to get his rifle up, aim, and shoot Castillo before Castillo shot him.

Luckily he had another option.

* * *

Mojo may not have been much of a shot, but he was one hell of a chunker. Mojo was the champion beer-bottle chunker of Culberson County. No Texas Highway Department sign was safe when Mojo was on the road. Mojo could dead-center a Highway Department sign from a speeding automobile with fantastic accuracy. Poteet had once bragged that Mojo could hit a highway sign with a beer bottle even if Mojo was too drunk to see the sign.

Mojo whipped the rifle forward with a sweeping underhand motion that would have been alien to any boy who had learned his throwing style from baseballs rather than beer bottles. The rifle spun once in the air. Twice. Three times. It caught Castillo on the forehead with a sharp crack. The rifle bounced one way and Castillo another. Castillo went down into the quagmire of folding chairs like a load of bricks.

The Reverend Jerry Lee Rutt peeked over the top of the chairs just as Mojo hurtled past. There was a bruise on his cheek and a long red scratch across his temple but his lacquered hair was still immaculate. "I'll remember you, motherfucker!" the Reverend Rutt screamed after Mojo.

Mojo and Juanita tore around the altar and under the goat's head and into the small cave, Mojo snagging a torch from a socket as they flew past.

"Hurry up!" the boy shouted. He was just inside the mouth of the cave, waiting for them. He had a second torch. Before Mojo could reply, the boy had turned and was pounding up the narrow passage.

Mojo and Juanita raced after the bobbing flame of the boy's torch, Narn right behind them.

14

Mojo and Juanita ran down the cave, following the boy's bobbing torch. They ran for some time, turning and winding and turning and running, following one passage after another. After a time Mojo lost track. The cave had more strands than a bowl of spaghetti. It was like traveling through a piece of Swiss cheese. As they dodged through one narrow tunnel after another he began to doubt whether even chain-gang dogs could have followed them.

"Slow . . . down . . . damn it!" Narn wheezed finally.

"Good . . . idea." Mojo slowed to a walk then halted, Juanita beside him.

The boy turned back. "What's wrong? Why are you stopping?"

"Why? I'll tell you why." Narn leaned against the

wall of the cave and took a deep breath. "Because nobody's chasing us."

Mojo listened. Narn was right. There were no pursuing footsteps. No voices. The cave was silent except for their ragged breath and the distant sound of water dripping.

"They're not?"

"Nope," Narn said. " We lost them somewhere, and I don't think we're gonna see them again anytime soon either. You made sure of that, buddy boy. I haven't seen that much juking and jiving since O.J. Simpson retired. They've got about as much chance of finding us as we do of finding them. Which is to say, slim to none."

"You're saying we're lost?" Mojo asked.

"Well, I don't know about you, but I damn sure am."

Mojo peered around. Beyond the small circle of torchlight the cave was a blank wall of impenetrable darkness. He couldn't have said which direction was north or east or whatever, never to mention which led back to the big cavern.

"I don't see that it makes any difference whether we're lost or not," Juanita said. "We couldn't go back to the lodge now even if we wanted to."

"Good point." Narn pushed himself away from the wall. "She's right. If we intend to leave this gar-hole alive, we're gonna have to find another exit. One that doesn't have Ray Castillo and his *pistoleros* waiting for us."

"But how?" Mojo wondered. There were several corridors near them, all branching off in different directions. Any one of them could have led out; any one of them could have led deeper into the maze of passageways.

"There're ways to find a trail. Even in a cave." Narn

told him. "If the air's circulating, then we can follow it to its source. And I suspect from the way those torches are flickering, there is circulation."

Narn stepped closer to Mojo. Eyed his torch. After a moment he pointed up one of the side corridors. "That way. The breeze is blowing from that direction."

Narn led them up the side passage, stopping periodically to check the soft cave breeze by studying the torch flames or by holding up a wet finger. They passed out of the passage and into a series of short connecting tunnels. Out of the connecting tunnels and into a new passage. Reached a dead end, doubled back, passed into yet another long corridor.

They entered a large cavern. Narn had Mojo extinguish his torch, saving it for later. The cavern was so big that the dim light of the single torch couldn't reach its walls. The cavern might have been the size of the one under the hunting lodge or the size of a football stadium or the size of a small ocean. There was no way to tell.

"Were you serious back there when you said they were going to sacrifice you to the devil?" Mojo asked Juanita as they picked their way across the huge cavern.

"Serious as a heart attack. It's how they pay him for the stuff."

"The stuff?" Narn asked.

"The cocaine. Castillo sacrifices people to the devil, and the devil gives him cocaine in return."

Mojo shook his head. So Grandmother was right after all. The devil really was behind the drug business.

"That's the damnedest thing I ever heard," Narn said. He glanced at Mojo and hesitated. "Well, maybe the second damnedest."

"But how did you know where I was?" Juanita asked Mojo.

Mojo quickly recounted Narn's encounter with the black Christ and his with the demon.

"A demon?" the boy, Rocky, asked dubiously.

"I know it sounds crazy, but believe me, it's real," Mojo assured him.

"I believe you," Juanita said. "You know that altar back there where all the chairs were? That's where Castillo planned to sacrifice Rocky and me. On that altar. He told me all about it. Bragged. Said they were going to cut our hearts out, and then, afterwards, a demon would come up out of this cave, up from Hell, and take our souls."

"This cave? This cave we're in now?" It sounded ominous to Mojo.

"Right." She nodded grimly.

"Come on." Rocky tugged at Narn's sleeve. "Let's get going."

They crossed to the far side of the cavern and—after searching along a limestone wall until they found an opening—passed into a long corridor with a sand bottom. Along that corridor into a longer one. Then a longer one still.

The boy's torch began to sputter. When its flame had dwindled to little more than a feeble blue flicker, Mojo relit his. Moments later the boy's torch died with a final wisp of oily grey smoke.

They reached the end of the corridor and descended into a narrow passage with a rocky floor and damp walls. The passage ended at a pile of loose boulders. Narn said the breeze was blowing from behind the boulders, so they climbed them. Mojo going up first and then helping the others. Rocky scrambled over last, bounding up the rocks like a monkey.

They squeezed through a crevice behind the boulders and into a tunnel so tight that they had to crawl most of the way. The passage finally opened up into a larger corridor with high, shadowy ceilings. The breeze grew stronger. At the end of the corridor there were several passageways. One of the passageways was faced with a row of gigantic black columns.

"What are they?" Mojo ran his hand down one of the columns. The column was smooth and hard and cold as ice. It was blacker than black. Unnaturally black. It seemed to absorb light rather than reflect it. It had veins like marble but it wasn't.

"A better question is: Why are they?" Narn stroked his chin and stared into the darkness behind the columns. "This seems like a rather peculiar spot to be building things."

"Maybe it's the entrance to Hell," Juanita suggested. "A gate."

"Hell?"

"Sure. If Castillo is bringing up drugs from Hell, then there has to be an entrance to it somewhere, right? Maybe this is it."

"You think so? You think this could be a gate to Hell?" Mojo wondered.

"Maybe. What else?"

Mojo had no idea. He peered through the columns into the cavern beyond. All he could see was blackness and the leading edge of a packed, level floor.

"But it really doesn't matter, does it?" Narn said. "The torch is almost finished. If we intend to get out of here alive, we've got to keep following the breeze.

And the breeze is blowing from in there." He pointed through the columns.

"Couldn't we at least check out some of these other passages first?" Mojo asked, not at all anxious to go to Hell if he could avoid it.

"Come on." Narn took the torch from Mojo and stepped between the columns. The boy followed. Mojo and Juanita had no choice but to follow as well.

They were walking along another black sea bottom. If the cavern had walls or a ceiling, they were too far away for the flickering torchlight to reach them. The air was colder here than in the other sections of the cave. The breeze was stronger. The flames of the torch arched like tree boughs in a gale.

They had been walking for about fifteen minutes when Narn suddenly paused. He lowered the torch and studied the floor for a long moment. Then stood back up.

"Footprints," he said over his shoulder as he resumed walking. "At least most of them were. Some of the others didn't look that much like feet."

Mojo swallowed. This was not the sort of talk Mojo cared to hear while walking through the pitch-black dark with only a slowly dying torch for light. He found Juanita's hand and squeezed it. Juanita, thinking he was trying to reassure her, squeezed back.

They walked on. They came to a pool of darkness that was blacker than even the bottom of a cavern should have been. Narn stepped to its edge.

"Pit. Deep one."

Mojo joined Narn. The pit was huge. The light barely carried to the other side. Narn held the torch over the open mouth but there was no bottom to be seen. Just sheer stone walls descending into darkness. A shaft straight down into the bowels of the earth.

Mojo felt air, a current rising from the pit. It brushed across his face. He sniffed. The rising air was hot and humid. It stank of rot and mildew and sweet nauseous decay.

Mojo shrank back from the edge of the pit. He had smelled that stench before.

"What's this?" Narn ran his hand along the ground.

Lifted it. His fingers were coated with a fine, white powder. He licked some off the tips. Frowned. Licked again.

"Cocaine," Narn said slowly. "I'm damned if it's not cocaine!"

"Don't! Don't put that in your mouth!" Mojo gasped.

Narn squinted at him. "Why not? This could be important. It confirms what the girl was saying. It's—"

"Just . . . don't . . . put any more in your mouth. Please," Mojo pleaded through clenched teeth. "It's not really cocaine . . . It's . . ." He couldn't say it.

"It's what? Poison? I agree, though I sure didn't expect to hear that from the likes of you. Now, come on. Let's get moving. That torch isn't getting any longer."

They skirted the pit and were only a short ways beyond when a light flashed suddenly in the darkness ahead. "There!" Narn shouted. They rushed eagerly towards it.

"Breeze's getting stronger!" Narn exclaimed as they neared the light. "Must be an exit!"

But it wasn't.

It was a lamp. An old-fashioned oil lamp. The lamp was balanced on the edge of a battered wooden table.

An old man was seated behind the table. He looked up as they hurried into the circle of yellow light.

"Well, well." The old man cocked a bushy eyebrow. "What have we here?" A deck of greasy cards was laid out on the table before him. A solitaire game.

"Man, are we ever glad to see you!" Mojo exclaimed. "We're lost. We're . . . we . . ." Mojo's voice trailed off. He suddenly realized the old man was not a man at all.

The old man grinned. He was very old. Older even than Narn. Older even than Grandmother. He had wrinkles so deep they seemed to cut his gaunt face to the bone. He had lips that were too wet and eyes that were too yellow and huge liver spots on his arms and hands the color of bloating fish bellies. He had a pair of small, ivory-colored horns protruding from his forehead.

"Who are you?" Narn asked. What he meant was: What are you?

"Me? Why, I'm old Aghastere. Didn't they tell you about old Aghastere?"

Narn wasn't sure who "they" were. "Well, no . . . nobody told us anything."

"They didn't tell you anything about old Aghastere?" The old man's eyes narrowed. "They didn't even mention my name?" He sounded offended.

"Look!" Juanita pointed to the side. "Another gate."

Mojo peered. She was right. There was another set of black columns set in the far wall beyond the table. Behind them were stairs. The stairs led up.

"No." Narn shook his head. "And now—if you don't mind—we'd better be on our way."

He stepped towards the doorway.

"But I do mind," Aghastere said, his voice suddenly hard. "I'm afraid I mind a lot."

Narn turned back with a frown. "What do you mean, you mind?"

"I mean I can't let you go. But you knew that, didn't you? That's rule number one down here, isn't it? No one is ever allowed to leave Hell."

"Hell? You're claiming we're in Hell?!"

"Well, an antechamber, but it's all the same as far as you getting out."

"You don't understand," Juanita protested. "We're not in Hell. We're just passing through."

"Just passing through? . . . Oh, I like that one!" The old man cackled, displaying broken, discolored teeth punctuated by gaps. "Just passing through! That's a good one!"

Mojo caught something in the corner of his eye. Glanced over his shoulder and saw a small shadow scurrying out of the far edge of the lamplight. The shadow touched the wall and then turned for the doorway. Rocky.

"Look, you can't keep us here. We're not damned." Narn tried to reason with the old man. "We're not even dead."

"Sure," Aghastere snorted.

Mojo watched as Rocky bolted out of the darkness and dashed between two of the black columns. For a moment Mojo thought the boy was going to make it. But then, just as Rocky's feet were disappearing up the stairwell, the old man wheeled around, reached leisurely out, and snagged the boy by the cuff of the neck.

The old man dragged Rocky back to the table and dropped him in a heap on the floor. "Damned gates," the old man muttered to himself. "Getting so weak they couldn't stop a mouse."

Mojo's eyes widened. It had all happened so quickly he wasn't exactly sure how the old man had done it. All he knew for certain was that Aghastere's reach was longer than his arm. Much, much longer.

Rocky scrambled back from the table, away from the old man, his eyes as wide as Mojo's.

"Now, then," the old man said pleasantly. "Now that we've established that none of you are going anywhere—any of you folks play cards?"

"Cards?!" Juanita sputtered. She took a step forward.

"Wait." Mojo stopped her. "Let me talk to him first."

"A what?" The old man wrinkled his nose.

"A bribe. A payoff," Mojo repeated.

The old man squinted at Mojo. The lamp gave his eyes a creeping cast, as if things were moving around inside them. "And what makes you think that I can be bribed?"

"Why not? There's nobody around but you and us. You could take a bribe and nobody'd ever know. We're not on any official rolls or rosters or whatever it is you use down here to keep track of people. You could let us go and no one would ever know the difference."

The old man leaned back in his chair. He smacked his too-wet lips. He rubbed his chin thoughtfully. "What're you offering?" he asked at length.

Mojo had a watch and twenty in loose bills.

Juanita had some silver jewelry and a rip-off Louis Vuitton purse.

Narn had two hundred in cash and a pearl-handled .45 pistol.

Rocky had three loose joints.

The old man considered it for a long moment.

Then shook his head. "You'll have to do better than that."

"Better than—? It's all we have!" Mojo objected. "What do you want us to do? Write you checks?"

Aghastere shook his head. "No." He smiled slyly. "Something much simpler."

Aghastere wanted their souls.

"Our souls?" Mojo frowned. He wasn't sure what a soul was or whether he had one or, if he did, what it would mean to trade it away.

"If we agree, you'll let us go?" Narn asked.

"Well . . . I'll let one of you go."

"One?"

"Here's my deal." The old man leaned forward. "The four of you draw straws. Short man gets to leave. I keep the other three."

"Deal? You call that a deal?" Juanita sputtered. "I call it a screw-job!"

Aghastere shrugged. "Take it or leave it. But you really don't have much choice. Moloch'll be coming up here as soon as it's dark topside, and Moloch, being a major devil and all, doesn't have to go through all this legal crap like I do. Not here. He'll just take your souls and that'll be that."

"Take them?" Mojo wondered.

"Rip them out," the old man said grimly. "He'll rip your souls out and cast what's left of you down into the pit where you'll be turned into worms and put to work on the farms."

Mojo blanched. A worm. In the pit.

"But that's not fair!" Juanita protested.

"Neither's Hell."

Mojo had an idea. He wasn't sure whether it was a good idea or a bad idea, but it was certainly a better idea than Aghastere's deal.

"Tell you what. You wanted to play cards; I'll do it. I'll play you cards for them," Mojo proposed.

"Cards?" The old man eyed him.

"Right. I'll play you cards for our souls. I win, you let all of us go. You win, you get all four souls."

The old man raised an eyebrow. "Hmmmm . . . Now, that is an interesting proposition. Yes, very interesting . . . What kind of game did you have in mind?"

"Poker?"

"Which poker?"

"Five-card draw?"

"Straight draw, huh?" The old man's grin widened. The yellow lamplight caught in his broken teeth. He motioned Mojo towards the table. "All right, then. We'll play. Straight draw. All or nothing." He began squaring the cards into a deck.

Mojo stepped forward towards the table.

"Hold on there!" Narn grabbed him by the arm. "I didn't hear any of the rest of us agree to this harebrained scheme!"

"Let him try," Juanita said. "Even if he loses, we won't be any worse off than we are now."

Narn considered it. "Well . . . I suppose that's true . . ."

"Come on," Mojo implored. "I'm pretty good at cards. With a little luck, I might even win."

Narn pursed his lips. Thought some more. Then shrugged. "All right. Why not? This old man has got us by the short hairs no matter what. And at least this way we got a chance. A slim-to-nothing chance, I grant you, but a chance nevertheless."

Narn released Mojo's sleeve.

"Shuffle," the old man said, pushing the deck towards Mojo.

Mojo and Aghastere had been playing draw poker for nearly an hour. They were using matches for chips. The matches were from the box the old man used to light his lamp. They had begun with twenty matchsticks apiece. After an hour Mojo had twenty-one sticks and the old man nineteen. Mojo hadn't cheated yet, but he was getting ready to rectify that.

Mojo shuffled the cards. He could feel them as they passed through his fingers: king of diamonds, deuce of clubs, ten of hearts. He directed them to where he wanted them with tiny flicks of his fingertips. He squared the deck, putting a crimp into it with the same motion. He pushed the deck across the table to the old man.

The old man cut at the crimp.

Mojo slapped the two halves of the deck back together.

He dealt.

Mojo set the deck down, picked up his hand, and looked at his cards. Four fat queens looked back. He had dealt the old man three tens. When the old man drew, he would pick up the fourth ten. It wouldn't be enough.

"Bet two." The old man pushed two matchsticks into the center of the table.

"Your two and one more." Mojo pushed out three matches.

The old man hesitated for a second. Then: "Call." He added another stick to the pot.

"Cards?" Mojo asked, picking up the deck.

"One."

Mojo resisted the temptation to grin. The old man was trying to be tricky. He was trying to make Mojo think he was drawing to a flush or a straight.

The old man flipped a card facedown onto the table. Mojo dealt him the fourth ten.

"And the dealer takes one." Mojo tossed away his non-queen and picked another card off the top of the stack. He slipped it in with the queens and made a show of studying the hand for a couple of seconds.

"Bet?" Mojo looked up at the old man.

"Bet ten." The old man pushed them out without hesitation. It was a steep bet, but Mojo would have done the same with a gut cinch like four tens.

Mojo paused for a moment, worrying the cards with his fingers. Then: "Your ten plus the pot."

Mojo pushed all of his matches into the center of the table. He could hardly keep from grinning. He had him now! "Call." The old man shoved the rest of his matches in. He leaned back in his chair. Smiled lazily.

A sudden sense of unease stole over Mojo. He didn't like that smile. Those sparkling eyes. He didn't like the way the old man had called so quickly. Aghastere just didn't look like a man should look who has just bet everything he has on one hand. Even on a hand as strong as four tens.

A cold knot formed in Mojo's stomach. Tightened.

"What'd you got?" the old man asked softly.

"Four ladies." Mojo fanned them out.

The old man nodded. "A very good hand. An excellent hand, in fact. But not this excellent.'' He tabled an ace. Then another. Then another. Then another.

Mojo sat up straight. He stared at the aces. His mouth fell open. The cold hard knot in his stomach ballooned to the size of a basketball.

''Four aces?!''

''Read 'em and weep.'' The old man grinned at him. His teeth were as wet as his lips. They shone in the lamplight. ''Luck of the draw, as they said.''

''Bullshit!'' Mojo blurted. ''You—!'' His breath was suddenly cut off. It took a second for him to realize that the old man had him by the throat, that the old man's too-long arm had stretched across the table and was choking him. He tried to pry the old man's fingers away, but he had a grip like steel.

''Time to pay up,'' the old man hissed. His eyes were even yellower than usual and Mojo suddenly realized that it wasn't just the lamplight.

''Not so fast.'' Narn stepped out of the darkness behind the old man. Mojo blinked. He had been so intent on the cards that he hadn't noticed Narn leave.

''This game's not over yet,'' Narn told the old man. ''There's still the big trump to play.''

> *This about R.K. Narn:* This wasn't the first time he had slipped behind someone. Narn was not a trusting person. The only person Narn ever trusted was his dog. And then only when he had the dog in clear sight.

''The big trump?'' The old man frowned. He tried to twist his head towards Narn. ''What'd you mean, the big trump? There's no trumps in a draw poker game!''

''There is in this one.'' Narn stepped up behind the

old man's chair. Suddenly the 12-gauge was in his hands. Its barrels were as big as open sewer pipes.

The old man whipped around . . .

"Ace of shotguns," Narn announced as he pulled both barrels.

The 12-gauge belched fire and thunder. Cards flew off the table in a blizzard of hearts and clubs and diamonds and spades. The old man shot up out of his seat. Blood and gore and grey hair flew everywhere. The old man's angular body somersaulted over the table and to the floor a few feet past. His head went bouncing off into the shadows near the far wall.

"Run for it!" Rocky yelled. And did.

The old man's body had already hit the floor and was lying there twitching and squirming like a severed worm before his hand released Mojo's throat.

Mojo leaped away from the table and spun on his heels. Rocky was already through the gate columns and disappearing up the stairwell. Narn wasn't far behind. Juanita was running after Narn and waving at Mojo to come on.

Mojo bolted after Juanita.

Mojo, racing towards the gate, passed the old man's head. The head was standing upright on the bloody stump of its neck and dragging itself across the floor, using the shredded flesh like tentacles.

The head glared as Mojo flew past. "Moloch!" it screamed. "Mo-ooo-loch!"

Mojo flew past the head and through the columns and up the stairwell. He could see the others ahead of him, their legs churning up the steps. There was a tiny square of sunlight high above them, just visible at the top of the stairs. The stairs looked as tall as the sky.

"Mo-ooo-loch!"

* * *

The stairs were even higher than they looked.

By the time they were three quarters of the way up, all four of them were gasping and hanging on to the stone side walls for support. Mojo remembered reading once about a race up the Empire State Building. Up the stairs of the Empire State Building. He felt he had acquired a new appreciation for that race.

"Just—a—little—ways . . . more," Narn panted.

Mojo glanced back. The stairs behind them were dark and empty. So far. Mojo was a little nervous about being the last in line. He would have much preferred that Narn be last. Or even the boy. He thought it was very impolite of Narn and the boy to climb ahead of Juanita. He thought they should move aside and let Juanita go to the front. And him with her, of course, since he was her unofficial protector. He would have complained about it had he had the wind to speak.

A dozen steps more.

Then half that.

They were almost there. The tiny square of light had become a gaping doorway. Beyond the doorway was a cave. Sunlight was streaming though. The actual cave entrance must be very close.

Mojo was just below the top step when he heard it.

The sound came roaring up the stairwell behind him. The sound of hard shell scraping against stone, of many legs, of clicking, clacking, trailing body parts.

Mojo didn't know where he found the breath to scream, but he found it. "Run!!"

The beast roared.

Adrenaline carried Mojo up the last step and into a narrow passage. He squeezed past a boulder and dashed up a slightly wider tunnel. A sun-flooded entrance was just ahead, the light blindingly bright after all the hours down in the deep caverns.

"Locked!" The boy's voice carried back down. "It's locked! We can't get out!"

In another moment Mojo arrived at the cave entrance and could see what the boy was shouting about. The entrance was secured with a line of heavy steel bars cemented into place. There was a door in the bars—very similar to a cell door—held by a padlock and chain.

The beast roared again. The sound reverberated off the tunnel's stone walls.

"I know this place. It's Indian Cave," Rocky gasped. "The Forest Service put these bars up last spring. They're set in concrete!"

Mojo hurried to the door. He pulled a piece of wire from his pocket and went to work on the padlock. It was a simple hasp. He would have had it open in seconds if his hands hadn't been shaking.

The creaking-door voice suddenly rattled up the cave. "Mojo. I am here, Mojo."

"What's that horrible smell?" Juanita asked, turning and wrinkling her nose.

Narn turned with her. "I'll be damned," he said after a moment.

Mojo had jumped at the sound of the voice and dropped the wire. Now he scrambled frantically to pick it up. As he raised up he glanced towards the rear of the cave. He could see it there: a maggot-whiteness hanging back in the deepest shadows. He guessed it was the sunlight pouring in the entrance that was keeping it at bay.

Mojo returned to work on the lock with a vengeance.

"The sun will be setting soon, Mojo," the creaking door creaked.

Mojo wormed the wire further into the lock.

"Ugly as hell, ain't he?" Narn stared at the beast, more fascinated than frightened.

"You will never get out of these mountains, Mojo. Not before dark."

"Why don't you leave Mojo alone and go screw yourself?" Juanita suggested to the thing in the back of the cave.

Mojo popped the lock open.

The door swung back with a rusty groan. Mojo and Juanita and Rocky and Narn spilled out of the cave and onto a rocky, wildflower-strewn slope. The slope fell away to a small valley with a narrow stream meandering down its middle. The mountainside opposite was covered with thick pines. The sun was hanging just above the mountain, feathering the tallest trees. Mojo opened his arms to the sun. He had never felt anything as warm and comforting in his life.

"Come on!" Narn grabbed Mojo's arm and pulled him down the slope. "We don't have time to be lollygagging around. You heard that fly-faced bastard. Soon as it's dark, he's gonna come after us!"

15

There was a well-beaten path beside the small stream. The boy led them down it. He seemed to know where he was going. The path followed the stream down the valley and around a rocky ridge. Mojo glanced back as they passed behind the ridge. He could still see the cave entrance, dark and silent behind them on the side of the mountain.

Mojo turned and hurried on.

The path made a jaunt around a finger of forest and then opened into a broad meadow. The meadow was sprinkled with wildflowers. The air hummed with bees and other insects. There was a large tent pitched in the meadow at the edge of the forest. The tent was a mass of patches. It looked as though it had been sewn together from remnants of other tents, some of which matched and some of which didn't. There was a clothesline running from the tent's center pole to one of the pine trees, with a pair of jockey shorts hanging from it. There was a small campfire in front of the tent with four figures huddled around it.

"Welcome to space cadet city," the boy muttered to Mojo as he led them towards the tent.

One of the figures from in front of the campfire rose as they approached. It was a woman. She stared at them for a long moment, then pointed. Then yelled. She ran towards them. As she came nearer she threw open her arms. She was wearing an ankle-length dress trimmed with fringe and beads. There was a scarf tied around her head bandanna-style with the peace sign painted on it. She had long braided hair that flopped behind her. She looked as though she had just stepped out of a time warp.

"Moonbeam! Oh, Moonbeam! Oh, thank God, you're all right!" The woman ran to Rocky and hugged him. There were tears running down her cheeks. Long streaks of grey in her otherwise sandy hair.

"Aw, Maw!" The boy tried to twist away. "I've asked you not to call me that stupid name! It's Rocky, Maw! Rocky!"

"We've been so worried, Moonbeam! When you didn't come back from Santa Fe, we looked everywhere! We didn't know what had happened! We even called the Forest Service in to help us search!"

"The Forest Service?" The boy stopped struggling. He looked suddenly worried. "The Forest Service has been snooping around up here?"

"They sent a helicopter, but after a couple of days without finding any trace, they quit. Your father was so angry with them!"

"Yeah . . ." Rocky looked relieved.

"Son." A man approached. He was dressed somewhat like the woman. That is, he looked as if he might have stepped through the same time warp. He was wearing granny glasses and faded jeans and a Pendleton shirt. He was going bald.

After the man hugged Rocky and assured himself that the boy was all right, he introduced himself to the others. His name was Soaring Eagle. He introduced the woman as "my eternal kindred spirit, Nefertiti."

There were two more kindred spirits back at the campfire. Their names were Big Judy and Willis.

Big Judy was big. She was a large blond woman with a full, smooth face and placid blue eyes. She was built like a side of beef, and not just of fat. She had arms the size of Mojo's thighs and those arms didn't jiggle.

Big Judy warmly greeted each of them in turn as "brother" or "sister," then gestured towards a tiny black man who was sitting immobile beside the fire. "And this is Willis," Big Judy announced with a proud gleam in her eye.

"Hello, Willis," Mojo said politely.

The little man didn't look up. Didn't even blink. He was staring vacantly into space. He wore a grey sweatshirt with "LSU Bengals" and some unidentified, multicolored stains across it.

"Pleased to meet you, Willis," Juanita tried, but Willis still didn't respond.

"What the hell's wrong with him?" Narn asked.

Big Judy took them aside and explained in a low voice that Willis wasn't ignoring them on purpose. Wasn't being impolite. Not at all. Willis was sick. Willis had had an unfortunate accident some years back. He had made a wrong turn while on an LSD trip and never come back.

After the introductions were over, Narn led Mojo and

Juanita and Rocky into the forest to gather firewood. Narn's plan was to build a bonfire that would last all night. A bonfire so big and so bright that the demon couldn't get near enough to harm them. He also wanted enough light to shoot the demon, but he didn't tell them that.

They located the bonfire in the middle of the meadow, as far away from the forest as they could get. The kindred spirits watched curiously as Mojo and the others hauled wood to the bonfire. They seemed to find the concept of work fascinating.

The stack of firewood grew higher as the afternoon grew shorter. By the time dusk had begun to settle over the valley and the woods were filling with deep shadows, the stack of firewood was higher than the tent.

Mojo was carrying a final load of dead pine branches through the greying twilight when Willis' drooping head suddenly snapped up.

"You need healin', man?"

Mojo peered down. The little black man's normally dead eyes were bright and alive and staring intently at Mojo.

"What?" Mojo asked, caught off guard.

"I said: Do you need the Lord's healin'?"

"Ah . . . No. Thanks. I feel fine."

"That's good, then. That's real good." The little man nodded once. Then looked away, the light in his eyes fading, his chin drooping as if a battery inside him had flared for a brief instant before running down again.

Big Judy smiled up at Mojo. "Just remember: If you need healing anytime, anytime at all, Willis'll be glad to help you. He has the gift."

"Yeah . . . well . . . sure . . . I'll keep that in mind." Mojo hurried on to the bonfire and dumped his load. He wiped the sweat from his forehead. He wasn't sure but that this Willis character was even weirder when his brain was in gear.

By the time the last sparks of sunset had faded from the sky and Narn had called a halt to the wood gathering, the stack of dead wood dwarfed Mojo. The stack of firewood was huge. It looked big enough to fuel a small freighter across the Atlantic. It looked like enough wood to cast light all the way up to the mountaintops. It looked like enough wood to last an entire winter instead of only one night.

Mojo was just sorry that it wasn't any bigger.

Night fell.

Night fell like a bucket of cold water on the small valley, extinguishing all light. The forested slopes on both sides were black, impenetrable walls. Even the ground was black. Only the high, narrow strip of sky above was even the slightest shade of grey.

Narn lit the bonfire.

Everyone gathered close around, huddling about the light and turning their backs on the darkness. The hot firelight colored their skin and danced on their faces: streaks of yellow, red, and white. Narn kept adding wood. Soon glowing coals formed. The fire grew hotter. Then hotter still.

The fire grew hot enough to peel skin. Mojo had to back away from it. "Couldn't we tone that down just a little?" Mojo asked Narn. "I'd almost as soon be ripped to pieces as be roasted to death."

Narn shook his head. "Not yet. Best to keep it high for now. We can't be sure it'll be enough as it is."

"Beautiful up here, isn't it?" Soaring Eagle sat down

beside Mojo. He leaned his head back and gazed up into the narrow sky.

Mojo followed Soaring Eagle's gaze. The first stars of evening were beginning to appear. The stars were bright and cold and distant. A million miles from Narn's scorching bonfire and centipede demons that came in the dark. Mojo only wished he could spend the night on one.

"Yeah . . ."

"We've been living up in these mountains for nearly twenty years now, and I never grow tired of it. I never grow tired of looking at the beauty that surrounds us."

"Twenty years? Really? Up here all alone? Just the five of you?"

"Oh, no." Soaring Eagle lowered his eyes. He shook his head sadly. "At one time we had over three hundred people in this valley. There were tents as far as you could see." He waved an arm expansively. "Tents and crops and livestock. We were a real tribe then. We had our own schools, our own laws, our own government. We were a free people. Not like now."

"Really? What happened?"

"The Gestapo," Soaring Eagle said bitterly. "The Gestapo came and persecuted us. Persecuted and harassed us."

"The Gestapo?"

"The Forest Service. They spread lies about us."

"Really? What kind of lies?"

"You know. The usual. The usual fascist lies. First there was the lie about syphilis—they said we had a syphilis epidemic up here—then after that there was the lie about herpes."

"Herpes too, huh?" Mojo tried to scoot unobtrusively away from Soaring Eagle.

"Yes. As if the lie about syphilis wasn't bad enough." Soaring Eagle shook his head and stared grimly into the fire. "They even tried to send their Nazi doctors up here to experiment on us. We resisted them, of course."

"Of course." Mojo scooted over until he bumped up against Rocky.

"Just another case of America oppressing its people."

"Hey!" Juanita ducked her head. "A bird! It almost hit me! Flew right at me!"

"Not a bird." Nefertiti laughed. "A bat."

"Bat?"

"Sure. The firelight attracts bugs, and the bugs attract bats. But don't worry, they won't hurt you. They may come close sometimes, but they won't actually fly into you. They've got a sonar that guides them."

"Yeah . . ." Juanita peered warily upwards. Nefertiti was right. She could see scores of the tiny black creatures, flitting rapidly in and out of the edges of the firelight.

Suddenly one of the bats broke from the edge of darkness and came rocketing down. It shot past Juanita, who yelped and ducked again, and nicked Willis on the side of the head.

Willis' hooded eyes jumped open.

The bat soared back up into the night.

"You think it's out there yet?" Rocky asked Mojo in a hushed voice.

Mojo glanced over his shoulder. Bright reflections of the bonfire danced on the face of the forest behind them. Farther up the side of the mountain, beyond the light, there was only blackness. "I don't know. Could be."

"You think the fire's enough to keep it away?"

"Sure." Mojo forced a smile. He tried to sound more confident than he felt. "It's like Narn said: We're completely safe as long as we keep our fire going."

"I can feel somethin' comin', uh-huh! I can feel somethin' comin' this way, uh-huh!"

Mojo glanced around at the sound of the voice. Willis was rising to his feet on the far side of the fire. His hands were clinched into tight fists. His face was turned up into the night sky.

"I can feel somethin' comin' around the edge of the world and shootin' across the seas and over the mountains and right down into this very valley, uh-huh! I can feel the hand of the Lord Himself comin', yessir! I can feel his mighty hand comin', yessir! I can feel the mighty hand of the Great God Jehovah Himself comin' this way, yessir!"

"Tell it, Willis!" Big Judy cried happily from her place beside him. "Give us the word!"

"Oh, shit," the boy said softly. "It's Holy Roller time in the Rockies again."

"I can feel somethin' out there, uh-huh! I can feel somethin' out there in the dark, uh-huh! I can feel somethin' out there in the dark heart of man waitin' to defy that great powerful hand of the Lord's, uh-huh!"

"Again? You mean he gets like this often?" Mojo asked.

"Just whenever the spirit takes him. Which is all the friggin' time."

"I can feel the dark heart of evil out there! I can feel the dark heart of sin out there! I can feel the dark heart of the devil himself out there in the darkness! I can feel him creepin' around out there, yessir!"

Suddenly Mojo could feel him too.

Mojo whipped around. It took a few moments of

searching before he found what he was looking for: high up on the side of the mountain, far back in the pitch-black darkness of the trees, peering down through the gloom. Railroad lanterns.

"Mojo," the creaking door boomed down from the mountainside. "I have come, Mojo."

Mojo gulped. Why him? Why was the damn thing always talking to *him*? Why not somebody else?

"Send back those you have stolen. Send the woman and the child back to me."

"Tell him to forget that," Rocky whispered emphatically.

"Is that the demon you told us about?" Nefertiti wondered.

"Send them back or I shall destroy you all." The voice rumbled across the valley like a slow freight train.

"Just stay calm. He's bluffing. He can't touch us as long as we stay by the fire," Narn assured them.

There was a long moment of silence. Then: "Very well. So be it."

Mojo didn't like the sound of that. It sounded too final to suit Mojo. He turned nervously towards Narn. "You've let that fire get too low. Put some more wood on it."

"Ten minutes ago, you were bitching about how hot it was."

"So I was wrong! Throw some more wood on it!"

"Gather, creatures! Gather, my bloodthirsty creatures!" the demon's voice rumbled down from the mountainside.

"Bloodthirsty? Vampires? Is he trying to sic a pack of vampires on us?" Mojo wondered.

"It's possible," Soaring Eagle said grimly. "There are vampires in these mountains. I've seen them. One of them even joined the tribe a few years back. You remember her, don't you, hon? The girl who stayed rolled up in her sleeping bag all day? The one from Fresno?''

''Gather, now! Gather!''

Something whined past Mojo's ear. He swatted at it. Missed. It whined past his other ear. He swatted again. Missed again. The something stung him on the neck.

''Mosquitoes!'' Narn shouted suddenly, slapping his arm. ''The sonofabitch has called up a mosquito invasion!''

Mojo could see them now. They were coming in from the darkness in clouds, spreading around the camp like a thin, grey fog. Thousands of mosquitoes. No, millions of mosquitoes! A flood of mosquitoes! Mojo dropped to the ground and crawled towards the fire, hoping that the heat and smoke would drive them away. He could feel mosquitoes descending on him, covering his backside like a blanket.

''There's a can of Off in the tent. I'll go get it.'' Big Judy staggered away from the fire, swinging her arms around her face in an impersonation of an electric fan.

''No!'' Narn screamed at her. ''Get back! That's just what he wants! If you leave the fire, he'll get you for sure!''

Big Judy hesitated for a second, then fled back to the fire, where she joined the rest in trying to root into the ground. Everyone was on his or her stomach by now, pressing into the soft earth to minimize the amount of exposed flesh. They were flopping and writhing and swatting on all sides of Mojo. Above their shouts and curses Mojo could hear the tiny insects buzzing. There were so many they sounded like a small aircraft revving up for takeoff.

Then something shot past Mojo's head. The something was very small and very black and very fast. Then another. And another and another and . . .

"Bats!" Mojo cried joyfully. "Bats are coming in!"

"Gather, creatures!" Moloch's voice boomed from the mountainside.

Mojo decided it was time to fight fire with fire.

"Gather, bats!" Mojo boomed back.

"Come, my thirsty creatures!!" the demon commanded.

"Come on, bats!!" Mojo answered.

The air was now so thick with bats that Mojo was afraid to lift his head. The wind from a thousand leathery wings fluttered across his neck. The stinging sensations along his arms seemed to be lessening, though he wasn't sure whether this meant there were now fewer mosquitoes or fewer nerve endings.

"They're eating them!" someone yelled. "They're eating the mosquitoes!"

Mojo kept his head down and prayed. He had never imagined he would be so glad to be dive-bombed by bats.

"Stay low! Wait it out!" Narn shouted.

They didn't have to wait very long. In less time than Mojo would have believed possible, the mosquitoes had been thinned down to a few buzzing stragglers. Mojo remembered watching a Discovery Channel program once about how many thousands of mosquitoes a bat could eat in an hour. He hadn't believed it at the time. He did now.

Mojo pulled himself up onto his hands and knees. Then his feet. Other people were doing the same, standing up and dusting themselves off. He rubbed his arms.

They were tingling from all the mosquito bites, but other than that, he felt fine. He took a deep breath. The night air was sweet. It was good to have not been sucked dry.

"It was pyramid power that saved us," Soaring Eagle said solemnly as he rose to his feet beside Mojo. He reached into his shirt pocket and pulled out a tiny glass pyramid. He pushed the pyramid under Mojo's nose. The glass sparkled in the firelight.

"See that? See that light? That's the internal spiritual energy source. I've got a half dozen of these babies hung in trees all around the meadow. They're what energized those bats." He readjusted his wire-rim glasses. "Nothing can harm us in this valley. No way. Not with pyramid energy to protect us."

"Gather, darkness!" Moloch roared angrily from up on the mountainside. "GATHER . . . DARKNESS!!"

"That's it? That's darkness?" Mojo wondered, looking up.

Narn nodded. "I guess it must be."

A huge black cloud had filled the sky above the valley. The cloud was growing. It had started out no bigger than a dot less than a half hour before. Now it covered the entire sky except for a few grey areas around the edges. The cloud was rotating as it grew. It spun around and around. White threads of lightning flickered in its center.

"I think maybe it's coming down," Soaring Eagle said. "Lowering. It's hard to tell in this light, but I'd swear it was higher a few minutes ago."

"What do you think it is? A tornado or something? Think it's going to suck us up?" Juanita asked.

"Gather, darkness! Gather!" the demon roared again from his place on the mountainside. It was the same litany he had been repeating over and over again for the last thirty minutes. Several bolts of lightning crackled in reply.

"Maybe he's trying to make it rain on us," Nefertiti suggested.

"Now, that's a cheerful thought." Mojo lowered his head. Staring up at the cloud was making his neck stiff. He glanced over at the fire. Jumped in alarm.

"Hey! The fire's going out!"

"What?!"

Mojo ran to the bonfire. It was smoldering. Thick black smoke hung over the charred wood. There were still flames, but they were low and flickering. "It's dying! The fire's dying! Come on! Help me fan it!"

Mojo grabbed a branch from the pile of deadwood and began swinging it over the fire, creating a draft. The flames flickered feebly in response. A few white sparks shot up. Then died away.

"Come on!"

The others came to help, but the fire continued to flicker and die in spite of their efforts. Mojo fanned until his arms ached, but it was no use. The white flames were slowly turning to blue, the blue flames slowly turning to red. The heat was dying along with the flames. The smell of smoke hung heavy in the night air.

"What the hell's going on here?" Narn panted as he swung a branch over the fire. "It acts like it's being smothered. Like somebody's holding a blanket over it or something."

Mojo stopped fanning. "That's it!" he exclaimed, suddenly seeing it. "It *is* being smothered! By the darkness! By the cloud!"

Mojo looked up. The dark cloud covered the entire

sky now. And it was definitely lowering. He could see it coming. It was falling down on them like some huge black curtain.

"We've gotta stop that cloud! That's what's putting the fire out! We've gotta stop it from coming any lower!"

"Stop it? How the hell can we stop a cloud?!"

A deep rumbling laugh rolled over the meadow. Mojo spun around. The firelight no longer reached to the trees. Nowhere near them. The light stretched only a few scant yards beyond where they were standing. Beyond those few yards there was nothing but black, unfathomable darkness. The laughter had come from that darkness.

"Damn! It's in the meadow!" Narn dropped his branch.

The laughter rolled again, coming closer.

Mojo stepped back until he was almost in the fire. The others pulled back with him. Even this close the light was dim and hazy. The ring of firelight that separated them from the darkness was shrinking. The light was receding as the fire died, coming back like a rug being rolled up.

"Did you really believe you could defeat me? Did you really believe that a pitiful little trick like those bats could defeat a Baron of Hell?"

The voice was so close that Mojo had to steel himself not to step backwards into what was left of the flames. He could hear the demon slithering towards them, crackling through the dry meadow grass. He could smell it. After a few moments the demon's yellow eyes materialized in the edge of the creeping darkness.

"Soon," the demon promised softly. "Soon the light will be gone."

"Do something!" Juanita yanked on Mojo's arm.

"Do what? What do you want me to do? Attack it? I don't even have a weapon."

"No. Something else. Stop it."

"That's all, huh?"

"You can do it! Think of something!"

Mojo had no idea how he could stop a giant centipede demon, but he was certainly willing to try. After a moment of reflection, Mojo stepped forward and spread his arms and turned his face to the black sky. "Scatter, darkness!" Mojo commanded the cloud, which was now so close above them that it was only discernible as a cloud when lightning ran across its face. "Go away, darkness!!"

He waited. Nothing happened.

"It's not working! Try something else!" Juanita demanded urgently.

"Gather, light!" Mojo tried. And then, in a louder, more desperate voice: "Gather, fire! Gather, light and fire!"

A brief flicker of lightning played over the cloud. It was, if anything, closer than before.

The demon chuckled. A deep, ominous sound.

The firelight flickered, settled, flickered again, grew dimmer.

"Try the bats! Call the bats back!"

"Gather, bats!" Mojo shouted at the top of his lungs. "Come on, bats!!"

After a moment a single bat swooped past Mojo, followed by a low grunt in Willis' direction. But that was all. They waited, but no more bats appeared.

The fire sputtered softly.

"One? That's it? That's all? Just one crummy little, sorry little bat?" Juanita wondered.

Narn shouldered his way past Mojo. "Stand back. I've got a special kind of magic for our friend there." Narn had a determined look on his face. He had the shotgun in his hands.

Narn stopped beside Mojo. Planted his feet and raised the shotgun towards the half-seen demon. "I've been waiting for this," Narn said softly. "Waiting for this chance ever since I first heard the damned thing back in West Texas."

Narn aimed and pulled both triggers. The triggers clicked. Narn paused. Pulled the triggers again. The triggers clicked once more.

Narn cursed softly under his breath. He broke open the gun, tossed out the two shells, and inserted two more. He snapped the barrels shut. Lifted the shotgun. Aimed. Fired. Again the hammers clicked harmlessly against the shells.

Narn lowered the shotgun. "Shit," he said.

The demon snickered.

"Soon," Moloch creaked softly. "Very soon now." He took another rustling, crackling step in towards the fire.

Mojo glanced over his shoulder. There were only a few pitifully small flames left. The thing was right. It wouldn't be long now.

"Out of my way!" A dark figure strode forward, pushing Mojo and Narn aside. The figure leaned out and pointed a pistol-like finger at the demon. "I hear you, sucker! I see you! I see you sneakin' around out there! I see your lyin' yellow eyes, you old devil! I hear your lyin' tongue!"

It was Willis.

Mojo stared at Willis, amazed. Mojo could hardly recognize him. Willis' shoulders were no longer slumped; his neck was no longer bowed; his eyes were no longer clouded. Willis stood straight and tall as he faced the demon. Pale blue firelight glistened on Willis' dark face and sparkled in his dark eyes. He looked like a different man. He sounded like a different man. The old confused, sleepy-eyed Willis was gone. This new Willis had an air of iron resolution about him. He had a voice like a brass church bell.

"Yeah, I see you, you lyin' devil!"

"I see you too, little man. And soon I will see you dead."

"Dead, huh?" Willis snorted contemptuously. "You want to wrestle with me, devil? Is that it? You want to try me, you old devil? Well . . . come on, then! Come on and wrestle with Willis, then! I ain't afraid! No, sir! Not one bit afraid! You see, I already wrestled with worse than you! I already wrestled with sin! I already wrestled with my own soul! I already wrestled with sin so strong and heavy and hot-breathed that it makes a devil like you look puny in comparison! I already wrestled with a soul blacker and eviler and heavier than you could find in a whole pack of devils! So come on, devil! Come on and wrestle with me 'cause I got God on my side now, yeah! I got God as my good right arm and can't no devil whip me! No, sir! Can't no devil scare me since I stood toe-to-toe with sin! No, sir! Can't no lantern-eyed, slack-jawed, shit-brained excuse of a devil whip me now that I got the Great God Almighty on my side!"

"You tell him, Willis!" Big Judy cried excitedly. "Tell that devil how it is!"

"You have a sharp tongue, little man," Moloch rumbled from the edge of the darkness. "But soon I will make you sorry that you were not born dumb. Soon I will drag you down to Hell!''

''Hah!'' Willis boomed. ''Don't try to lay no 'what I'm gonna do to you' shit on me, devil! No, I'll tell you; I'll tell you what you'll do to me, old devil! I'll tell you what you'll do! Shit! You won't do shit to Willis! You won't do shit to me because you're nothin' but a dried-up, fucked-up, toothless old limp-dick of a devil!''

The demon growled angrily. It was a grating sound worse than a hundred pieces of chalk being scraped across a blackboard all at the same time. The demon took another step in towards the fire. He was so close that Mojo could smell his kerosene breath.

''Now, there's some who say a devil can't be beat,'' Willis said, turning calmly towards the others and ignoring the demon, who was now less than ten feet away. ''There's some who say a devil just can't be beat. There's some who say that a devil is just too strong, that a devil is just too old, that a devil is just too wise, that he's just too much of a devil for a mortal man to beat. But I say they're wrong! I say they're dead wrong! I say fuck them! I say a devil can be beat! I say we can beat this devil! I say we can send this old devil packin'! I say we can send this old limp-dick devil packin' right back down into that cold dark pit he crawled up out of! Yessir! All we need is faith! Yessir! All we need to kick this old devil's ass is faith!''

''Amen, brother! Amen!'' Big Judy shouted.

The fire behind Willis stirred: a sudden red sparkle, a quick white flash.

The demon growled ominously in the darkness.

''No, sir! No, sir! Can't no devil pull me down, no, sir! Not while I got faith! Can't no old cold devil jerk me around, no, sir! Can't no old, cold, no-souled, lyin' motherfucker of a devil pull me down and jerk me around while I got my faith!"

"That's right, that's right!" Big Judy cried. "Oh, don't let that old devil turn you around, Willis!" she pleaded.

Mojo saw a flash of light and glanced back. Flames were popping up all over the bonfire. Bright white flames. Mojo turned back. Willis was advancing on the demon, the light from the flames casting a towering shadow in front of him. Willis shook his fist at the demon, who was slowly retreating before the light.

"No, sir! No, sir! Can't no old devil turn me around, no, sir! I got the power right here, yessir! I got the power in the blood right here, yessir! I got the power of faith in the blood right here, right now, yessir! I got the power and can't no old devil face that power! Can't no old devil turn me around!"

Mojo felt a sudden flash of heat on his back. Light leaped out from the fire behind him and lashed across the blackness. The light struck the demon. Mojo could see the demon clearly. The demon reared up on its long legs in the light. It opened its sideways mouth and gnashed its white fangs. The demon screamed like a banshee. It screamed and twisted for a moment in the sudden bright light, then turned so fast that it was no more than a blur and raced off into the darkness.

"Yessir, yessir! You'd better run, yessir! You'd better get your evil devil ass out of here right now, yessir! I got the power of faith right here, right now, yessir! I got the power of faith that no half-brained, half-assed, full-ugly devil like yourself can ever stand up against right here, right now, yessir!"

The bonfire roared behind Mojo. Its flames leaped to

the heavens. Its light surged across the meadow and broke over the forest. Its heat seared across Mojo's back and curled the hair on the back of his neck. Mojo stumbled away from the burning heat of the bonfire and out into the grassy meadow. When he was far enough away from the fire that it no longer felt like an open oven at his back, he stopped and looked in the direction Moloch had gone.

Mojo spied something big and fast running up through the pines on the mountainside. He spied a huge black shadow dodging up through the forest, whipping around the tree trunks, running pell-mell, racing just ahead of a wave of rapidly spreading firelight that seemed to be chasing after it.

"Hallelujah!" Big Judy shouted from somewhere near Mojo. "Look at that! Look at that old devil run! Glory, hallelujah!"

"Hallelujah! Hallelujah!" Mojo shouted with her, caught up in it.

The huge black shadow gained the top of the mountain and flew over it and disappeared just before the light flared and lit the entire mountainside like a ring of spotlights. Mojo watched for a few moments longer, but the demon didn't reappear.

Mojo turned around. The bonfire was so white and bright that he could hardly bear to look at it. Whatever was burning in it certainly wasn't wood. The bonfire was casting so much light that Mojo figured they could have played night baseball in the valley and still had enough light left over to illuminate a half dozen shopping-center parking lots.

"Look!" Narn was pointing skywards. "The cloud is breaking up!"

Mojo looked up. It was true. The black cloud was on

fire. White-hot flames from the bonfire were running across its face. Smoke billowed from around the white flames. As the wind blew the smoke away, Mojo could see stars shining through the holes.

A few minutes later and the cloud was gone.

A few hours later and the bonfire was still burning without even adding any wood to it.

Many hours later and the sun came boiling up out of the east. Sunlight struck the bonfire. The bonfire gave one last blast of white light before smoking down to a cold black smudge on the valley floor.

16

"Get up." Narn gave Mojo a not-so-gentle kick. "The Queen of the Nile has breakfast for us."

"Wha—?" Mojo rolled over and opened his eyes and blinked at the bright sunlight. He moaned softly. His back ached. He rubbed it. He couldn't imagine how these people could stand to sleep on the ground every night. If going back to nature meant sleeping without mattresses, Mojo wanted no part of it.

"Come on. We've got to get out of these mountains and do something about that heart before it's too late." Narn grabbed Mojo's arm and hoisted him up.

Juanita was waiting for them at the patched tent.

The breakfast Nefertiti served was nutritious. The breakfast was nourishing. It was healthy. It was some of the worst stuff Mojo had ever tasted.

"Do you like it?" Nefertiti asked Mojo.

"Oh, yeah." Mojo fished around with his spoon and plucked a few sunflower seeds out of the mess in his bowl. Sunflower seeds were one of the few ingredients he could recognize. "Really different."

"I serve only healthy foods," she said with pride. "Natural foods. None of that poison like you get back in the fascist state."

Mojo slipped the seeds into his mouth and chewed enthusiastically like he had taken a bigger bite than he actually had.

"Guaranteed to keep you regular too. That's the secret to health, you know. Regularity."

This sounded ominous to Mojo. He wasn't sure he wanted to be regular in a place that didn't have commodes.

Mojo swallowed and smiled at her. "Filling too," he said. "Very, very filling."

"Come on." Narn set his bowl down and wiped his mouth on the back of his hand. "We need to get on the road."

"I'm ready," Juanita said.

"Me too," Mojo said gratefully.

After they had finished telling everyone goodbye—including Willis, who was lucid enough to nod if not speak—Narn took Rocky aside.

"You should go to school," Narn said. "I know you don't want to leave your folks, but it's not right for a boy your age to live up here like some kind of damn animal. I could talk to your father. I could arrange for you to attend this boarding school in El Paso. It's run by some Sisters who owe me a favor."

"Nuns?!" Rocky looked appalled. "You want to turn me over to nuns?"

"You want to be an ignoramus?" Narn growled. "You want to spend your life washing cars?"

"Look." Rocky lowered his voice. "You don't understand. I can't leave. These dorks would starve to death in a week without me. You think they live off the fat of the land up here? The bounty of the earth? No way! They live off canned tuna the same as everybody else. Even that swill this morning came from a health food store in Santa Fe, and you wouldn't believe what it cost me! No, without me, they'd be chewing grass in a week. I can't leave them."

"Where does a boy your age get the money to support five people?" Narn asked suspiciously.

"Well . . ." Rocky looked evasive. "Let's just say I've been real successful with my vegetable garden."

"Your garden . . . I see." Narn scowled.

"Come on." Mojo pulled on Narn's arm. "You said we were in a hurry." Mojo wanted an early start. He didn't want to take any chances on being caught up in the mountains at night again.

"And I suppose those loose joints you had in your pocket back in the cave were stuffed with fresh lettuce?"

"Come on." Mojo began to drag Narn away. "You can discuss this some other time."

Narn came reluctantly.

Narn and Mojo and Juanita followed the path beside the stream down the valley. The path led them through another meadow and down a canyon and back out into a third meadow. The path veered away from the stream on the meadow's far side and cut through a willow grove and then wound back to the stream again at a spot where two logs had been laid to form a bridge.

There was a small animal sitting on the log bridge waiting for them. It was a sleek fat rat with a long pink tail. As Mojo approached the log bridge the rat stood up on its hind feet and began to squeak. It hopped about. It flipped its long nose from side to side.

"Look!" Juanita stepped up beside him. "It's Mr. Rat!"

"Is it?" Mojo moved closer. All rats looked alike to Mojo.

"Of course it is," she said. "Do you think rats normally dance for anybody who comes along? It has to be."

The rat scampered to the far end of the bridge. Stopped. Turned expectantly towards them.

"I think he wants us to follow him," Juanita said.

"Should we?" Mojo looked longingly down the trail that Soaring Eagle had assured him led back to the bright lights of civilization. "I mean, what if he takes us back to the hunting lodge or something?"

"Oh, go on." Juanita gave Mojo a shove. "I'm sure Mr. Rat wouldn't lead us anywhere dangerous. He just wants to help us. He probably knows a shortcut back to where you two parked your car."

Mojo wasn't so sure about the rat taking them on a shortcut, but he stepped onto the bridge anyway.

The rat trotted off down a poorly defined trail, disappearing behind some drooping pine limbs. Mojo and Juanita and Narn crossed the bridge and followed.

The rat led them through the woods and up a rocky ridge on a narrow, slippery path covered with loose rock. They crossed the crest of the ridge and went down a somewhat better trail into a valley on the far side. As they neared the bottom of the valley they could see two figures through the trees. The figures were seated beside a small stream. It was Grandmother and Captain Benegas.

"Juanita! Child!" Grandmother rushed forward to hug her. "I was so worried about you!"

"What are you doing here?" Narn asked Grandmother.

"What am I doing here? I am here because of the most wonderful thing! The most wonderful thing that has ever happened to me!" Grandmother said exuberantly. She released Juanita and stepped back. "The Child of Atocha appeared to me in a vision! Yes, the Christ Child himself! He came to me while I was speaking with Captain Benegas here." She gestured towards the old man. "And gave me a vision! The child granted me a vision of this place in the woods. This very spot! He didn't speak a word, yet I knew with a certainty to take the heart and the captain and come here!"

Juanita smiled. "That's wonderful."

"Did you see me?" Mojo asked.

Grandmother frowned, puzzled. "See you?"

"In your vision. Was I there? With the child? Did you see me with him?"

"Listen," Narn said impatiently. "We don't have time to be standing around. We're supposed to take the heart back to the Madonna. And I'd like to get it done today. Before nightfall," he added significantly.

"You're right. We must hurry." Grandmother nodded solemnly. "We must return the heart to the Madonna as soon as possible. The child showed me this also. We must take the heart to the old mission."

"But how can we?" Juanita asked. "Captain Benegas told us the mission was lost. That nobody could find the trail. Or did the child show you the way?"

Grandmother shook her head. ''No. He didn't show me the way to the mission. I believe it must be too far and too difficult for that. But he did send me a miracle to aid us in finding it. A miracle that will allow Captain Benegas to guide us there.''

''What kind of miracle?''

''Eyes.'' Grandmother turned and gestured triumphantly at the old man seated on the tree stump behind her. ''Captain Benegas has eyes now.''

Mojo peered at the old man. There was a big black crow sitting on the captain's shoulder. The crow stared at Mojo with bright eyes. ''Caw,'' the crow said.

''But I have some bad news as well.'' Grandmother picked up a large straw basket from beside one of the tree stumps. Reached inside. ''There seems to be something wrong with the heart.''

''What's wrong with it?'' Juanita asked worriedly.

''See for yourself.'' Grandmother pulled the pickle jar from the basket and held it up. ''See? See how weakly it's beating? And look here. At this spot around the bottom.''

Mojo looked. The black stain now covered almost the entire bottom half of the heart.

The crow or Captain Benegas or maybe the two of them together—Mojo wasn't sure how it worked—led them up through the woods. There wasn't a path, and they seemed to spend as much time wandering around deadfalls and skirting ravines as they did climbing in a straight line. They crossed one ridge, went down into a valley, and then up another ridge. Mojo had the sense that all the ridges were part of one big mountain, but it was hard to tell from underneath the thick canopy of pines.

"How much further?" Narn asked as they broke from a tangle of brush and into a small meadow bright with tiny red flowers.

"I'm not sure," Benegas said as he, aided by the crow, who chattered incessantly into his ear, led them across the short meadow and into another dark wall of trees. "I'm fairly certain we're on the right path, but as to where the mission is exactly, I can't say. I only remember that it was very high up. Near the tree line."

"We will find it," Grandmother said confidently. "We must have faith."

They were resting near the crest of a steep ridge when Mojo looked down and saw a line of men crossing a meadow in the valley below.

"Damn!" Mojo leaped to his feet.

"What is it?" Juanita asked in alarm.

"Castillo. He's on our trail."

Narn joined Mojo. A line of men was snaking its way across the meadow, heading towards them. Castillo was leading, his silver hair easily recognizable. Mojo counted eleven more. They all had guns slung across their backs.

"We'd better get going." Narn spun on his heel. He picked his shotgun up off the ground. "They're moving fast. A lot faster than we can. We'll need all the head start we can get."

Mojo hesitated. "Wait. I've got an idea. Give me your gun."

"My shotgun? Why?"

"Because there's no way we can outrun those guys with Grandmother and the captain along. Give me the shotgun and I'll wait here. Ambush them."

Narn stared at him. "They'll kill you," he said.

"I don't think so. I don't intend to fight them, not really stand and fight them. More like delay them. If I take a few potshots at them and then leg out through the woods, they may even follow me instead of you."

Narn thought for a moment, then nodded. "Okay. That makes sense. Might even work." He turned to the others. "Come on. We'd better make tracks."

"I'm staying with Mojo," Juanita said.

"And do what?" Mojo asked. "Throw rocks at them? No, you can't do any good here, and you'll be safer with the others. Besides, the heart's the important thing. You should stay with the heart. Don't worry about me, I'll be okay. I don't intend to take any unnecessary chances; I can promise you that."

"I'm staying." She sounded determined.

"Joseph is right." Grandmother took Juanita's arm. "You must come with us. You're the only one besides Joseph who is young enough and fast enough to carry the heart to the mission if worse comes to worst. If they catch us, then you will have to take the heart on up alone."

"Alone? I couldn't even find it alone," Juanita protested.

"We must have faith that you would be shown the way. Now, come along, there is nothing you can do here."

She hesitated for a long moment, then went to Mojo and put her arms around him. "Be careful," she whispered.

"Hey, you know I will. You know there's no way I'm gonna let myself get shot. You can bank on that." He tried to sound more confident than he felt.

Mojo found a loose boulder in a rocky outcropping not far away. Using a dead pine branch for a lever, he dislodged the boulder and rolled it over to the head of the trail. Then settled in to wait. The shotgun was in his hands. There were no sounds but the drone of insects and the soft sigh of the wind.

He waited for what seemed a long time. Then he heard voices coming up the trail.

Mojo braced his shoulder against the boulder. His plan was to send the rock rolling down the trail and then, while Castillo and his men were scrambling to get out of its way, open up with the shotgun. What would happen after that was a little vague, but at some point he intended to make a run for it.

The voices drew closer. Booted feet crunched in the trail's loose gravel. Mojo tensed. He dug in for the shove that would send the boulder crashing down.

The voices and the footsteps slowed. Stopped.

Mojo remained pressed against the boulder. He felt beads of sweat gathering on his forehead. He wiped his hands on his Levi's. Listened. Waited.

Mojo waited a few minutes longer, and then, when he still couldn't hear anything, raised carefully over the top of the rock and peeked down the trail.

The trail was empty. There was no sign of Castillo or his men.

Mojo realized immediately something was wrong. He backed quickly away from the boulder, the shotgun tight in his hands. He hadn't gone far before he backed into something hard and round and cold that jabbed into the small of his back.

"Drop it, shit-for-brains!"

Mojo hesitated for a moment, then dropped the shotgun. It struck the ground with a clatter.

"Now, get your hands in the air and turn around."

Mojo turned. It was the Reverend Jerry Lee Rutt. The Reverend Rutt had an automatic rifle pointed at Mojo's stomach. He had a big grin on his face. The grin was full of the whitest, straightest teeth Mojo had ever seen.

"Party's over, dog-breath," the reverend told Mojo.

"I don't know where they went. Honest."

Mojo was hanging upside down from a tree branch, strung up like a gutted deer. He felt dizzy and disoriented. He could feel his heart laboring.

"Let me have him." A short, stocky Oriental stepped up beside Castillo. At least Mojo thought he was Oriental. It was difficult to make out facial features when hanging upside down.

"Give me twenty minutes, and he'll tell us everything he knows," the Oriental promised.

"We don't have twenty minutes," Castillo told him. Then: "Forget this boy, he's nothing. We've wasted enough time with him already. We need to get back on the trail. After the others. After the heart." Castillo wheeled away from Mojo, his face floating like a bird in an upside-down sky.

"You're just gonna leave him? Without even taking a knife to him?" the Oriental asked plaintively.

"Hell, Ray, listen to the man!" a new voice protested. "Come on, be a sport! Old frog-face is on his way. He'll take care of the heart for us." It took Mojo a second to recognize the voice as the Reverend Rutt's.

"We can't rely on that. Not when there's this much sunlight," Castillo said. "No, we can't take the chance. We have to make sure ourselves." His voice was receding, moving away from Mojo.

"At least let Bigthumb stay behind, then. Thumb can

get the truth out of him, then catch up with the rest of us later."

"All right." Castillo was on the other side of the clearing now. "You heard the reverend, Thumb. You stay here and work on the boy. Come after us in thirty minutes whether you get anything out of him or not."

Someone—presumably this Bigthumb—acknowledged the order with a low grunt.

Many footsteps receded, moving away from the clearing and into the woods.

A single set approached Mojo.

A broad face floated into Mojo's view. The face was dark and grinning. Its upside-down eyes had a dull yellow glint.

"Afternoon. I'm Hubert Bigthumb."

"Er . . . hi. Nice to meet you," Mojo said politely.

"I got the mountain power. Know what that means, boy?"

Mojo shook his head dumbly. He had no idea.

"It means I'm a full-blood Apache. And that means," Bigthumb continued, leaning in towards Mojo, "that you're gonna be a long time dying. Maybe all day. Maybe two days. I can't tell yet. It depends on the man, depends on how much *cajones* he has. But just looking at you, I wouldn't be surprised if you didn't go quick. I hope not, but I wouldn't be surprised."

"All day? But . . . you've only got thirty minutes! That's what Castillo said!"

"Don't pay any attention to him. I don't. I told you I was Apache. And the Apache take their time. The Apache do these things right."

"Right? What do you mean right?" Mojo gulped

nervously. He realized this was a man who took great pride in his heritage.

Bigthumb moved away from Mojo. He began gathering twigs and dry pine needles from the forest floor.

"What're you doing?" Mojo called.

"These are for the fire. You don't want anything bigger than little sticks in the fire. Big pieces give off too much heat."

"The fire?"

"Right. The fire I'm gonna build under your head."

Mojo's mouth would have fallen open if gravity hadn't prevented it.

"The whole idea is to build a fire that cooks slow," Bigthumb explained as he returned and arranged the twigs underneath Mojo. "It's gotta be real low. You get too much heat or too much smoke, your victim'll go too quick. But if you get it just right, where the fire's just hot enough to burn without being hot enough to kill, then it's the best torture of all. Pain from slow, steady burning never lets up. Just keeps on getting worse and worse without ever making you pass out. Apache invented it, of course," he added.

Mojo twisted in the ropes. All he succeeded in doing was making himself even dizzier than before.

"Yeah, you Anglos are always going on about how we used to cover you with honey and stake you out on anthills or cut off your eyelids and make you stare into the sun or peel you with sharpened sticks. Minor stuff like that. You're so ignorant that you think those were the worst we had. What you don't realize is that your real Apache, your real old-time Apache, never used anthills or that other junk unless they were in a big hurry and didn't have the time for anything else. When they had plenty of time, like you and I do now, the old-time

Apache always used fire. Mainly this brain roasting that I'm gonna do to you. Brain roasting was their favorite. It's a whole lot more painful than any red-ant hill and it'll keep you alive and suffering a whole lot longer.''

Bigthumb brought a second handful of twigs over and added them to the pile underneath Mojo's head.

''You seem to know a lot about it,'' Mojo said slowly, finding it somewhat difficult to speak. ''Torture, I mean.''

''Well, I can't say I've had a lot of chances to practice, but I suppose you could say I was an expert anyway. As near to an expert as there is nowadays. I've studied the old ways a lot. I consider it a sacred trust to try and keep those old traditions alive.''

''I don't suppose I could talk you out of this, could I?'' Mojo asked.

Bigthumb chuckled.

''Buy you off? In cash?''

Bigthumb snorted contemptuously as he wheeled away.

''A car?'' Mojo called after him. ''My uncle has a Cadillac.''

Bigthumb returned with another handful of twigs. He added them to the pile. Then wiped his hands on his Levi's. He reached into his shirt pocket and brought out a matchbook. Struck one.

''Women? Drugs? Microwaves? A cellular telephone?''

Bigthumb held the match down to the tiny stack of kindling. A white feather of smoke drifted up past Mojo's nose.

''Oh, shit,'' Mojo sighed.

* * *

Time passed with Bigthumb adding small handfuls of twigs at regular intervals. Finally, with the tiny fire burning nicely, he retired to the side and pulled a bottle of vodka from a backpack. He took a seat on the ground and began to drink noisily.

Bigthumb wiped his mouth on his shirt sleeve, then peered up at Mojo. "Hey, boy! You're being awful quiet. You hurting much yet?"

"Hell, yes, I'm hurting!" Mojo croaked. "I can't breathe! I'm being asphyxiated! You built the fire wrong!"

"Wrong?" Bigthumb squinted.

"Hell, yes, it's wrong! It's—" Mojo stopped to cough. "It's too smoky! You said I'd last all day, but I'm gonna be dead in the next ten minutes if I don't stop breathing smoke! And that's only if my heart doesn't give out first from having to pump blood uphill!"

Bigthumb eyed Mojo for a long minute. Then took another pull off his bottle. Then shook his head. "Naw," he said. "You still got a long ways to go. Hell, the coals aren't even built up yet. As the coals start to build, the smoke'll die down and the heat'll rise. You'll see. Fact is, I figure we got at least another hour before the real fun even starts."

Mojo didn't find that encouraging.

17

"Gotdamnsummabitch!" Narn couldn't believe his eyes.

"What is it?" Grandmother, just behind him on the narrow trail, tried to peer past.

Narn wheeled around. "Get back! Into those bushes over there!" He herded them back down the trail towards a dense thicket.

"Is it Castillo?" Juanita asked as she ducked into the thicket.

"Worse."

They barely had time to conceal themselves before what Narn had glimpsed burst through the trees and into clear sight: a demon, a gigantic thirty-foot demon with blasted black skin and bulging frog eyes. The demon was humpbacked and spraddle-legged. His wet, sucking breath hissed and groaned like an old steam boiler as he lumbered towards them, sweeping pine trees from his path like matchsticks.

Juanita peered through a break in the bush. This demon was different from the one the night before. Much more humanlike. He had two arms and two legs and all the other usual apparatus. He was definitely not human, however. In addition to his outrageous size, his body was twisted and contorted in ways no human could have survived. He looked as though he had been crushed in a pneumatic press while being hosed down by flamethrowers.

The demon strode down the path, headed straight for their hiding place. His reptilian eyes were narrowed to slits. He moved in the slow, hesitant manner of a man stumbling through darkness. Whenever a particularly strong shaft of sunlight struck him, thin smoke rose from his skin like mist off a marsh.

Juanita crouched lower to the ground, cowering underneath the brush. The demon drew level with the thicket, and a vile, putrid stink washed over her. It was all she could do to keep from gagging. The demon smelled as bad as he looked.

Then, just when Juanita had decided the thing couldn't help but see them, the demon was past, lumbering away without even a side glance.

No one moved for a long time. Not even after the sounds of branches breaking and trees falling had faded to an occasional distant crack. Finally Narn stood up and stared silently down the path in the direction the creature had gone.

Benegas joined him. "Beelzebub," Benegas said softly. "I recognized the stench. He's come back."

The crow floated down from a tree and lit on Benegas' shoulder.

"Come back? You know this creature?" Grandmother asked, prying herself out of the thicket.

"Yes," Benegas said. "I met him on the river, not long after I'd driven the Madonna away and found the heart in my saddlebag." He sighed heavily. "I was crushed, you see. Dejected. I knew what I'd done, what a terrible sin I'd committed. But I didn't know what to do next. What to do to rectify it. I didn't know what to do, so I did nothing. I just sat.

"I sat by the river for the next two days and waited for the Virgin to return and claim her heart. I waited, but she didn't come. I know now I should have saddled my horse and ridden for the mission, but at the time I was afraid. I was afraid that the murders of the friars had been discovered, and that I'd be arrested if I went back.

"On the second night this demon, this Beelzebub, came to me. He squatted in the darkness beyond my campfire and offered to buy the heart from me. He offered my weight in gold. I refused. He offered three times my weight in gold. I refused again. I told him that I intended to return the Madonna's heart to her.

"Beelzebub became angry. He stepped out of the darkness and came for me, promising to tear me limb from limb.

"I grabbed the saddlebag and ran. I ran to the river's edge. And then, with no place left to run and seeing he would have me in seconds, I threw the bag into the waters.

"The demon screamed. He cursed me. He rushed past me after the bag, but the river had carried the bag away. The demon ran down the bank after it. For a long time I could hear him crashing through the brush, following the bag downstream. Then I couldn't hear him anymore.

"I returned to the campfire and sat down and waited for the demon to return and kill me, but sunrise came before he did. I got up and saddled my horse and rode for Mexico. And I've wandered the earth ever since. It wasn't until over three hundred years later when you came to me in the old church"—he nodded to Grandmother—"that I learned that the heart had somehow escaped."

"And now this same demon, this Beelzebub, is back, seeking the heart again?" Grandmother asked.

"Yes. It must be the heart he's after. And if we don't find the mission before nightfall, he'll get it. He's weak now, in the daylight hours, but as soon as the sun sets he'll track us down and destroy us along with the heart."

Juanita glanced through the trees. The sun was already falling towards the west.

"Wake up!" Someone was slapping Mojo's face. At first the slapping seemed distant, removed, like it was happening to someone else or in a dream. Then suddenly it was real and close and painful. Mojo opened his eyes. Everything was spinning and swimming around him. He felt disoriented. He could taste smoke.

"Come on, man. Get up." Mojo allowed himself to be picked up and placed on his feet. The spinning slowed. He peered around. The rope he had been hanging from was dangling loose from the tree branch. Its end had been cut. There was a black, burned smudge underneath the rope. Bigthumb was sprawled beside the smudge. His eyes were closed and his mouth open. The vodka bottle was lying on the ground by his side.

Mojo turned shakily towards his rescuer.

"What's happening, man?" Chuy asked. "That *pendejo* Indian trying to roast you? He some kind of weird cannibal?"

"It was a vision, man. A real vision. And I'm not talking about a face on a tortilla! No way! It was the Man of Sorrows himself! Appeared in my bedroom big as life. Hovered over the foot of my bed, all lit up, like a chopper with a laser concert going behind him!'

"The Man of Sorrows?"

"That's straight, man. He's the one who sent me."

"He sent you up here to help me?"

"You?" Chuy frowned. "Naw. He never mentioned you. He sent me up here to help Grandmother. I just noticed the smoke and stopped off to see if she was here."

"Oh." Mojo felt vaguely disappointed.

"Geronimo over there didn't want me to cut you down." Chuy nodded at the comatose Apache. "So I had to talk him into it." He lifted his hand. His baseball bat was in it.

"Come on." Chuy took Mojo's arm. "We'd better get moving. I got my wheels right over here."

Chuy had an ATV. A three-wheeler.

"An ATV?"

"All-terrain vehicle, man. You can go anywhere on this sucker: over sand dunes, through the woods, across a swamp, even. There's no place this baby can't go."

Mojo peered closely at the strange contraption. It looked like a cross between a Harley hog and a tricycle.

It had huge balloon tires that raised the chassis a good three feet above the ground.

Chuy slipped his baseball bat underneath the lip of a carrying pack, then vaulted into the seat. "Come on, man." He scooted up to leave room for Mojo. "Let's go find old Grandmother."

Mojo hesitated. He had seen these things before. On a cable special about dangerous consumer products.

"Ah, don't these three-wheelers roll over kinda easy?"

"No prob, man! No prob! I been driving this sucker since I was a kid, and I haven't had more than two or three really serious crack-ups in all that time! And I know this mountain too. I been coming up here for years. I probably know every trail on this mountain. Hey! I'm not gonna crack up on a mountain I know like the back of my hand!"

"But . . . there's not even a trail."

"Sure there is. ATV trail, man. Goes all the way to the top. I told you, I ride up here all the time. It's against the law, of course. Fucking Forest Service law. But, hey! It's my land, you know? They stole it from me. I got the right to ride on my own land, right?"

Chuy revved the engine. It sounded like a berserk lawn mower.

Mojo got on anyway.

It was better than an amusement-park ride.

And worse.

Riding on the back of Chuy's three-wheeler was like riding a runaway water balloon. Mojo kept bouncing and slipping and sliding off the back of the seat. If it hadn't been for the death grip he had around Chuy's waist and his own keen sense of self-survival, he would have been thrown off several times.

"Slow down!" Mojo shouted over the roar of the engine. They were flying up a vague trail, bumping heavily over logs and holes and rocks.

"Slow down? Shit. We're barely moving."

Chuy maneuvered the ATV around a tight turn, one of the big rear wheels raising off the ground. Mojo leaned desperately in the direction of the wheel, and the tire fell back to earth.

"Hey! You're doing all right," Chuy yelled over his shoulder. "Really starting to get the hang of it."

The only thing Mojo wanted to get was off. "How much further?" he shouted as they blasted their way up a dry runoff bed, pebbles rattling in their wake.

"Not far. The tree line is at the top of this next ridge."

Mojo tried to look ahead, but the three-wheeler was bouncing so badly that all he could see were blurs of green and brown and grey. He ducked his head. He promised himself that if he survived this he would never get on or in anything with less than four wheels for the rest of his life.

They powered their way up a steep, rocky slope and shot out into a grassy meadow. They were almost across the meadow and into the woods on the other side when Mojo noticed the log cabin. The cabin was hidden in the shadow of some towering pines. It had a small cross affixed to its roof. There were several people standing in front of the cabin. One of them was waving madly in his direction. It was Juanita.

"It's them!" Mojo shouted over the roar of wind and engine. "Turn around!"

''Who?''

''Them! Go back!''

''Thank goodness you found us!'' Grandmother took Mojo's arm as he stepped shakily down from the ATV. ''We need you to open the door. It's locked.''

''Place is like a goddamn fortress,'' Narn told Mojo as they walked around to the back of the tiny church. ''Foot-thick walls and no windows. We tried to batter down the door with a dead log, but the log broke before the door did.''

Narn led Mojo to a door set in the mission's wall. The door was built from sections of sawed logs. There were no visible hinges. Near the left edge of the door was an ancient iron lock set deep into the wood.

''You must hurry,'' Grandmother said. She pulled the pickle jar from her basket and held it up in front of Mojo.

''Look,'' Grandmother said. Mojo did. The black stain had spread. Now it covered almost all of the heart. All but a tiny white splotch near its top.

Mojo pulled his piece of stiff wire from his shirt pocket and went to work.

''What's wrong?'' Juanita frowned over Mojo's shoulder. ''What's taking so long?''

''It's this lock. It's old, all rusted up. Even the inside is rusted. If I had some WD-40 or something, I might be able to loosen it, but without anything but a piece of wire . . .'' Mojo shrugged helplessly.

''Well, you'd better find a way. And soon. It'll be sunset in a few minutes.''

Mojo glanced to the west. She was right. The sun was hovering on the crest of the farthest ridge. The light was already beginning to fade.

Mojo returned to the lock with renewed vigor. He managed to chip away most of the rust from the outermost sections of the lock, but there was still a long ways to go. He wormed the wire down into the keyhole and closed his eyes and fished for the tumblers.

A distant shout.

A gunshot.

Another.

Narn came racing around the corner of the mission. "It's him! It's Castillo!" he cried.

Mojo wiggled the wire frantically but the lock wouldn't budge.

> *This about Mojo Birdsong:* He was a wizard because his mother was a witch.
>
> Mojo didn't know his mother was a witch, didn't know much about his mother at all. His mother had deserted him when he was still a child and he hardly remembered her. All Mojo could recall about his mother was her long blond hair and her snake tattoo and how she had always thrown things at him. Mojo didn't know his mother was a witch nor who his real father was. If he had, he would have known why the demon always spoke to him and not to the others. He would have known why he had such peculiar talents. He might even have known how to open the rusted lock.

Mojo had always had a talent for locks and keys and spoons and dice, had always been able to open, bend, and manipulate them, but without ever knowing exactly how he did it. It had something to do with geometry, he knew, but it wasn't any geometry he had been taught at Van Horn High.

When Mojo bent things, he did it by picturing the things in his mind as three-dimensional objects and then folding or unfolding the objects until he had them in the shape he wanted. He had the idea that it was space itself he was folding and unfolding, but he wasn't really sure.

There were rules. Things couldn't just be folded any which way. There were a few basic transformations that would work and no others. To turn a wad of orange peels into an orange with no center, for example—a trick that always made the girls ooh and aah—Mojo couldn't just pull the peels apart and mold them back together again into the shell of an orange. He had to leave the peels in a wad and then unfold rectangles of minuscule width to shift the peels around a minuscule bit at a time until they had all been shifted into a hollow sphere.

Forming hollow oranges was hard. It was long and tedious. Keys were much easier.

To turn a piece of wire into a key, all Mojo had to do was fold the wire into all its possible permutations. One of these permutations was bound to fit the lock. This was much easier to do than to explain. All he really did was set the wire to vibrating in a certain way. Once set to vibrating, waves ran down the wire like plucked guitar strings. These waves came so fast that it normally only took a few seconds until the right sequence of waves struck the tumblers and opened the lock.

Normally.

But not this time.

* * *

Mojo closed his eyes and concentrated. He felt the wire quivering in his hand. He felt slick sweat between his shoulder blades. He had to open this lock.

But he couldn't.

Mojo opened his eyes. It just wasn't going to work. There just wasn't enough room inside the lock for the wire to vibrate properly. There was too much rust and dust and crap compacted inside and no time left to clean it out.

A bullet whined over the roof of the tiny church.

"Come on!" Juanita tried to grab his arm, but he pushed her away.

There was one more chance.

Mojo closed his eyes again. He pictured a line in his mind. The line was the wire. He expanded the line. The line grew at an exponential rate. The line ballooned up through Mojo's mind in the same way that Mojo and the Child of Atocha had ballooned up through the universe. It only took a few seconds for the line to grow so large that Mojo's mind could no longer hold it. In only seconds the line had reached the point the child and he had reached when the universe could no longer hold them and they had floated out into the white haze of the spinning egg.

And then the line was gone.

The line had floated out of Mojo's mind.

At first Mojo thought he had lost it completely. Had failed. Then he saw it again: an almost invisible crease in a corner in his mind, a shadow of a line that was now as small as it had been huge only a few seconds before. He concentrated on the crease and it began to grow. When it was almost the size of a hair but not quite, he stopped it.

Mojo opened his eyes. The wire between his fingers

was so thin and so fine that he had to turn his head and look at it in a certain way to even see it. It was no more than a glint running between his fingers and the lock. It made dental floss look like a fire hose.

"Come on, Mojo!" Juanita threw her arms around his waist and yanked. "We've got to get into the woods!"

Mojo held his ground. He set the wire to vibrating. The lock shook slightly. There was a low crackling sound. Flecks of rust puffed out. The lock clicked open.

"Follow me!" Mojo shouted as he pushed open the heavy door and stumbled into the church, dragging Juanita in with him.

Grandmother and the others did. They followed.

"Hold it right there!" a voice demanded just as Mojo was reaching back for the door.

Fat chance.

Mojo slammed the door and bolted it shut.

18

It was dark as a drive-in back seat inside the church.

Something struck the door. Mojo jumped away from it. It struck again, a heavy, hollow thud.

The hollow thuds became a steady pounding.

A match flared. "Phew! Smells in here!" Chuy snorted.

Chuy held the light higher. They caught a quick glimpse of long, narrow wooden walls bordering two rows of rough-hewn log benches before the match sputtered out.

A bullet thwanged off the door's heavy lock. Then a succession of bullets popping like grease in an iron skillet. Mojo held his breath. In a moment the popping stopped. The door remained shut. Mojo resumed breathing.

"Light another match," Grandmother instructed

Chuy, her voice disembodied by the darkness. "I have a candle in my bag."

Grandmother led them up the aisle between the log benches, the dry, ancient flooring creaking ominously underneath their feet. They passed a skeleton lying sprawled in the middle of the aisle about halfway to the altar. The skeleton was dressed in the decayed rags of what had once been a monk's robe. Benegas made the sign of the cross and muttered something as he stepped over it.

They mounted the altar.

They found the santo.

Mojo stepped onto the altar and faced the santo of the Madonna. The Madonna stood on a simple pine pedestal just to the right of a rickety altar table. She glistened in the soft candlelight. She was dark-eyed and dark-skinned. She had a long, aristocratic face that was as beautiful as it was sad. Golden tears sparkled on her face. Golden threads glittered in her long blue robe. Her hands were raised beseechingly. There was a gaping hole in her chest with wine-colored stains around it.

Grandmother set the basket down in front of the santo and pulled out the glass jar. She turned to Benegas. "You must do it." She held the jar out to him. "You must be the one to return what you stole."

Benegas shrank back from her. "No. Please. I . . . I'm afraid." His face was pale. His lips trembled. He looked as old as he was. "What if she won't accept it from me?"

"You have to do it," Grandmother said firmly. "It's the only way."

Grandmother pressed the jar into Benegas' hands. He took it reluctantly.

"Go on," Grandmother prompted.

Benegas unscrewed the lid and reached into the jar and pulled out the heart. The heart lay limp and lifeless in his hands. It shone with a slick, greasy sheen. It was completely black. There was no light coming from it. No movement.

"Something's wrong! I can feel it! It's . . . dead!" Benegas exclaimed, horrified.

The heart looked dead to Mojo too. A sudden sense of sadness, of loss, swept over him. Juanita must have felt it because she reached over and squeezed his arm.

"Do it anyway," Grandmother said commandingly. "Replace the heart in the wound." Her expression was grim.

After a few seconds of indecision, Benegas nodded. "All right, but you'll have to help me."

Grandmother guided the old man to the Madonna. He placed the black heart carefully into the wound in her chest. They stepped quickly back.

The heart lay still and unmoving for a long moment. Then a tiny blue spark appeared above it. Then another. The two sparks rose to meet one another. The two sparks circled together above the heart. Three more appeared and joined them.

"See?!" Grandmother pointed triumphantly. "Do you see them? She has reclaimed her heart!"

But even before Grandmother had finished speaking, the sparks began to slow and fade. Suddenly there were only three sparks circling over the heart. Then one. Then none.

Grandmother gasped.

There was a long silence.

"What happened?" Mojo asked, confused.

Grandmother shook her head. "I don't understand it.

We've done everything the child ordered me to do. What else could we—"

The roof raised.

There was a loud crackling sound that drowned out Grandmother's next words. Mojo jerked his head up. The church roof was shooting up into the sky, spinning around and around as it ascended. Mojo stared after it, dumbfounded. He didn't see a tornado, but he wouldn't have been surprised if Dorothy herself had leaned over the edge of the rapidly dwindling roof and waved down to him.

And then there was someone leaning over him, only it definitely wasn't Dorothy. Mojo had to look twice to make sure the dim twilight wasn't playing tricks on his eyes. It wasn't. It really was a thirty-foot hunchbacked demon with bulging frog eyes who was leaning over the church and grinning down at him.

Oh, shit, Mojo thought.

"Beelzebub," Juanita whispered.

An intense blue light flashed in Mojo's face.

". . . free."

Mojo rubbed his eyes, trying to clear away the blue flash. When he could see again, the Madonna was standing in front of him. Only she wasn't a statue anymore. She was real. The tears were gone from her cheeks. The sadness was gone from her face. There was a glowing heart of pure gold burning in her chest. She was peering down at a yellowed, crumbling skeleton at her feet. The skeleton was dressed in Benegas' clothes.

The Madonna looked up at them and smiled. "He is free now," she said. "The curse is finally lifted."

Mojo wasn't listening. It wasn't Benegas Mojo was worried about. It was the grinning demon.

"Lo-look," Mojo managed, pointing, "at that!"

The Madonna glanced up. Her smile turned to a frown. "You. You shouldn't be here," she told the demon.

"Wrong. You're the one who doesn't belong here. Not anymore," the demon rumbled from somewhere in the pit of his enormous belly.

"You must return," the Madonna said softly, her voice lilting with soft music. "There is no place for you now that Grace has been restored to the world."

"Too late for that grace crap," the demon snarled.

"It's never too late for Grace," the Madonna replied. She spread her arms and rose towards the demon in a revolving halo of light.

The halo of light swirled around the Madonna as she floated upwards. Mojo blinked, and suddenly the Madonna was no longer an Indian. The Madonna rising towards the demon had alabaster skin and pale blue eyes and long blond hair that swayed across her back. She was dressed in a long white gown that covered her feet. There was a crescent of golden stars above her head.

Mojo blinked again. Now it was a dusky Virgin with almond eyes and a sharp nose who was rising towards the demon in a cloud of light.

Mojo blinked a third time and now the Virgin was as black as coal with full red lips and a great puff of black hair. She was wearing a red robe with blue stripes. Her willowy arms were covered by jangling copper bracelets.

The black Virgin floated up until she was in front of the demon's huge face, suspended in the air some thirty feet above Mojo. He had to crane his neck to see her.

"I order you to return," the Virgin said, raising a thin, delicate arm and pointing it at the demon. She had coffee-and-cream skin. She had midnight-black hair piled high on her head and held by ivory combs. She had long, oriental eyes and tiny hands and feet.

"You order me?!" The demon's protruding eyes protruded even further.

"I order you," a diminutive Virgin with white lips and glossy green vines for hair repeated.

The demon rolled his head back onto his hump and laughed. It was a huge, deafening sound. Suddenly the laughter stopped. Cut off. His head snapped forward and a gigantic fist flashed downwards. The fist smashed into the front wall of the church. Someone screamed. Logs flew. The remaining walls creaked and settled ominously. Mojo turned just in time to see Castillo and several others scurrying away from the ruins of the wall.

"You order me? You? What kind of power do you think you have over me?!" the demon demanded to know.

"The power of light," a santo of Our Lady of Mercy with the hilt of a silver dagger protruding from her ruby-red heart said evenly.

"The power of light," the demon mimicked scornfully. "Is that something like the power of music? Or maybe the power of love? Is that how you plan to do it? With your bright lights and your sweet music and your pretty little pictures?"

"If you don't return voluntarily, I'll be forced to use my power against you," a burnished brown Virgin carved from mahogany with orchids in her hair said.

"Your power? Don't make me laugh. You don't have any power," the demon said contemptuously. Then: "You want to see power? You want me to show you some real power? I'll show you real power! I'll show you what power is, all right! I'll rip this pretty little world of yours into specks of fly shit! I'll turn your pretty music into a funeral dirge!''

Mojo was edging towards the fallen front wall, pulling Juanita along with him, when the demon suddenly raised a clenched fist high into the air. He knew immediately that the time for edging was over.

''Run!'' Mojo yelled, bounding over a pair of outstretched legs as he shot through a gap in the wreckage. He burst through the gap, Juanita in tow, and spilled out into the meadow beyond. Narn and Grandmother were right behind him. Chuy, his arms pumping furiously, brought up the rear.

Mojo spotted a grove of pine trees just ahead. He sprinted for it, the others following. The demon's fist fell with a tremendous crack. Small pieces of splintered wood peppered their backs as they raced into the grove. Larger chunks whistled through the boughs.

They scrambled for safety behind the trunks.

''Man!'' Chuy wheezed.

''Damn!'' Mojo agreed with him.

When a few minutes passed without further bombardment, Mojo took courage and peeked around a low limb.

''Why do you always struggle against the light?'' a porcelain Virgin with white skin and white hair and white eyes was asking the demon. She seemed sad rather than angry.

Beelzebub growled in reply. His hand whipped up faster than a striking snake. Faster than Mojo could follow, the demon's enormous fist shot up out of the gathering twilight and into the Virgin.

The fist passed through the Virgin. The fist passed

right through and out her other side trailing streamers of tumbling sparks.

The demon roared angrily. He jerked his fist back. The Virgin was floating exactly where she had been floating before. Not even a hair was out of place.

"I can help you if you'll let me," a stained-glass Virgin with cobalt eyes told the demon. "I can make you whole again."

"Help yourself to Hell, bitch!" Beelzebub leaped at the Virgin, his mouth flying open to reveal row upon row upon row of tiny razor-sharp teeth. He bounded up and over her, wrapping her in his great arms. It didn't work. He passed right through her again and tumbled heavily to the ground, crushing several small pines and what was left of the mission's eastern wall.

The Virgin revolved slowly in the air and looked down upon the demon, who was lying stunned on the ground.

She smiled gently.

She began to sing.

The song the Virgin sang was light as well as sound.

The song drifted over the meadow towards Mojo in a great, slowly revolving wheel of light. It passed over him, submerging him on the bottom of a sparkling sea. The song had no words, and yet it was about time and space and love and a thousand other things. It was a song like no song Mojo had ever heard before. He wasn't even sure if it was really a song. It had a peculiar undulating rhythm: a rising, falling, rising cadence. It had an incredible range: The high notes soared far beyond Mojo's ability to hear them, the low notes rumbled down to a slow thunder that he felt more than heard. As the song progressed he realized it was as huge in scope as it was in range. It was a song of songs. Somewhere within the Virgin's song was every song that had ever been written and every song that would be written and every song that could be written. Mojo suddenly realized that the song—if that was what its was—was somehow akin to his trick for opening locks. He realized that the Lady's song contained all the possible permutations of all the possible musical notes. It was truly and literally the song of songs.

And yet it was even more than that.

The song had the power of all music played all together at one time and yet understood separately. The song had the power to turn men's minds and hearts. It was certainly turning Mojo's mind and heart. Mojo closed his eyes and let the music swell up around him. The music swelled, and Mojo swelled with it. As the Virgin's song rose up and up over ever-ascending scales, Mojo rose with it. Mojo rose up in ecstatic harmony with the song. He felt the song rushing through his blood like a warm sweetness. He felt himself and the music becoming one. Mojo sighed in ecstasy as he rose with the song. It was like sex, only closer and tighter and drier. All thought left Mojo's mind. He let himself rise upwards with the Virgin's song, upwards into a dazzling night of stars and through that into a black void of galaxies and through that into a swirling fire storm of galaxies of galaxies of galaxies.

And then—at the very height of the song, at the ultimate peak of the ultimate note that encompassed all possible notes, at the highest high Mojo had ever reached—the song shifted.

The song shifted with a disconcerting suddenness.

Suddenly the rising sweetness was gone. Suddenly the song was descending, falling back, running back down the scales it had just ascended. Suddenly the song was falling at such a speed that it sounded like the garble generated by spinning a radio dial. Mojo's stomach heaved. He felt the blood leave his face. The song was degenerating into a discordant, chaotic squeal as it fell. The squeal grated in Mojo's ears. It was the most horrible thing he had ever heard. He yelled and threw his hands over his ears. It did no good.

Mojo's knees buckled, and he had to catch himself to keep from falling. He was in pain. Pain was stabbing through Mojo's mind and descending through his body as the song that was now a squeal descended through the scales. The pain was everywhere and nowhere, a nonspecific generalized ache.

Mojo drew his shoulders in and huddled against the pain. He was in a black depression as well as in pain. He clenched his fists and gritted his teeth and glanced over at Grandmother. Then back again. He stared in disbelief. Grandmother was not in any pain. Grandmother was not even depressed. No. Grandmother was in ecstasy. Grandmother was beaming. Her face glowed like one of her pictures of the saints. She was holding her hands out towards the Virgin and singing along with her.

Mojo looked past Grandmother to where Narn and Juanita and Chuy were huddled behind an ancient pine. Narn didn't look ecstatic. Not at all. Narn looked like Mojo felt. Maybe worse. Narn was propping himself against the pine with both hands. Sweat was pouring from his forehead. His head was hanging down. He looked green around the gills.

Juanita was standing beside Narn, helping to support him. Juanita looked better than Narn, but nowhere near as well as Grandmother. Juanita's face was pasty. Her hands were clenched. Her mouth was set in a grim, determined line. She apparently wasn't suffering as much from the Virgin's song as Mojo and Narn were, but she certainly wasn't singing along with it either.

Neither was Chuy.

It took Mojo a moment to find Chuy, and when he did, all Mojo could see of him were the soles of his shoes, the rest of him having rooted underneath a bush.

Mojo heard a low moan from the forest behind him. Then an entire series of moans as if a chorus of the damned had been raised to accompany the Virgin. Mojo turned. The moans were coming from a low thicket near the forest's edge. A head popped out of the thicket. Then an upper body. It was the Reverend Jerry Lee Rutt. He looked terrible.

The Reverend Rutt rose out of the thicket and stumbled over to a nearby tree. He grabbed the tree and clung to it with the desperation of a man caught in a hurricane. He leaned over some bushes and dry-heaved. His face was mottled and contorted. His eyes were unfocused. Threads of spit clung to his lips. He looked like the last day of a two-week drunk.

Now more figures emerged from the thicket. Many were on their hands and knees. They were all crawling or staggering, trying to reach the deeper woods, trying to get away from the song. Mojo spotted Castillo stumbling through a thicket. Castillo's jacket was torn and muddy. He was dragging one leg behind him. His head was bobbing like a doddering old man's.

Castillo disappeared into the shadows just as the song bottomed out and began to rise again. The song rose slowly at first, then faster, then faster, gaining momentum. Like a passenger on an emotional roller-coaster ride, Mojo rose with the song. Mojo rose out of the depths of pain and despair. Mojo rose up through happiness and contentment to the edge of ecstasy.

And then the song ended.

"NO!!"

The cry rolled across the meadow like a clap of thunder. Beelzebub was climbing back to his feet. A tornado of golden light was spinning around him.

"You can't do this to me!" He surged towards the Virgin, the bright tornado moving with him.

"Why do you struggle?" a santo of Our Lady of Remedies sighed as one of the demon's clawed hands passed harmlessly through her. "Surely you know that you only struggle against yourself."

Mojo stared at the demon. The demon was in bad shape. He was being ripped to pieces. Flecks of black flesh were being pulled from his body by the tornado. The flecks swirled around the fringes of the tornado like candy wrappers.

The demon turned away from the Virgin. He swatted at the tornado. He twisted about, trying to free himself from it, but without success. The tornado was closing in around him. Larger and larger pieces of burned, black flesh were being torn from him.

The demon screamed as he struggled with the tornado.

Then screamed again.

Mojo frowned. Peered closer. Something weird was going on. Where the black flesh had been torn from the demon's body, light was shining through. There was something shining underneath the blasted black exterior of the demon. There was something underneath that twisted exterior that shone with the same bright light that encircled the Virgin.

The demon spun away from the Virgin and tried to

run, but the tornado had him now. The demon staggered to his knees, the tornado wrapping itself around him, growing ever tighter, pulling and tearing at him.

The tornado ripped off the demon's hump. The hump came away in one piece like a turtle's shell. It flew through the air and struck the ground and broke into a dozen smoking pieces.

The tornado whirled faster and faster around the demon.

More chunks of black flesh flew.

The demon screamed with rage.

"Now you need not return," the Virgin said. "Now you have a second chance. Accept it. Accept the Grace," she urged.

"I accept nothing!" the demon roared. And suddenly he was shrinking. As Mojo watched transfixed, the demon shrank rapidly down to the size of an elephant. Then to the size of a man. Then a rat. Then a horsefly. And then he was gone completely, the center of the tornado a swirling, empty void.

The tornado slowed as if confused.

The Virgin sighed heavily and shook her head.

Mojo stepped out from behind the tree.

Mojo stared dumbfounded at the spot where the demon had been. He could hardly believe it. It didn't make sense. The humpbacked demon was gone, but not before Mojo had gotten a good look at what his hump had concealed: a pair of bright shining wings. Golden wings. The same kind of wings you saw in stained-glass church windows.

A demon with angel wings?

19

Narn's picture was in all the newspapers. In one picture Narn was squatting by a towering stack of white plastic Baggies. In another picture he was standing outside the federal courthouse in Albuquerque with a squad of DEA agents. In a third picture—and the only one Mojo ever saw—Narn was leading Raymundo Castillo down a gauntlet of reporters at the El Paso International Airport.

Mojo's picture did not appear in any newspaper. Neither did Juanita's. Juanita and Mojo were not invited to Washington to receive a commendation from the DEA as Narn was. But then, Juanita and Mojo were not arrested as Castillo and the Reverend Rutt were either, even though they could have been.

They were married instead.

Mojo and Juanita had a real Mexican wedding. The groomsmen wore ice-blue tuxedos with pink pinstripes and matching pink carnations. The bridesmaids wore pink ball gowns with ice-blue ribbons and matching blue carnations. Trumpets played when Mojo and Juanita walked down the aisle. Balloons were released. A chorus sang and a mariachi band played.

Narn came to the wedding and sat in a rear pew.

Chuy sat in a front pew with Lupe.

Grandmother sat between Chuy and Lupe and cried copiously and swore that she could feel the presence of the Dark Lady herself presiding over the ceremony.

Uncle Ort found a seat in the back near Narn and smiled contentedly as he fingered the crisp new check in his shirt pocket. The check was from Mojo. It covered the deductible on the Cadillac plus five hundred more for the damage to the store plus another five hundred for Uncle Ort's trouble.

It wasn't until after Mojo and Juanita left on their honeymoon that the check bounced.

Golden wings.

Mojo took a sip of champagne and considered it. It was too bad the Madonna had disappeared shortly after the devil. Maybe she could have explained it to him.

Mojo shook his head. A devil with golden wings made no sense to Mojo who knew what little he knew from watching cable TV. John Milton had never appeared on cable TV. Or, if he had, Mojo had missed him.

Not that Mojo was totally ignorant of the history of Western civilization. Some of the greatest figures of the past were on cable TV regularly: Abraham Lincoln, John F. Kennedy, Jack the Ripper, Buddy Holly, even

Hitler. Especially Hitler. Hitler was on cable TV so much that Mojo could have picked him out of a football crowd.

But not John Milton. Mojo had never heard of John Milton or of any paradises being lost. He did not know Milton even in the sense he knew Taiwan was a city in Europe and Aristotle and Plato were men's colognes.

But why sweat the small stuff?

Mojo set his champagne goblet down and fluffed his pillows up and kicked back, sighing with contentment. Look on the bright side, he told himself. Things were going good. Things were going even better than he had imagined they might.

Mojo was lying on an opulent round bed in an opulent honeymoon suite in the opulent MGM Grand Hotel in Las Vegas, Nevada. The suite had everything. The suite had red velvet curtains and a well-stocked bar with its own refrigerator and a bubbling hot tub and a wall safe filled with fifty thousand dollars in casino chips Mojo had won shooting craps the night before.

It was only the tip of the iceberg.

Mojo had a talent for craps.

Mojo sighed again. He had it made, all right. Made in the shade. He resolved he would send Uncle Ort another check first thing in the morning, a good one this time. And if his luck at the tables held out—and he had every reason to suspect it would since it wasn't luck at all—he would buy Grandmother a real house with walls made of Sheetrock instead of scrap lumber. And an ivory statuette of the Virgin for Chuy. Maybe even a new Stetson for Narn. What the hell. Mojo was not the sort to let cash lie idle in his pocket, and the principles behind CDs and savings accounts had always eluded him.

Mojo turned and snuggled up to Juanita. Juanita stirred in her sleep: a slow, languorous stretch. Mojo bent down and kissed her throat. He bent further and kissed the tiny red rose that was tattooed above the nipple on her left breast.

Juanita smacked her lips softly. Opened her eyes and lifted her hand to admire the glittering diamond ring Mojo had bought her the night before. The diamond was huge. Brilliant. It shimmered like a salt flat at high noon. She smiled up at the dazzling ring. Then at Mojo. She rolled over and pressed the length of her body to his.

The refrigerator hummed.

The hot tub gurgled.

The sheets whispered: a snap, a cinch, a piece of cake.